"I hope you don't mind my borrowing one of your shirts..."

Oh my God, Jackson thought as Dallas entered the main room of the jail, clad only in one of his tan uniform shirts. The tails flapped around her bare thighs, teasing him with a glimpse of golden-tanned skin. "What the hell are you doing?"

"It got too hot in here for the sweat suit."

Jackson heard the innocent words, but then noticed the sly smile teasing the corners of her mouth.

"If you think this is hot, you ain't seen nothing yet," he muttered.

"It fits pretty well, don't you think?" She pirouetted for him. "Of course, if you mind," she said as her hand reached up to the buttons, "I can take it off."

"No!"

"No?" she said, inching away, backward. He was drawn along with her, following her like a lovesick puppy. "No, as in you want me to leave it on? Or no, as in you want to do it for me?"

He closed his eyes and swallowed. "No, as in there's a man outside claiming to be your husband."

ABOUT THE AUTHOR

Jenna McKnight started writing stories when she was nine, as an antidote for schoolwork. A few years ago, her husband and teenage daughter encouraged her to leave her physical therapy practice and pursue writing professionally. Much to her satisfaction, her books have not only appeared on the Waldenbooks bestseller list, but she also recently won the Holt Award for best short contemporary romance for her book *The Bride, the Bachelor & the Baby*. Jenna loves to hear from her readers, who can reach her at: P.O. Box 283, Grover, MO 63040.

Books by Jenna McKnight

HARLEQUIN AMERICAN ROMANCE

426—ELEVEN YEAR MATCH
512—ALLIGATOR ALLEY
539—THE BRIDE, THE BACHELOR & THE BABY
605—THE COWBOY HIRES A WIFE

JENNA McKNIGHT

TWO WEDDINGS AND A FEUD

Harlequin Books

TORONTO • NEW YORK • LONDON
AMSTERDAM • PARIS • SYDNEY • HAMBURG
STOCKHOLM • ATHENS • TOKYO • MILAN
MADRID • WARSAW • BUDAPEST • AUCKLAND

ISBN 0-373-16628-1

TWO WEDDINGS AND A FEUD

Copyright © 1996 by V. M. Schweiss

Chapter One

It was another great day *not* to have a wedding.

And the weekend hadn't even begun. At noon on Thursday, Jackson Ridgefield wondered if it was possible the flood had been sent to keep the Ridgefields and the McKanes as separate as they had been for over seventy years.

Then again, he could be punchy from lack of sleep. He'd poured enough caffeine into his system since dawn on Tuesday to keep the whole National Guard awake. He stared at the river for a long moment, letting it lap at the toes of his boots. It should crest tomorrow if it didn't rain anymore. He could sleep then.

His dark brown eyes glazed over; he needed more coffee. He forced one foot in front of the other, climbed behind the wheel of his truck, and reached for his thermos. Empty. The bench seat stretched out beside him, so tempting. He tugged on his short, dark hair with exaggerated roughness; anything to stay awake. He slapped himself, one hand right after the other. Hard, stinging his cheeks, opening one of the many nicks he'd gotten from shaving all week in the ancient, cracked mirror hanging over the jail's sink.

He turned his truck away from the swollen river. The narrow gravel road to Green Valley was little better than mush as it wound through the back regions of the national forest. Long, slender branches, their tender green leaves heavy with spring rain, drooped low and whipped against his windshield.

Fallen trees forced him to weave the truck along as if he were drunk—which reminded him to keep an eye out for Otis and the other two moonshiners, Elmer and Jasper. No sense letting them take advantage of a little thing like a spring flood to increase their business.

The route to Martha's Diner should have taken him fifteen minutes. It took forty.

He could smell strong, black coffee—Heaven!—even before he opened the front door. A blend of pipe tobaccos permeated the air. Martha didn't allow any other vices in her domain, but she loved the smell of a good pipe. Several men sat scattered around inside, two and three to a wooden table, a couple at the Formica counter.

Greetings of "'Morning, Sheriff" and "'Morning, Jackson" echoed around the room. Everyone sat up a little straighter, although it was an unconscious reaction on their part. Their shoulders would never be as broad and square as his.

"'Morning, boys."

"You look like hell, Jackson." Martha craned her neck to look up at him as she pushed a wisp of gray hair back toward its bun. She draped a dish towel over her shoulder and rested her hands on her ample hips, daring him to deny it. In spite of all the rain, he'd somehow managed to acquire a tan during the hours of patrol and cleanup between storms, but it didn't make up for the hours of lost sleep.

"Why, thank you, Martha." He grinned as he thumped his thermos onto the counter. The damp weather had taken the razor edge off the creases in the tan shirt and brown trousers of his uniform, and he steeled himself for her comments on that fact.

She squinted her eyes and took an unusually close look at his face. "Been in a fight with a bobcat?"

He didn't dignify her taunt with an answer, but he did pick up a paper napkin and dab at the new scab on his jaw, just in case it was still bleeding. "You can't imagine what a pleasure it is to receive such a warm welcome."

"I suppose you're here for more coffee."

"I'm not here for a haircut."

She swatted the front of his shirt with her towel, struggling to scowl at his sassiness but failing miserably. His hair was as regulation short as always. "When's the last time you ate?"

He knew the caffeine was wearing off when he had to stop and think about the answer to her question. It should have been right there on the tip of his tongue. He looked at Chuck McKane sitting two stools down the counter, but he puffed on his pipe and offered no help at all. A McKane wouldn't.

"That's what I thought." Martha reached behind her into the pass-through window from the kitchen and set a plate of bacon, sausage, steak, and three fried eggs in front of him. "Eat."

He stared down at the food and cringed at the thought of all that fat headed for his arteries. "Whose is this?" He didn't think he'd ordered it, but it was possible he'd dozed off there for a couple minutes.

"Who do you think? You eat it, and I'll have Leon fry him up another order." Using her well-padded hip as a bumper, she blustered through the swinging door into the kitchen.

"There'd better not be any chicken on it," Elvin Brooks called after her. He leaned forward and hovered a couple of inches above the seat of his chair, the way he always did when he contemplated rising.

Jackson took the plate of hot food and set it on the table in front of its intended target, along with a bottle of catsup.

"How do you eat all that and stay so..." He couldn't call the man skinny. And no man wanted to be labeled small.

"Healthy?" Brooks demanded. He didn't wait for Jackson to assure him that's what he'd meant. "I don't eat no chicken. Damn, miserable, filthy animals."

Brooks teetered for a minute, then creaked back down onto the seat. He unrolled the paper napkin slowly, spilling his utensils noisily onto the wooden tabletop as he did so, and tucked it into the V of his flannel shirt.

"I hear the wedding's off." He bent to his food without sparing another glance at Jackson.

It wasn't easy for Jackson to keep a straight face. He bit the inside of his cheek to keep from grinning. Brooks wouldn't notice if he gloated, of course, but there were others in the diner studying every nuance of his behavior. "You heard right."

"Good." Brooks shoveled a sausage link into his mouth, signaling that his part of the conversation, such as it was, was over.

"Jackson Ridgefield," Martha complained as she returned with his thermos and a plate, "you were supposed to eat that."

"It was his." He glanced at the rapidly disappearing meat and hoped Martha wasn't bringing an identical order for him.

"He moves so slow, he wouldn't know the difference." She set a plate of apple pie à la mode on the counter. "Here. This was supposed to be your dessert. You might as well start on it."

Jackson eased himself gratefully onto the swivel stool. He hooked one boot heel over the bottom rung and let his other leg stretch down to the floor to keep the stool still. There was a twinkle in his eyes for the older woman. "Did you used to give your kids pie for breakfast?"

"Don't change the subject."

If they'd been discussing anything, he was more tired than he thought. "What subject?"

"You know darn well what subject. We were talking about the wedding." Martha raised up on her toes and leaned her short, plump body forward over the counter in a conspiratorial fashion. "Jackson, won't you reconsider?"

"Me?"

"Don't go sounding all innocent with me, Mister. I've known you since you were in diapers."

He tried to concentrate on his food, but she didn't budge out of his face. "It wasn't my decision, Martha."

"Hmphf! Fine time for you to realize it, after sticking your nose in where it didn't belong."

The cook placed another plate in the window behind her. Martha slammed it down in front of Jackson and took the uneaten half of his pie and ice cream away in a single swipe.

"Hey!"

"Eat your breakfast before it gets cold. Then go home and go to bed."

"I can't. The water's still too high to get to my cabin."

"Then get on over to the jail and take a nap."

"Not till I finish my pie."

With a cross look that had never had any effect on any of the Ridgefield boys, Martha gave in and returned his pie.

"Thank you."

"Don't thank me. I'm just trying to get you to go get some sleep before you drive your truck into the river."

Jackson ate his fill and left the diner with the full intention of going back to the jail for the prescribed catnap, but he had one more back road to check and a full thermos of black coffee to keep him awake. He headed west out of town, driving right past the jail without a second thought.

Flood stage for Green Valley was twenty-one feet. The Green River was already at thirty. The main part of town sat up on a knoll and had never flooded, but the surrounding fields looked like an endless lake. A lot of the bottomland farmers had moved in with kin up on higher ground to wait it out. They were a river-valley community; this wasn't the first time they'd been this wet, and it wouldn't be the last.

He left his truck, Twain County Sheriff's Department emblazoned on the dark green door, sitting in the middle of the gravel road. Its front tires rested mere feet from the muddy, debris-filled river. Binoculars in hand, he climbed up on the roof of the truck to survey the scene. Sticks, branches and whole trees that had been yanked out of the ground—roots and all—were adrift. The fifty-foot tree that passed in front of him lurched and dipped in and out of the water like some imported sea monster.

To his relief, there were no signs of canoers or campers in distress. None of the trees out in the middle of the swollen river had anyone hanging on them, calling for help. He carefully scanned the areas where debris had gotten hung up, now littered with driftwood and a smashed washing machine.

"What the—"

He took a closer look upstream. And almost missed it. Might have if it hadn't been for the orange-red sweatshirt. Looking like a pile of old rags dumped on a tiny island, an immobile body lay crumpled in a wet, muddy heap. Possibly a teenager or young adult. Dead or alive, male or female, he couldn't tell.

The island was minuscule, barely bigger than the body. When the water rose two more inches—and he was sure it would—the body would be covered.

NOISE. All around her was a roaring noise. It sounded as if she were sleeping on a Florida beach during a storm with one wave crashing right on top of another. But she knew that was only a dream. It didn't smell like the ocean; it smelled like dirt.

Her eyelids fluttered open to a sight straight out of a disaster movie. In an area as wide as a football field, brown water gushed no more than a foot from the tip of her nose. It roared its objection to trees and boulders in its path, sending up torrents of white water.

The ground beneath her cheek was rough. Rocks dug into her skin. Long, sopping hair hung over half of her face. Her sweatshirt clung to her body and chilled her to the bone. The cutoff shorts did nothing to warm or protect her legs.

She focused on her fist, clenched in front of her face. Other than a blue tinge, it lacked all color. Scratched and raw, embedded with gravel and dirt, it looked as if it had been to hell and back.

She eased up slowly, pausing on one elbow at first, testing the ground for a soft spot with her sore hands, still praying this was all a dream—a nightmare that would go away as soon as she was fully awake. Then, suddenly sitting in inch-deep water, she knew it was only going to get worse. She clawed her way to her feet, ignoring the stiffness throughout her body, trying to locate the nearest land and the quickest, safest way to reach it.

Land was forty feet away on one side, more on the other. The current raged past her. If she set foot in it, she knew she'd be skewered on partially submerged trees. Or, if she somehow made it past the trees, she'd be smashed on the bluffs waiting beyond.

The water rose to her ankles. Thick tree branches swept by. Foam cups and beer cans bobbed on the muddy surface, then disappeared below. She scanned both shores, hoping to see someone she could call out to. Someone who might be able to rescue her.

There was no one. They wouldn't have been able to hear her anyway. Rescue would be impossible without a helicopter.

A dead animal floated by, possibly a raccoon; it was difficult to tell at this point.

At shin-level, a violent surge in the current almost carried her away. It had only been a couple of minutes since the water had barely covered her toes. She didn't know how long she'd been in this mess or how she'd gotten there. At the moment, she didn't care. She just wanted out.

Almost knocked off her feet by a thick, twenty-foot tree branch, she struggled to keep her balance.

At knee-level, the river sucked her right off the gravel bar.

IT'S A WOMAN! It wasn't the mud-colored, shoulder-length hair that confirmed it, but the rounded curve of her hips and the shape of her long, bare legs.

Jackson stripped off his jacket and gun belt and tossed them onto the hood of the truck. He had just finished tying a rope to his bumper when he saw her pulled along by the current on a trajectory which hopefully would bring her within range. If he didn't act fast—and get very lucky—she would soon be gone.

"Hold on!" he yelled. He wanted her to know that help was at hand, but his voice was immediately swallowed up by the roar of the rushing water. He charged into the swift current, knowing it could knock him right off his feet. He'd grown up on this river and fully understood its power. He hoped she had enough presence of mind to aim toward shallow water.

He knew immediately when she saw him.

He couldn't believe with all the muddy water in her eyes that she could see anything, but she looked right at him, making the connection. She turned in his direction, ever so slightly, but it could be the advantage they needed. Her arms were barely visible; he knew her wet sweatshirt was dragging her down with its weight.

He moved quickly, gauging the distance between them. It didn't look good.

He was able to tell when she momentarily touched on a submerged log. There had been a fleeting second of hope on her face. It vanished as she was pulled, like a rag doll, back into the current.

"No!" he roared. The river was pulling her too fast. He wouldn't be able to reach her in time.

He would remember her face for the rest of his life. The brief look of hope when she'd seen him.

Just as Jackson thought it was all over, the woman was jerked backward and held in place. She was caught, bobbing up and down, even more helpless as the possessive current threatened to tear her in half. She thrashed in panic, unable to swim, unable to float. As he watched in horror, dirty water filled her nostrils and mouth. The current pointed her downriver, relentlessly holding her stretched out in that position.

"I've got you!" Jackson yelled triumphantly in her ear when he reached her. "Hold on to me!"

She sucked in a rasping breath of air as he lifted her head and shoulders out of the thigh-high current. She threw up brown river water and gasped for more air, then grasped his thigh with every ounce of energy left in her.

"Put your arms around my waist!" When she didn't respond, he yelled over the roar of the water, "Let go! I've got to be able to move my legs!" Without her cooperation, he was forced to peel first her right arm, then her left, from their death grip on his thigh.

"My leg's—" she gasped and heaved, then continued "—caught!" After another spasm, she tried again. "I'm caught!"

Jackson slipped, and his body shifted with the force of the current. She dug her fingers into him with surprising strength, anchoring him, enabling him to get his footing. He fought both the current and her viselike grip, not sure which was harder to deal with. The river was up to his thighs and he had to fight to keep his balance. Every move he made was hampered by her panic-stricken grip.

Knowing she had floated freely before, he attempted to push her backward until she came loose from whatever had snared her. It was a gamble. He didn't know exactly what was caught or how, and he didn't know whether she was snagged on a branch or wedged into a fork. It could even be something else entirely, something he didn't have time to consider.

The current hit his legs so hard, he could barely stand. Each step he took had to be carefully placed to avoid slipping and falling. Each foot had to be firmly positioned before he picked up the other. Submerged debris—rocks, branches, bottles, anything the powerful flood waters could pick up and toss about—banged into his legs beneath the surface.

He continued to move her, inch by inch, praying that a tree wasn't on its way downriver right now. If so, they were both goners.

"Okay!" she shouted.

"You're free?"

She nodded her head against his belt buckle.

"Hang on until I can get you to shallow water."

He carefully picked his way across the rocky, shifting bottom until they were in water up to her shins.

"Can you stand up now?" He hoped she could conquer some of her fear and help him help her.

Her feet took a minimum of her weight as they waded toward shore, her death grip on Jackson's waist never weakening. Her right leg lagged behind, dragging something, and her cheek remained pressed to his buckle as she stumbled along, hunched over.

Jackson never saw what hit them below the surface. His legs were swept out from beneath him. His balance was gone. He lunged for shore.

At the last possible moment, he twisted his body. They were going to fall hard, and he didn't want to land on her. She was much smaller than he. There was no telling what was already broken or bleeding. He hit the gravel on his back and dragged her down on top of him. It was the best he could do.

"You all right?" he asked between gasps of air.

"Oh, wonderful."

He laughed from sheer relief at the dry tone in her voice. They were both alive and safe. He lay still, breathing heavily. Resting. Enjoying her weight on top of him, her legs tangled with his. He was surprised to find her warming him from the inside out.

She shivered in his arms.

"Cold?"

When she didn't reply, he raised his head. Her face had turned pale, ghostly. Her lips were blue. He lifted her until he could slide out from under her, then propped her against the back tire of the truck.

She clenched her arms to her chest, shivers racking her slender body. "T'ank you," she said, then repeated it at least fifty times, as though it were a litany, before he pulled himself together and left her side.

"Here." He held out his jacket when he returned, but she didn't move to accept it.

She was no longer aware of his presence. The stream of "T'ank you's" began again as he crouched beside her and physically bundled her into his coat, forcing first one cold, stiff arm and then the other into the sleeves.

"Was there anybody else?" He scanned the river, looking for another victim. He could radio downriver if she'd had a companion that had been swept away ahead of her, or upriver if she'd been swept away from somewhere else.

"T'ank you so 'uch," she said through lips that were too numb to enunciate clearly.

He retrieved a blanket from his truck and wrapped it around her upper body, then briskly rubbed her bare legs to get the circulation going, careful to avoid the worst of the cuts and gashes. Nothing felt broken, but it was difficult to be certain.

"Thank you."

"Yeah, I know." His first consideration was to get her warm. Hypothermia was a real danger.

"Really," she said quietly.

Jackson looked closely into her dark green eyes and found them focused on him. Much to his relief, the toneless "thank you's" had finally ceased.

"Are you okay?" He touched her face lightly, his finger tracing a cut across her cheek and up to her temple. So lucky. His gut tightened at the thought of what might have happened to her if he hadn't come along when he did. It just validated his earlier resistance to give in to sleep.

Thunder rumbled in the distance.

She thought she must be in shock when she felt a tingle from his touch. Otherwise she was numb, glad to be alive, and starting to realize how lucky she was. Her teeth chattered. Her lips trembled. She stuffed her raw and bleeding fingers between her cold, wet thighs, trying desperately to warm them.

"I'm so cold," she confessed in the quietest of whispers, her energy sapped.

"The truck's warm. Let me get you untangled first, then we'll warm up in there while I take you somewhere dry."

He lifted her battered right leg gently, watching carefully to see if she was in any pain. "Okay?" he asked.

"Okay," she said through gritted teeth, feeling as though the extremity must be nearly dislocated. "What's on there?"

He unwound a chain from her leg, then held up a stringer with bits and pieces of raw fish dangling from it. "Two...four...six rainbow," he counted aloud. Then he grinned. "It seems you're over the limit."

"So arrest me." Surely, in spite of his uniform, he wouldn't do such a thing. She stared at the stringer, wondering where it had come from and how it had gotten wrapped around her leg.

"Come on." He half helped, half pulled her to her feet. "It's raining again."

"Good." She sniffed her sweatshirt and wrinkled her nose. "The rain's cleaner than where I've been."

She felt momentarily disoriented as his arms closed around her back and legs, then lifted and cradled her against his hard chest. As cold and wet as they both were, she still could feel warmth emanating from his body as he held her closely.

She no longer worried about being in shock. No one in danger of shock could feel so alive in this man's strong and capable arms.

He set her on the passenger side of the bench seat, retrieved his gun belt and rope, then climbed in beside her and shut the door. They sat thigh to thigh as he turned on the ignition and the heater, then reached down on the floor for a thermos.

"Let's get some hot coffee into you," he coaxed as he poured a capful of steaming coffee. "Can you hold this?"

She nodded. It took both hands to grasp the cup, though, and she was amazed at how much she shook. He lent a steady hand.

"Careful, it's hot," he warned.

She let the liquid burn all the way down. "It feels good." So did his large hands covering hers, warming them, distracting her even more than his wet thigh plastered next to hers.

He offered her more.

She shook her head. "No, you drink it. You must be freezing." She fingered his leather jacket with some guilt, knowing he could use it, but unable to part with it herself. "Here," she said as she moved stiffly. "Share the blanket with me."

Innocent enough words in context, but they rang through the truck like a wish spoken aloud. She was inordinately grateful that he didn't seem to notice, but why would he? She didn't need a mirror to tell her she was no mermaid today.

His hand stilled hers. "Keep it. You need it more than I do."

She grew dangerously warm all over from the power of his smile. His smile! Of all things to think about in her condition. She was disgusted with herself. Heaven help her if the man should laugh or say something nice to her. She probably would fall down on one knee and kiss his hand. Surely this attraction happened to other victims who were rescued from a life-threatening danger and would go away when she was warm and dry.

"I'd better let people know you're all right." He reached across her for the radio, his weight pressing against her leg and distracting her further. "What's your name?"

"I . . ." She hesitated, then stared at him as if she'd just noticed he had two heads.

He jerked back quickly, whacking his head soundly on the windshield. "Did I hurt you?" He ignored any pain of his own as he lay a hand tentatively on her thigh where he'd leaned on her.

"My . . ."

He shoved the edges of the blanket aside to check for himself. With a gentle touch, he ran his hands over her legs, working his way up from knees to hips. He frowned, his concern for her evident. "Where does it hurt?"

She struggled to catch her breath as his thumbs skimmed over the sensitive skin of her thighs. She pushed his hands away. "Everywhere."

His gaze was so intent, so tender and gentle as he captured her eyes and wouldn't let go. He gauged her every reaction, making her feel like a bug under a microscope, and all she wanted to do was hide.

"Tell me what I can do to help."

There was tenderness in his voice, the desire to help her any way he could. But it didn't help. How could it?

"Tell me."

A tear escaped and slipped down her cheek. Or was it a stray drop of river water dripping from her hair?

"Here?" he asked, and lay a hand gently on one knee.

Her voice was barely above a breath. "No."

She watched, mesmerized, as he raised his other hand to her cheek. Gently, tenderly, he wiped a tear away with his thumb.

"Where, then?"

She shook her head and looked away, racking her brain for the answer to his question. Surely this was momentary.

"I can't help you if you don't tell me."

She looked back at him, a blur through her tears. Could the day get any worse?

"I can't remember my name."

Chapter Two

She was soaking wet, smelled like dead fish, had mud and twigs in her hair, and Jackson wanted to engulf her in his arms and make it all better.

In his years of law enforcement and emergencies, he'd seen plenty of people forget everyday information. When faced with an injured child, parents tended to forget phone numbers, addresses, even their children's birth dates. It seldom lasted for long. He hadn't seen anybody forget their own name before, but he was confident it would fit a similar scenario.

This was the first time, though, that he wanted to look deep inside and pull the information out of nowhere.

He reached for her, telling himself it was to bundle her more snugly into the blanket. "I'll take you somewhere warm." The neighboring county had turned a high school gymnasium into a shelter for flood victims. It was large, impersonal and lacked privacy. The jail in Green Valley was a lot closer, smaller and definitely more personal. The fact that it was in his county—and he could see what she looked like when she dried out—was a plus.

He levered himself over her and eased into position behind the steering wheel, careful not to bump her battered legs as he moved. "More coffee before we go?"

The rain's tempo picked up, beating on the roof of the truck cab like a drum. Lightning in the distance promised more.

She shook her head, wanting nothing more than to go home, have a hot bubble bath and forget everything that had happened since . . . since she didn't know when. She wanted to wash away the smell of the river. She wanted to forget the feel of his hands wrapping the blanket around her shoulders and across her chest.

Most of all, she wanted to forget sitting next to him and liking it. Certainly remembering her own name was a higher priority than being attracted to the first man she met after a near-death experience.

"I'm Sheriff Jackson Ridgefield." His Ozark drawl sounded deep and rich in the close confines of the cab as he drove carefully along the rutted road. "This is Twain County. Missouri," he added.

"Missouri?" she repeated slowly, testing the sound on her lips. It didn't ring any bells.

He glanced at her often as he drove. She would have told him to keep his eyes on the road but, at their snail's pace, it would sound ridiculously silly.

"Where are we going?" She wanted to get away from him before she embarrassed herself by saying something stupid and gushy—like how grateful she was that he'd jumped in after her, and how she would do anything to repay him. Anything. With his muscular build, dark brown eyes, and even darker hair, he probably got enough of that anyway.

"Green Valley's the closest town."

Her body was no longer numb; she could feel every rut in what apparently passed for a road in this part of the country.

"I can't believe I don't remember my own name," she mumbled more to herself than to him.

"We should call you something." His gaze raked over her cocooned form. "How about Red?"

She glanced down at the blanket. It was army green without a trace of red in it. She wiggled an arm free and pulled a long lock of dark hair over to the corner of her eye. "Red?" It was dingy and muddy at best.

He grinned. She tried to ignore how such a warm expression, one that spread all the way up to light the golden flecks in his dark eyes, could be so at odds with his military-style posture.

"Your sweatshirt."

She frowned at her soggy sleeve, nearly hidden inside the jacket. Her inability to put a name to its present color had little to do with amnesia and everything to do with the amount of dirty water it had soaked up. "I'll take your word for it."

"Well, if you don't like Red, there's something on your sweatshirt."

"Yeah. Half the river."

His chuckle rumbled up from deep within his chest and sounded warm and inviting—two things about him she was trying very hard to resist right now.

"Besides half the river."

"Front or back?" she asked.

"Front."

She struggled to wiggle her other arm free. "I feel like a mummy."

He reached over with his right hand and tugged at the blanket, loosening it enough for her to pull her sweatshirt partway out. She thought she'd started to warm up until the back of his fingers grazed her collarbone. *That* was pure heat, and she had to take a breath and gather her wits before she spoke.

"I can't read it." She turned slightly toward him, self-consciously plucking the heavy fabric away from where it molded itself to her breasts. Then she felt like an idiot. He couldn't possibly have such a warped mind to be interested in a river rat like her.

He slowed the truck to even more of a crawl. "Dallas," he read with a nod of approval. "It'll do."

Her eyebrows arched. "You're going to call me Dallas?"

"Hey, it could have said Niagara Falls."

A curious thought filled her mind. "You think maybe I'm from Dallas?"

"ARE WE ALMOST THERE?"

Dallas was bone tired, and the comforting warmth of the truck heater made her eyelids heavy. She suspected she'd dozed off several times in the last thirty minutes, only to awaken to find herself still trapped in a bad dream.

She'd rather find out she was Meryl Streep. Then a director could yell, "Cut!" and she would be free to go home and soak in a hot tub with a tall glass of Chablis.

"Our destination's right up ahead. Sorry it took so long." Jackson raked his fingers impatiently through his short brown hair, clearly as put out by the delay and detour as she was. "We've never flooded this deep before. I didn't know Possum Trot would go under so fast."

Possum Trot was spelled just that way and clumsily hand lettered on a crooked, wooden sign with the *S*'s backward. The fact that she found the crude sign humorous was her first clue that she wasn't from around here. *Thank God.*

"Welcome to Green Valley," he announced. He turned to her and smiled, clearly proud of his community.

Green Valley was anything but green, but it was safer for her to study it than to ogle him. Rain fell steadily, churning up topsoil already soaked beyond its limit. The gravel road changed abruptly to blacktop when they reached the town, but even it was covered by a layer of brown runoff.

They drove slowly uphill through the short, straight town. There was a small barber shop and a beauty parlor, a red brick bank, a drugstore which advertised fountain sodas, and a general store with a porch—complete with wooden chairs and a pickle barrel. A sign over the local greasy spoon proclaimed it to be Martha's Diner.

Jackson parked in front of a small, cinder block building, and Dallas opened her door. By the time she gathered the blanket around her so she wouldn't trip over it, he was there to help. He slipped his arms under and around her blanket-clad form, lifting her from the truck and holding her firmly against his broad chest. She struggled to resume normal breathing and slow her racing heart.

"Relax." He sounded completely unperturbed.

"I'd rather walk."

"I doubt you have the strength."

"Put me down."

He didn't even break stride. "You want to fall flat on your face on the sidewalk?"

"I don't want to be carried around like—" *Like a woman being swept off to bed by her lover?* "—like a child."

He stopped and pinned her with a gaze that even hardened criminals would find unnerving. She certainly did, but she glared right back.

"Okay." He set her on her feet. "Just remember you asked for it."

Dallas's hip ached from being yanked when the stringer had caught under water. Every other joint in her body felt stiff after sitting motionless in the truck for so long. All her cuts and scratches burned and her wet clothes chafed under her arms and in the thigh area. But being carried only served as a reminder of her helplessness.

"I'll just keep a hold on you until I'm sure you won't fall."

He kept his hand on the blanket near her elbow, and its presence burned all the way through to her skin. There were two steps leading up to the door, and she had to place both feet on each step as if she were a toddler. She muttered curses beneath her breath with each slow-going step.

At first glance, the inside of the building appeared to be a single large room. Then she saw a holding cell on the left. "This is a jail!"

He nodded.

"I was kidding about your arresting me."

"I assumed so. Make yourself at home."

To the right was a tidy desk, with tall file cabinets, built-in bookshelves and a communications center behind it. A wood-burning stove stood straight ahead, near the far wall.

"Bathroom's straight back, behind the stove. Get out of those wet clothes, and I'll find you something dry while you wash down. Use plenty of soap."

Hampered by the blanket and sore beyond belief, she waddled across the hardwood floor toward the hidden bathroom. "I'm a big girl. I know how to wash."

"Sometimes there's raw sewage in flood water—"

"Oh, yuck."

He swallowed his grin. "I suggest you wash better than you ever have in your life."

Dallas limped to the bathroom and felt around on the wall for the light switch. Nothing. She looked on the outside wall without success. There was no window to provide light in the small room, and she wasn't about to strip with the door open—no matter how bad she smelled.

"Sheriff?" She limped back into the main room and found him stuffing wood into the stove. His wet shirt clung to his broad shoulders like a second skin. His trousers outlined hips and thighs that only gave her more reason to think this was a dream—and this wasn't the nightmare part. She promptly forgot what she wanted to ask.

"Need something?"

Seconds seemed like hours as she tried to remember why she was standing there staring at him as if he were some movie star. "Ohh." *Oh, yeah!* "How do you turn on the light in the bathroom?"

He gave her a puzzled look as he straightened up. For the first time, she noticed how very tall he was.

"I'm sure the electricity still works. Did you pull the chain?"

Dallas groaned in frustration and turned away. "Never mind," she said as she retreated. She hadn't thought of a chain.

With difficulty, she stripped out of her wet clothes and teddy, and rewrapped her freezing body in the damp blanket. She was chilled to the bone. Her teeth continued to chatter. She had doubts that she would be warm all the way through anytime soon.

Letting the blanket drop a little, she examined her shoulder. A bruise was already visible, covering her upper arm, shoulder, and shoulder blade. The raw spots in that area would most likely dry into ugly scabs.

In the mirror, she examined several scratches, one of which ran clear across her cheek and up to her temple. No wonder her face had tingled when he'd touched her. He'd been examining the scratch, probably to see if she needed stitches.

She surveyed her other injuries. Her fingers were scraped and raw, as were the backs and palms of her hands. One elbow was bruised, both knees, and her shins were both bruised and cut. Nothing major, all in all—she could have had several broken bones—but she wouldn't be running any races for a while.

Her shoulder-length hair was muddy, but undeniably auburn. She leaned over the sink and scrubbed it with the bar of soap, then rinsed every strand thoroughly. She pulled out leaves, twigs, something slimy she didn't want to identify, and tossed them all into the trash can under the sink. She rinsed again and again, making good use of a stained coffee mug until she got rid of as much grit as possible. There was a drain in the floor, and she stood over it and washed her body next, completely past caring that she'd run out of warm water.

JACKSON STEPPED OUT the back door and looked for a spot to strip down and hose off before changing into a clean uniform. On the other side of the cinder block wall, he could hear water running in the bathroom sink. Dallas was taking his advice.

When he'd first seen her on the tiny island, he couldn't tell if she was male or female. But, when he'd reached out and grabbed her in the rushing water, he'd discovered she was indeed very much a woman. He hadn't had time to enjoy grabbing her then. Everything had happened so fast. He wouldn't mind another chance—under more pleasant circumstances.

He heard a different sound inside. He knew when the water ran freely and when she interrupted the flow by sticking her hand under the faucet. Or maybe filled the coffee mug he ordinarily left on the sink. And he knew if she was using the mug, she was probably rinsing her body. Try as he might to remain professional, he knew she was naked just five feet away.

The cold water from the hose was just what he needed.

TWENTY-FIVE MINUTES. Jackson checked his watch again. He knew women could take forever getting ready to go somewhere, but all Dallas had to do was wash. A few more minutes, and he was going to see if she needed his help. The slam of the front door surprised him; he should have heard a truck drive up.

"Hey, big brother." Roman Ridgefield shucked out of his slicker and hung it on a nail on the wall, then finger-combed his hair as best he could.

"You look like you slept in your uniform," Jackson commented crossly.

"Martha said you haven't gotten any sleep in two days, and I'm supposed to ignore you."

"Is that so?"

Roman raked Jackson from head to toe. "Don't you ever relax? No, don't answer that. Martha sent me to make sure you were in bed. I'm supposed to relieve you."

"Is she signing your next paycheck?"

"No, but she's feeding me regularly." His grin was smug. "Until Julie and I can get our wedding back on track, anyway."

Jackson checked his watch again. Thirty minutes. "You found Otis's still yet?"

"Nah." Roman lounged in Jackson's desk chair, leaning way back and putting his feet up on the oak desk. "There's no still. It got washed away."

"Says who?"

"Otis and Jasper and Elmer."

"You believe them?"

"Why wouldn't I? You know, Jackson, you're very close-minded. You think just because those old men have spent their entire lives in the hills that they're some kind of backwoods hillbillies, when in fact they're very well-read gentlemen."

"You must have been sampling their shine. They've been running a still and lying about it for most of their eighty years."

"Well, I trust them."

"You'd trust a—" He cut himself off before he regretted it. Roman was, after all, his little brother.

"A what?" Roman's feet hit the floor with an angry thud.

"Nothing."

The heavy desk chair slid backward and hit the file cabinet as he stretched up to his full height, an inch shorter than Jackson. "Go on. Say it. I'd even trust a McKane, right?"

Jackson sighed, not sure how he'd gotten involved in this again. "I was just trying to point out that once someone lies, they're likely to lie again."

"I can read between the lines, Jackson. I know you're talking about Julie, and she's not like that. Our wedding might have been postponed because of this damn flood, but, like it or not, we *are* getting married."

He grabbed his slicker and slammed the door on his way out.

A SUDDEN, unexpected rap on the bathroom door made Dallas jump. Silently she cursed the aches produced by the quick movement.

"Are you all right in there?"

His deep voice sounded very near. Dallas stifled the urge to pull the blanket around herself for privacy. He may have saved her like a superhero, but he couldn't possibly see through the door.

"Yes, I'm fine, Sheriff." It had taken her forever to get clean; no wonder he was worried.

"Good. I've got a clean blanket for you here. Hand out your clothes, and I'll rinse them with the hose."

She gathered up her sweatshirt and cutoffs, but paused as she reached for her teddy. Dirty as it was, it undeniably had been a flaming red at one time. She couldn't just hand something so personal out the door to a man she'd met only an hour ago.

"Dallas?"

It sounded so strange to be called Dallas, and she tried again to remember a name that would sound familiar. Nothing came to mind. She huddled behind the door where she'd remain out of sight, opened it a crack, and gingerly handed him her other clothes.

"Is this all?" he asked as he passed the dry blanket to her waiting hand.

"Well..." She hesitated to have him think she hadn't been wearing any underwear at all.

"Come on now, pass it all out. I've seen ladies' underwear before."

She hesitated. He may have seen someone else's, but hers had never been hung on display in a jail before. "I think I'll just rinse it out and hang it up myself, Sheriff. If you don't mind."

"No, I don't mind."

Dallas couldn't see his face from where she stood, but if a smile could be heard, she knew he'd been grinning from ear to ear when he'd answered.

"Just leave the wet blanket on the sink when you come out. I'll take care of it later."

It took a couple of minutes for it to dawn on Dallas that she was expected to parade out into the jail in nothing more than an army green blanket. She fumed and mumbled about that while she rinsed out her teddy and hung it on the back of the bathroom door. If the smell didn't improve with a good airing out, it would have to be trashed, anyway. She wrapped herself up in the dry blanket, pulled it snugly across her breasts, took a deep breath for courage and ventured out into the main room.

"Finally," Jackson said when he saw her.

That one word spoke volumes. With his change of uniform and his hair freshly combed, he looked as though he'd never set foot in the river. She wondered if he'd used a shower somewhere while she made do with a faucet and a floor drain.

"Did you find a place to hang your . . . things?"

She nodded and looked away, but didn't say where. He'd find it soon enough. At least she wouldn't have to be anywhere near him when he did.

"Good. Come on over here and sit down." With a little wave of his hand, he indicated his desk chair. "I'll do what first aid I can before I find you some clothes."

Dallas gathered the blanket around her more tightly. "Isn't there a doctor in this town?" It wasn't him she didn't trust; it was the lightning bolt she felt whenever he touched her.

"Sure, we've got a doctor. I'll tell him you're here, but let me see what I can do first."

Dallas stood her ground. "How about a nurse?"

Jackson drew himself up tall and took a deep breath that expanded his already broad chest even more. "I've had first-aid training."

Afraid he would think she was hysterical and making a big deal out of nothing, Dallas gave in. She was practically covered from head to toe in an ugly blanket and intended to stay that way. She sat down in the heavy oak chair.

Jackson held out a hand. Dallas stared at it, but she didn't move.

"Give me your hand." His tone was professional, his manner impartial. "Come on," he coaxed in a tone that would convince the most recalcitrant child.

She was amazed to discover it worked on her, too, as she held the blanket with one hand and surrendered the other to him.

"That's good." He studied the back of her hand, then turned it over and examined her palm. His touch was gentle yet firm as he held it and a brown bottle over the wastebasket. "This might sting a little," he warned.

Dallas wasn't sure what she felt. Electricity from his touch? Stinging from the hydrogen peroxide? She snatched her hand back.

"Now the other one," he coaxed again.

She was at a loss, her thoughts all jumbled, her feelings confused. She needed a good night's sleep in her own bed before she'd be able to cope with the likes of him.

"Here, let me help." He reached toward the blanket, right where it was folded across her chest.

She jerked backward, away from his touch. He paused, then calmly gathered the folds of the blanket together while she switched hands. His knuckles grazed the skin over her collarbone. If she'd had the energy, she'd have vaulted out of the chair from the sheer power of his gentle touch.

"There," he said as he treated the second hand. "Anywhere else?"

"No!" She knew she said it too quickly, too forcefully, but she'd die before she dropped the blanket and showed him anything else.

Amusement showed in his eyes as he crouched in front of her. "How about your feet? I noticed you were barefoot." He reached down and picked up her left foot.

Dallas clutched the blanket at her knees.

"Let me raise it up a little." His touch was gentle as he held her foot over the wastebasket and disinfected it. "Does it sting?" he asked as she jerked it back.

"No. Not much."

He reached for her other foot, only to find it firmly anchored to the floor. He wiggled it as he looked up at her. "Relax."

Easy for him to say. He wasn't the one sitting there naked beneath a blanket with a gorgeous member of the opposite sex touching every exposed inch of skin.

"Come on," he coaxed again.

With a deep breath, she unclenched her sore muscles enough to let him do as he asked. She was half afraid he'd work his way up the injuries on her shin, half afraid he wouldn't.

"Anywhere else?" he asked again.

She shook her head.

"Well," he drawled doubtfully as he rose to his full height in front of her. "I'll leave the bottle in the bathroom in case you find anything else later. I can let the doctor know you're here, but he's busy, and it'll take awhile to make connections."

After her experience, Dallas could only imagine. "I don't think there's anything he can do for me that a bottle of aspirin won't take care of." She studied the injuries on her hand. "And some time." It would take weeks for the cuts to heal. It would take even longer for her to forget the feel of his touch.

He handed her two aspirin and set a mug of coffee on the desk in front of her.

She stared at the tablets in her open palm. "Wow. A full-service jail."

"Don't knock it."

He was rewarded for his efforts with a hint of a smile that tugged at the corners of her lips. Wrapped in a bulky blanket with her hair slicked back from her face, she didn't look old enough to take full-strength aspirin, but he knew her appearance right then was deceiving. He'd seen her legs.

He'd felt what they did to his libido when he sat beside her in the truck. And that hadn't been all sweatshirt filling his hands when he'd grabbed her in the river.

His well-tuned ear picked up a radio transmission meant for him, and he left her side to attend to business at the base station. When he was done with the call, he put out a bulletin on Dallas. Surely someone was missing her already. Giving her description into a piece of machinery wasn't easy; for the first time, it seemed so impersonal.

"Brown hair, shoulder length."

His expression softened as he turned and studied her. She'd fallen into an exhausted sleep right there in his chair, her fingers still clutching the blanket.

What color were her eyes? He had no trouble remembering. "Green eyes." They were more of an emerald, but he wasn't saying that on the air. "Five-five, 120 pounds." It would sound average to others. He saw nothing average about her, but he couldn't broadcast auburn waves and emerald eyes. He signed off.

Careful not to wake her, he scooped her gently into his arms, though he doubted an earthquake would disturb her. She was exhausted, battered and chilled. One look at the narrow cot in the cell he had thought to let her use, and he turned toward the back room. His bed would be more comfortable, give her more room. In the cell, she might bump the wall. With all her injuries, that could only be painful. He could rationalize reasons all day to give her his bed and know he was making excuses. He was still going to do it.

He tossed back the cover and lay her down. She instantly rolled onto her side and curled up with a whimper that made him instinctively reach out and touch her shoulder to comfort her. His hand lingered, as much for him as for her. She seemed to relax then, but he noticed the blanket was far too scratchy for her delicate skin.

He'd never known rationalization was a latent character trait in him, apt to pop out twice in five minutes after laying dormant for thirty years.

He pulled the sheet over her, then reached under for the blanket. Easier said than done. He whispered in her ear for her to release her grip on it. He pried her fingers apart. He couldn't see what he was doing. Frustrated, he tugged the sheet back down.

She'd scream bloody murder if she woke up and found him taking away her only covering. He made quick work of it, noticing she had a lot more injuries to pour peroxide on, trying not to notice her firm breasts, her flat stomach—

She groaned. Her eyelids fluttered. He covered her with the sheet in a split second, as though he'd been a schoolboy nearly caught studying pictures in a girlie magazine.

"I'm so cold," she murmured.

He lay the blanket over her sheet-covered form. "Is that better?" he asked softly.

"Freezing." Her teeth chattered.

Hypothermia could be a real problem. He could lie down with her and see that she stayed warm. He'd been on his way to take a nap anyway. Suddenly he felt very tired. The past sixty hours of work suddenly hit him like a sledgehammer.

Dallas shivered in his bed.

He was free to slip in behind her. He told himself this was only for a short while; he'd be out of there before she woke up.

THE GRAPEVINE in Green Valley was made up mostly of CBs, of which there was one in nearly every vehicle. By late afternoon, Jasper and Otis were sitting in the rain in Jasper's truck, celebrating their good fortune. Elmer sat between them, wondering what was so good about it.

"That'll keep 'em busy for a while!" Otis, by the passenger door, reached across Elmer and tooted the horn to celebrate.

"Let's go give that mash a stir." Jasper turned the key in the ignition.

He drove to a remote location, then pulled off the road as far as he could without getting stuck in the mud. They grabbed their fishing poles out of the truck bed—what they considered a likely disguise in case one of the deputies happened to show up and ask what they were up to—and hiked a mile through the woods to the mash barrel. It was a plausible story; their still was located near the edge of the water.

"I don't know why we're botherin' with this batch. We won't be able to find half our reg'lar customers," Elmer bemoaned the fact that the rising river had relocated a good portion of their clientele. He trudged through the woods behind his two cohorts anyway.

"Lord, what fool this mortal be!" Jasper quoted dramatically.

"Knock it off," Elmer griped.

"They'll find us," Otis assured him.

"They better bring jars, then. Ours is all busted."

"You don't have to split this one with us," Jasper said in plain English. "Me 'n Otis can do it ourselves."

That kept Elmer quiet, but didn't deter him. It wasn't like he had a regular job to support himself. He and Otis removed the branches and board covering the mash barrel. Jasper stirred.

Thunder rumbled nearby, drawing their attention to the fact that the rain fell increasingly harder. Lightning struck nearby, toppling a tree in the woods.

"You boys keen on hikin' back out through this?" Otis asked with a frown. "Or is the cave lookin' good to anybody else?"

"Lookin' better all the time," Jasper agreed, not wild about the idea of a tree landing on his head while he was sober.

They closed up the mash barrel and hiked the short distance to the cave.

"Hold on," Elmer cautioned as the other two rushed toward the dry entrance.

They stopped dead in their tracks and listened to see if they could hear whatever Elmer had. "What is it?" Otis whispered.

Elmer picked up a softball-size stone and hurled it into the cave. He moved to the side of the entrance.

"What the hell'd you do that for?"

"I ain't keen on stumblin' across no sleepin' bear."

Jasper threw his arms up in the air, muttering, "Dang fool. There ain't no bears in Missoura."

Otis and Elmer followed him inside. The cave wasn't deep, extending not more than thirty feet into the hillside, but it was relatively dry and several degrees warmer without the wind whipping at them.

Jasper kicked some stones out of his new bed, aiming Elmer's missile toward his spot with the toe of his boot, then lay down with his slicker still on to hold in his body heat. The floor was hard, cold, and he was going to have a devil of a time limbering up his old bones in the morning.

An hour later, an animal paused at the cave entrance, lingering outside in the dripping rain. It crouched there for long minutes, before creeping inside. Jasper woke up to the sound of it sniffing him from the feet up. He feigned sleep until he knew what it was. Too large for a skunk, he hoped, but he couldn't be sure without looking. It curled up behind his back, slowly adding its body heat to his. He'd take his chances and enjoy it until morning. Chances were whatever it was would leave at first light. Hopefully it wouldn't leave anything memorable behind.

"Misery acquaints a man with strange bedfellows," he murmured.

"Jeez, Jasper, shut up, will ya?"

THE RIVER REACHED for her. She struggled against it. Far more powerful than she, it enveloped her effortlessly. And just as she thought she would die, it spoke to her in hushed tones.

"Shh," it crooned. "Go back to sleep. You're safe now."

Warm body heat enveloped her from the back. It felt comfortable, secure, and very male. It felt right, as if waking up spooned in front of him was something she had always done.

Her eyes drifted open to a spartan room bathed in early morning sunlight, but the soothing heat behind her held her in a dreamy state that she wasn't ready to dismiss. She gave in and let her heavy lids block out the light for a while longer.

She rolled over, ignoring aches and pains that threatened to disturb this decadent luxury. She snuggled in closer, chest-to-chest, curling one leg over his thigh. She couldn't get close enough. His arm lay heavily across her. His hand stroked her bare back absently, soothingly, in his sleep.

The sensation was heavenly. Her toes curled, then stretched. She opened her eyes slowly, languidly, to see a well-tanned neck. The top button of his tan uniform shirt was open, revealing a white undershirt in the V. The patch on his sleeve bore the circular emblem of Twain County.

She frowned. Something wasn't right. She wiggled away from him slightly, trying to remember how she'd gotten here.

"Shh," Jackson crooned again. He pulled her back to him and nestled his chin in her hair. His hand continued to stroke her back. He snored quietly, peacefully.

Dallas was suddenly very aware that somehow he'd gotten her into his bed—naked. Ignoring all aches and pains from the sudden movement, she got a hand free to show him just what he could and couldn't expect of her.

"Why you low-down, conniving, backwoods . . . !"

She let loose with everything she had.

Chapter Three

It had been a long time since a woman had spent the whole night wrapped in Jackson's arms. Not that he was a saint, but with him being the sheriff and his father the judge, it had been impressed upon him by the community that he had an image to uphold.

Dallas had slept soundly, spooned in front of him, his arm draped over her protectively. It wasn't supposed to be an embrace, but it sure was easy for him to pretend so in a haze of sleep with her bottom pressed up against him. When she rolled over, he guided her close again to keep her warm.

His hand brushed lightly over her back to soothe her. His other arm was numb from sleeping on it, but he hadn't wanted to move it and risk disturbing her. His legs shifted to allow her room to flex. He didn't mind at all when one of hers came to rest on his thigh. She'd been restless off and on for the past several hours, and he wanted to make her feel safe.

Not that that's how he was feeling. He actually felt quite dangerous at the moment. He didn't want to just lie there and hold her, memorizing how her dark curls tickled his chin. He wanted to caress her all over, see just how her breasts fit into the palms of his hands, stroke her until she grabbed his shirt and ripped it off his shoulders, popping the buttons until they flew in every direction.

He'd never felt such emotion so vividly before. It was almost as if she were really doing it, right then and there. He felt her hand stroke his chest. It didn't feel as if it were undressing him with unbridled passion, though. It shoved— hard—and it was followed by immediate contact with his face.

"What the—" He jerked up, leaning one elbow on the pillow. He stared at her, his eyes open wide, his mind only half-alert, trying to make sense of how they'd gone so fast from lovemaking to retribution. His fingers traced the side of his face where it still burned. "You *hit* me?"

He kept a wary eye on her as she skittered to the other side of the twin bed, only inches away. She clutched the sheet above her breasts with one hand and kept the other free as a weapon. It hovered in the air, ready to take aim.

"Get out!"

"I can't believe you hit me."

"Believe it, Jethro."

This was the woman he'd been dreaming about? A woman full of heat and passion? Well, she'd demonstrated that all right, just not in the way he'd been imagining. Still, passion was passion, and now that he knew she had it in her, he hoped to see a whole lot more of it. In a kinder, gentler fashion, of course. And he'd make damn sure she knew whom she was with first.

"The name's Jackson." He rolled out of bed and onto his stockinged feet, careful to leave the sheet with her. "I was keeping you warm."

"I trust I didn't keep you from anything important," she said with sugarcoated sarcasm.

Safely out of her reach, he stretched his arms up over his head and worked out the kinks he'd gotten from lying on one side for too many hours to count. He was rewarded with her wide-eyed appreciation of his body, which promptly made him forget the pins-and-needles feeling in his hand.

"You're not big on gratitude, are you?" As soon as the words were out of his mouth, he wished he could pull them right back in. They drew her attention away from his body and back to the fact that she was displeased to have found him in her bed. He'd rather have flexed a few more muscles for her first, to see whether he could raise some of that passion in a more . . . appropriate manner.

"Where's the blanket I had wrapped around me?" Her quick rebound made him wonder if, in his hazy state, he'd imagined her visual appreciation of him.

"It's on top of the sheet."

"As I recall, I had a pretty good grip on it when I went to bed."

"You didn't 'go to bed.'"

"I didn't?" Her eyebrows puckered in a frown that made him want to smooth it with his fingertips.

"No, I put you there." And he thought he'd like to do it again sometime when she was wide awake and as interested in him as he was in her. "And I had to pry it out of your fingers."

"Ah-hah!"

"It's pretty rough and scratchy. I figured you were in enough pain."

"Oh." The fight went out of her face, and with it some of the fire. Her eyes roamed his body without apology, assessing that he was, indeed, fully clothed. "I see."

Her eyelids fluttered downward, setting his body on fire before she looked away. She slipped her legs out of the far side of the bed while she gathered up the sheet and wrapped it around herself. Instead of wrapping it under her arms and tucking it above her breasts as he would have liked, she covered every inch of skin from her shoulders to her shins.

In spite of what he wanted, he couldn't very well follow her around all day, waiting and hoping for the sheet to slip. "I keep some old clothes out in the cabinet. I was going to give them to you after I doctored your cuts, but you fell asleep. I'll be right back."

The temperature in the main part of the jail felt ten degrees cooler, but he doubted that was the case. It wasn't the bedroom alone raising his temperature. Funny he'd never thought of it as a bedroom before. It always had been just the back room in the jail, a place where he slept on rare occasions. He never would be able to sleep in it again without thinking of Dallas, wanting to curl his arms around her and hold her close.

He retrieved clean jeans, a flannel shirt, and a pair of gray socks out of the bottom drawer of the file cabinet. He kept them on hand for nights when he brought in a messy drunk. It was invariably raining when that happened, and he couldn't just lock him up in his damp clothes and hope he didn't catch pneumonia. The clothes were soft from frequent washing, and he hoped they didn't hurt Dallas's cuts and scrapes.

"Here you go—" He ran into her just inside the bedroom door and automatically reached out to steady her. His hand closed around her arm, nothing more than a thin sheet between his skin and hers. The temperature in the room went right back up, and he acknowledged that it had nothing to do with anything that mercury could detect.

At the same time, she said, "I was just on my way to the bathroom."

Her smile was tentative, testing his reaction to her as she looked up at him. Her green eyes were dark, heavily lashed, still burning with a little of the fire that she'd exhibited upon awakening. He continued to hold her, and he knew she wasn't thinking of slapping him again. In fact, under different circumstances, he could almost think, maybe, if he was lucky—

"You can let go now, Sheriff."

"Oh. Sure." But he didn't want to. He wanted to kiss her. Hell, he'd already been smacked for something he didn't do. Might as well risk the real thing. He put a couple of inches between them as he held out the folded garments. "Think you can carry these?"

She wiggled a hand free of the sheet, maintaining a firm grip on it with the other one, and scooped the clothes up against her chest. That took care of her free hand—he didn't particularly care to get walloped again.

"Sorry I don't have any underwear for you." He was rewarded with a lovely shade of pink coloring her cheeks. "Got a good hold on them?"

"I think so, Sheriff."

He wouldn't have chosen to have her arm and a pile of old clothes between them for their first kiss, but he wasn't planning on making a big production out of it, either. "It's Jackson."

"Thank you, Jackson."

How wrong could he be? Hearing his name on her breathy whisper went straight to some deeper force inside him. He pulled her into the circle of his arms, crushed her against his chest, and captured her with a kiss that did more to jump-start his heart than getting socked in the face earlier. Her lips were softer than he'd dreamed. And, even better than that, they moved gently beneath his as first she hesitated, then kissed him back.

The bedroom of the jail had never seen a simple kiss, much less such an evocative one.

Dallas had never been kissed like that, she was sure. Even if she couldn't remember her own name, she knew that was fact, without a doubt. If she'd ever been kissed like that, it would be etched indelibly on her brain, if not on her heart.

Her arm was pinned between them, so she couldn't have slapped him if she'd tried. If she'd wanted to, which she certainly didn't. It seemed as though she'd lost use of every single muscle in her body except the ones in her lips, and they were feeling their way against his with an intense longing that warmed her in spots she hadn't been thinking about.

His lips were firm on hers, yet gentle enough to make her seek more contact. Her arm was pinned between their chests, yet she longed for it to be free so she could run her hand over his strong back and up into his dark hair—and so she could feel his heart beat against her breasts.

"Oh, my," she said when he finally introduced a couple of inches of air between their bodies. A couple inches too many, in her estimation.

His hands remained on her arms long enough to make certain she could stand on her own two feet, and he seemed certain of that long before she was. Then he backed away slowly, looking every bit as dazed as she felt.

"I guess I'd better go... do something," he stammered.

It seemed like several minutes before she could put her feet into forward gear and continue on to the bathroom. She'd seen a teasing flicker in his eyes right before he'd kissed her. When his lips had touched hers, she'd expected a light peck, maybe a little more. Something to get even with her for punching him, she knew. At any rate, she suspected his intention hadn't been to get her all hot. But, if that was a playful kiss, she was grateful it hadn't been a serious one. One of those would have her melting in a puddle at his feet.

In the bathroom, she dressed like an automaton, barely aware of how her fingers and legs had stiffened overnight.

When her heart rate finally returned to normal, she made use of the cracked mirror over the sink. Her hair was long enough that she already knew it was dark brown with some red highlights. And she could tell it was curly. But looking into a strange pair of green eyes staring right back at her gave her goose bumps from the top of her head all the way down both legs. It was downright unnerving, like looking through a foggy window and finding a Peeping Jane scrutinizing her. And feeling as though she knew her from somewhere. If only she could remember.

It was much less disconcerting to study the wild way in which her hair had dried. It stuck out everywhere. She couldn't have done that with a whole can of mousse if she'd tried. It needed wetting down if she was ever to face Jackson again. He might kiss her once looking like that, considering she'd just gotten out of bed, but there wouldn't be any excuse for scaring the poor man later. She turned on the water and stuck her fingers under the faucet, then yanked them back out when the water burned into her cuts like a million tiny needles.

She checked in the mirror again. The decision was simple—look like a witch or stick her fingers back under the water, bear the pain and do something with herself. She went for the pain, but suffering in silence wasn't one of her strong points.

She glanced down at her new outfit and amended her picture of herself to that of a scarecrow. The jeans were way too big and hung on her hips. All they needed was a little straw sticking out of the waist and legs, and she could take up residence in the nearest cornfield. She knotted the tails of the red flannel shirt around her waist, but it was still quite evident that it was big enough for three of her. Or one of her and one of Jackson.

A gentle knock sounded on the door. "Dallas? Are you all right in there? It's been half an hour."

She could hear concern in his voice. "I'm fine, Sheriff—"

"Jackson," he reminded her gently.

"Jackson." She liked the sound of his name on her lips.

"If you need a woman's help, I could go get Martha."

"No, I'm ready." *As ready as I'll ever be.*

She wrapped her fingers around the knob to open the door, then found it required both hands because they were so sore. She grabbed for the jeans as they started to slip off her hips. He followed her out into the main room, making her nervous as he adopted her slow pace for his own.

"I can cut you a piece of clothesline to hold those pants up," he offered. He pulled a skein out of a cabinet, unwrapped a length, then stepped in front of her. "Here, let me measure."

She hadn't thought they'd be this close again for a while, and he took her breath away as he reached forward. His hands slid along her waist as he slipped the line around behind her. His arms brushed along her ribs as he grabbed it with his other hand and pulled it around. She thought she saw him fumble as he cut the line with his pocketknife.

"There you go." He held it out to her, and she saw concern cloud his eyes when he noticed how red and scratched her hands were. "Maybe I'd better do it for you."

She was sure he fumbled when he started to thread it through her belt loops and couldn't get it on the first attempt.

He covered up well with a soft, low laugh. "I'm not used to doing this on someone else."

Fortunately, it didn't call for a response, because she had none. She just wondered how much longer she could enjoy this sweet torture.

THE RAIN CONTINUED in Green Valley, sometimes a drizzle, sometimes a downpour. Dallas stared out the front window of the jail, hoping to find a patch of blue sky opening up. There was something about rain that troubled her deeply, but she couldn't put her finger on it.

Not that she wanted to. Right then, she'd rather be staring at Jackson. He sat at his desk, his back straight beneath his fresh uniform shirt, his dark head bent over his paperwork, one ear attuned to the incessant crackle of the base station behind him. He'd been that way for an hour, and she wondered if he always had such perfect posture or if he actually relaxed in bed.

Not that thinking of him in bed was relaxing for her. Quite the contrary. But he'd told her to make herself at home, and she took that to mean she should go find something other than him to look at. So she chose the window.

Two women crossed the deserted street and headed toward the jail. The short, plump one, bundled up in a yellow slicker and hood, carried a basket in each hand. The other, younger and taller, wore a blue raincoat that failed to button across her very pregnant belly. She waddled along, holding a black umbrella over her head with one hand and a canvas bag in the other.

Dallas turned to Jackson, pleased to be able to speak to him again without worrying about disturbing his work. "You've got company coming."

He dropped another completed form on top of a basket labeled Out and set his pen on top of a stack yet to do. Dallas watched, fascinated, as he raked his hands through his short, perfectly combed, dark hair and wondered what it would feel like to have those same fingers running through her curls.

"I hope it's a social call. Any more official business and they'll have to elect me to another term just to finish the paperwork."

She hoped it was a social call just to relieve her boredom; it was making her think crazy thoughts that involved her and Jackson and that desktop. She needed to get out of here soon, before she did something foolish. Surely somebody would have missed her by now. Jackson had done his part in getting the information out. How many petite, auburn-haired, green-eyed, white women could be missing in Missouri, for heaven's sake?

She took a deep breath and willed herself to speak without a catch in her voice, which might betray her thoughts. "Looks social enough. It's two women. One short, one pregnant."

"Is the short one carrying anything?"

"Two baskets."

"Hallelujah." He shoved the rest of his paperwork away, clearing a spot on his desk and rubbing his hands together in anticipation. "That's Martha, then. And where there's Martha, there's food. Good food, too. I hope you're hungry."

Funny how they were both thinking of putting *something* on that desk. She waited for him to say who the pregnant woman was, but he just let her identity hang in the air as he rose from his desk and headed for the door.

"Food's good," she agreed. "I get cranky when I'm hungry."

One hand on the knob, Jackson turned and looked at her, surprise written clearly on his face. "You remember that?"

She nodded. "I guess...so." As soon as she realized she'd remembered that tidbit, however, any and all others flitted back into the recesses of her mind. "But that's all."

When the two women were close enough for their laughter to be heard inside, Jackson started to open the door, then paused. "You might want to put your hands in your pockets," he warned.

"Why?" she whispered back.

"Trust me." He opened the door wide, his free hand jammed firmly into the pocket of his uniform trousers. When he closed the door behind them, his other hand followed suit.

"I thought you might be hungry," Martha greeted him. She turned toward Dallas with a warm, friendly smile. "And you must be our newest resident."

Dallas was caught up short at the change in Martha's expression. It was easy enough to read shock on someone's face, especially when that someone was as expressive as Martha. Her eyebrows arched as her eyes widened. She raised one basket as she pointed mutely in Dallas's direction.

Dallas's hands flew to her hair to smooth down any spikes that might have popped back up. Her hair felt fine. She tugged her jeans up a little higher, the knot in her shirttails lower. She pasted on a smile. "Sorry about how I look."

Martha glanced over at the younger woman. "Julie..."

"It's uncanny!" Julie remarked. She made a half circle around Dallas as she scrutinized her from every angle, from head to toe and back. "She looks just like her."

"Like who?" Dallas and Jackson demanded together.

"Oh, it must be a coincidence," Martha said with a dismissive wave of her hand, and the basket.

Julie's voice trailed off as she wavered, unconvinced, "I don't know."

"Who?" Jackson demanded, his attention directed fully at Martha.

"Why, the Budget Lady, of course."

"Of course," he muttered. "Why don't I get right on the radio and let everyone know we found the Budget Lady?"

"Don't go getting sassy with me, Mister. I brought this food over here and I can take it right back." Martha's threat carried little weight as she hung her slicker on the wall hook.

The Budget Lady? Dallas didn't know if she liked the sound of that. Who or what the heck was a Budget Lady? She couldn't say much for the cutoffs she'd been wearing, but that teddy she'd washed out in the sink hadn't looked like a budget item to her.

Martha and Jackson continued to harangue spiritedly over which was going to come first, food or information.

Julie's eyes moistened as she said, "Martha's been helping me plan my wedding. We were using the how-to book you—or the Budget Lady—wrote on how to do it, you know, on a budget."

Dallas didn't know whether to jump for joy that someone might know who she was, or to apologize for whatever was making this young mother-to-be so sad. Something about her book?

With a start, she realized she'd already accepted the fact that it *was* her book. Boy, she must be desperate for an identity if she'd grab at one as boring sounding as the Budget Lady. If that's what she did for a living, she wasn't in any hurry to go back. She'd rather stay here and give some more thought to whether Jackson relaxed a little in bed.

"Come on. We can snack and cook and talk about it all at the same time," Martha ordered. From one basket, she extracted a plastic container of vegetable sticks, a plate of cheese cubes, and a bag of chips. "I didn't bring any coffee, Jackson. I figured you'd be on your third pot by now."

Julie grinned good-naturedly at Dallas. "We'd better do as she says. Martha gets mean if people don't enjoy her food."

"I heard that," Martha squawked.

"What a pair you two make," Jackson said to Martha. "Dallas says she gets cranky when she gets hungry."

Her hunger pangs vanished at his teasing tone. While he stood as straight and tall as a ramrod, she noticed a warm glow in his eyes, turning them a deep, chocolate brown.

"Dallas?" Martha asked with raised eyebrows.

"Well, I have to call her something. What's the Budget Lady's name?"

Martha and Julie stared at each other. Julie was the first to respond, shrugging her shoulders as she said, "We always just refer to her as the Budget Lady."

Martha set four potatoes and a wire basket of brown eggs on the desk, then unwrapped a thick slice of ham. Her eyes raked over Dallas's slender figure as if she were grossly underweight. "You'll never put on any weight staring at it." She urged her into a chair and dropped a bag of chips onto her lap. "Eat those while I cook you a good meal. Jackson, mind your manners and get Julie a chair."

"Where's the book now?" Jackson asked Julie in the first words he'd spoken to her. Both of his hands remained in his pockets, and Dallas still hadn't a clue as to why.

"I lent it to—" Julie began, but was cut off as a horn blared outside. Jackson, very businesslike, turned away from the women and the food and headed for the door.

Martha quickly tested the temperature of the antique stove with a fingertip. "Bring some wood back in with you," she called out just before he closed the door behind him. "We'll wait on him for a bit." She perched her plump body on the chair in front of the desk.

Julie dragged over the chair out of the cell. "I lent the book to my sister," Julie told Dallas. "The flood was making everything so inconvenient that Roman and I decided to postpone our wedding."

"Damn shame if you ask me," Martha commented.

So now Dallas understood Julie's misty eyes.

"And I don't know where the book is now. My sister got flooded out of her apartment and moved in with a friend. And then they got flooded out of there, too."

The Budget Lady. Dallas turned it over in her mind to see how it fit. It didn't feel at all familiar.

"I'm sorry I can't help," Julie apologized.

Her wedding had been cancelled and she was apologizing for not having a book on hand? The forlorn look in her eyes made Dallas feel as if she'd slapped a cute puppy. "Sorry about your wedding," was all Dallas could think of to say.

"I could stay home and be depressed," Martha interrupted them crossly. She held the cheese cubes under Dallas's nose until she took two. "Show Dallas what you brought her."

Julie's expression lightened as she reached into the canvas bag balanced on what was left of her lap. She pulled out a folded garment and held it against her chest for a brief moment.

"When I heard Jackson had rescued a woman from the river, I thought you might be able to use this." She held it up by the shoulders, letting it unfurl to reveal a peach-colored dress with a delicate floral print, cap sleeves, and tiny pearl buttons all down the front. "I hope it fits."

Dallas stared, wide-eyed. It was brand-new and far too good to give away to a complete stranger. A polite refusal was on the tip of her tongue.

Julie's eyebrows puckered and her smile disappeared. She took a second look at the dress, as if maybe she'd misjudged her choice. "You don't like it?"

"I love it! But it'll look beautiful on you."

"Trust me, I'll never get into this dress again." She laughed and rubbed her hand across her belly. "Oh, he's doing cartwheels again." Before Dallas could react, Julie grabbed her hand and spread-eagled it across her rounded belly. "Feel it?"

"Uh...yes," Dallas said politely. The truth was, it felt wonderful, and she wished she could remember if she'd ever felt it from a mother-to-be's viewpoint.

"It's pretty enough to wear to a wedding," Martha hinted blatantly.

"Well, I certainly hope Dallas can get home before I get my wedding pulled together. Here. Take it, it's yours." She held it out until Dallas had no choice but to accept it.

She rose to her feet and held it up in front of herself, certain it would fit, glad it was long enough to hide most of the cuts on her shins. She'd wear it tomorrow.

"Just your color, too. Shame there's not a wedding to wear it to," Martha continued without restraint. "Oh, I know it's been postponed because the liquor store was flooded, and we're having trouble getting food delivered regular." Her voice faded out at the end, then came back stronger. "'Course, with the Budget Lady's expertise, an' all—"

"Martha, hush!" Julie's cheeks turned red at Martha's brashness. All the same, she looked hopeful.

Martha had brought enough food to keep Dallas fed for days. Julie had given her a pretty dress to replace her scarecrow outfit. What could she say to Martha's shameless hint and Julie's waiting, hopeful expression? No?

Of course not. Nor did she want to. All the same, there was one major problem.

"But I don't remember writing any book on weddings. How much help could I be?"

The two women perked up, their faces and hands animated as they both started to talk at once.

"I'm sure once you got started—"

"It's not likely something you'd forget—"

They laughed together like two longtime friends, even though thirty years separated them in age. Dallas was somewhat dazed with the energy they put out between them.

"I don't know how long I'll be here."

"Oh. Well," Julie said with a sigh, sounding resigned to the worst. "I understand."

Dallas quickly added, "I mean, if I'm going to help, maybe we'd better plan to do it soon." She didn't want to add to Julie's distress over a wedding that wasn't coming together as she'd hoped. "Someone could come for me anytime."

"That's true," Martha said, slapping a hand down on her knee with finality. "How many days do you think we'll need to pull this together?"

"How much have you already done?"

"I have my dress made," Julie replied eagerly. "And so do the bridesmaids."

"I have some food set aside in the freezer. And I can whip up a cake in an afternoon."

"Flowers?" Dallas asked, pleased that she had enough wits about her to think of that.

Julie shook her head, but Dallas was relieved to see that she didn't get all teary-eyed again. "We can't get a delivery into Green Valley right now. Your book gave instructions on how to make some out of tissue paper, though."

Dallas hoped Julie had read the directions carefully, because she sure as heck didn't know where to start on something like that. "Where were you planning on having the ceremony?"

"The church," Julie answered. "I'm sure it'll be free whatever day we pick. It's not like there's a rush right now."

"Tuxedos?"

"The men can wear their Sunday suits," Martha said.

Sunday suits, tissue flowers, and homemade dresses. Dallas got a clear picture of what the budget book was all about—keep it simple—but she didn't think it was her memory kicking in.

"Do you think we can be ready in two days?" Martha asked.

Dallas nearly fell out of her chair. "Two days?" She was so dazed by the timetable that she didn't even notice Jackson come back into the jail.

"Two days for what?" he asked. One quick glance at Julie, and his hands retreated into his pockets again.

Dallas wasn't so dazed that she didn't notice the light go out of Julie's eyes at his brusque tone. Julie's posture stiffened noticeably as she pointedly kept her back to him.

Martha, with a twinkle in her eyes, had no intention of keeping silent, however. "Two days to get ready for Julie and Roman's wedding."

"I thought—"

Martha jumped to her feet and stretched to her full four feet eleven inches right in front of him but well below his firmly set chin. "I know what you thought, Jackson Ridgefield. But this is Julie and Roman's wedding. It has nothing to do with you."

"The hell it doesn't. He's my little brother."

"He's twenty-one. He's old enough to do whatever Julie tells him."

Dallas stared back and forth between the two of them, watching the sparks fly as neither of them backed down.

"There won't be any wedding," Jackson said with finality through gritted teeth.

Chapter Four

Martha was one of the kindest people Jackson knew. She could also be the most infuriating. Like now.

Imagine her thinking she knew what was best for his little brother. Roman should be in college, but he'd dropped out and returned to Green Valley as soon as he'd found out Julie was pregnant—which was long after the rest of the town knew.

Julie struggled to ease her bulk, stomach first, out of her chair. Dallas jumped up, reached out a helping hand, and pulled. He knew it had to hurt her injured fingers to do so, but she didn't complain. He watched in silence as Julie waddled full-speed across his jail, wiping tears off as they trailed down her angry red cheeks. She yanked open the front door, letting it slam back against the wall by her umbrella, which, in her haste, she left on the floor.

Martha bestowed a dark, quelling scowl on him, as if he'd sprouted an extra head, and she would be the one to knock it off. She yanked her slicker off the wall and punched her short arms into the sleeves as if they were his chin. If a cold glare qualified as assault, he'd have more than enough grounds to arrest her.

Having vented some of her anger, she turned a kinder eye to Dallas. "Would you like to come back to the diner with me?"

The crackle of the base station reminded her that she was hoping for news. "If it's all right with Jackson, I'd like to stay by the radio."

Martha looked from her to Jackson and back again, and she didn't look as if she bought the radio story. "Maybe it's just as well. At least there's a bed here so you'll be able to get a nap. You're looking a bit peaked."

Dallas smiled weakly.

"But you have him bring you over to my place tonight. Now, be sure and cook yourself a good breakfast." She raised her voice so Jackson couldn't miss hearing her. "You don't have to cook for *him,* though, if you don't want to."

And just as suddenly as company had arrived, Jackson and Dallas were left alone, listening to the reverberating slam of the front door. He stared out the window, wondering how to defuse the situation. He looked around the room, anywhere but at the umbrella or the door. He noticed a peach-colored dress draped over the back of one of the chairs and meandered toward it.

"Nice dress," he said, testing the waters. Women, in his experience, always liked to talk about clothes.

He wasn't surprised when she didn't answer. He'd seen his mother give his father the cold shoulder a time or two. Dallas had the same look on her face; unable—or unwilling—to speak, she stared at him the same way Martha had, as if he had two heads.

He sidled closer to the dress, mentally gauging whether she could reach anything dangerous to throw at him. Not because he deserved it, but because, after years of dealing with domestic violence, he knew that's what an angry woman often did.

And she certainly looked angry. A frown puckered her eyebrows. Some very attractive golden sparks lit up her green eyes. Her arms were folded like a barricade across the red plaid, flannel shirt. Her lips formed a thin line instead of the luscious mouth he'd grown accustomed to.

She hadn't been in Green Valley long enough to understand the intricacies of his county; he'd have to explain them to her. But maybe he'd wait until she looked a little less angry and a little more receptive.

He stroked the fabric over the back of the chair, testing it with his fingers. It was soft and smooth, and would feel good against her skin. The tiny green flowers sprinkled over it would bring out the emerald color in her eyes. Pearl buttons ran from top to bottom. He wondered if she'd button all of them, or leave a few open—the top ones to show some skin beneath the delicate arch of her neck, the bottom ones to show off some leg.

"Martha has good taste," he said. Though not as good as the woman who wore a lacy, flame-red teddy to the river and hung it in his bathroom, Jackson thought. Knowing that suggestive piece of lingerie was there—and that *she* was here—had made it all but impossible to concentrate on his paperwork.

"You sound surprised."

He shrugged his shoulders, pleased that he'd been successful in giving her a few minutes to warm up to him again. She looked so much more approachable without that ugly old frown. Now if he could just do something about the rest of her body language.

"Martha seems more the utilitarian type to me."

"Me, too," she agreed softly, and he relaxed his guard. "I guess that's why *Julie* brought it."

His scowl was automatic. Unfortunately Dallas's eyebrows puckered in response, and that wasn't his goal. "She just met you. Don't tell me she already wants you to be in her wedding.''

Her lips stretched into a smile that Jackson didn't think he was supposed to like.

"No, she didn't ask me to be in her wedding."

He let out a breath of relief. "Thank goodness for that."

He was getting nowhere with the dress or the wedding as a topic of conversation. He spied the food and decided to change tactics. He lowered himself into his desk chair and helped himself to a carrot stick. He raised it to his lips and nibbled, running an assessing glance over her slender form as he did so, picturing her in the dress and him nibbling on her ear.

She sat in a chair catty-corner from him, crossed her legs, and swung one foot as though she hadn't a care in the world. "She asked me to help her organize her wedding."

He paused, caught off guard for only a moment, though he couldn't get back the picture of him nibbling his way down her neck. "I wouldn't spend too much time on it if I were you. There's not going to be any wedding."

"But—"

"Trust me, Dallas. There'll be no wedding between my brother and a McKane."

"Why not?"

"Because McKanes can't be trusted."

As he saw it, he had two options. One, turn on the charm and get to know her while she was in Green Valley waiting to hear who she was and where she belonged—a mighty fine option to his way of thinking. It could take days with the way the flood was playing havoc with everything. Or two, get her out of town immediately before she did exactly what Julie wanted and organized a wedding between the feuding clans in two days.

Normally, he wouldn't be worried about anyone pulling that off. The Ridgefields and the McKanes had been at odds for over seventy years. But she was the Budget Lady, and he'd heard enough about the damn Budget Lady and her damn book from his brother Roman to make his head ache. It seemed to be general consensus that the lady in question could accomplish anything with very little.

He shuddered. He couldn't imagine anything worse than a roomful of Ridgefields and McKanes. Except maybe Dallas never speaking to him again. And what better way to keep her talking to him than working together to find out her identity? Finding out she was the Budget Lady couldn't be giving her very much satisfaction.

"Maybe the library's got a copy of one of your books."

She didn't respond as he'd hoped. Instead of the bright-eyed "Really?" he'd hoped for, she said, "You didn't have to make Julie cry."

"She's a big girl." He could see he was going to have to work harder at this. He forged ahead while she remained speechless at what she apparently considered a very insensitive remark, if her openmouthed stare was any indication. "I figure if your picture's in your books, there's probably a biography, too."

Dallas's foot stopped swinging. She uncrossed her legs. Two very good signs as far as Jackson was concerned. That image of him nibbling on her neck was coming back.

"Maybe we could find out where you're from, at least, and narrow our search a bit. And I could get word to your publisher that we need to know who you are."

She sat up straight and unfolded her arms. Was it possible that within the next hour she might know something about herself?

"Do you have a library here?" She heard a slight, trembling hint of hope in her voice, saw it reflected in Jackson's eyes. She also felt a little like a traitor as her concern over Julie took a back seat to the immediate prospect of finding out who she was.

"It's a half mile or so down the hill."

"And you think they might have a copy of my book?"

"Books," he corrected. "You have a whole line of them."

"I do?" She thought he sounded personally acquainted with her work and she began to hope she really was the Budget Lady. To think he'd held something in his hands that she'd created, before they'd ever met, was mind-boggling at the very least.

He leaned toward her, his dark eyes once again as soft as warm chocolate, and she forgot they'd been at odds a moment ago. She couldn't even remember what they'd been arguing about.

"My mother used the one on how to make slipcovers for furniture."

"Your mother has a copy?" That seemed so personal. His own mother was more acquainted with her than she was herself.

"She donated it to the library when she was done. You're pretty popular among thrifty-minded ladies with good taste."

He grinned, and she wasn't sure she was ready to leave Green Valley. Yes, she wanted to find out who she was and go home, but she also wanted to get to know him well enough to know whether she wanted to pack, turn around and come right back.

She popped up out of her chair. "What're we waiting for?"

He rose in front of her, still wearing that grin and moving far too slowly. "I don't know about you, but I'm waiting for someone to cook me a hot breakfast."

Cook? "Not now!"

"I wouldn't want you to get cranky or anything," he teased.

"I don't even know if I know how to cook. Let's go to the library first."

He raised his hands to stop her. "Look, I don't even know if the library's open."

"What time is it?"

"It's not the time. It's the flood. Our librarian may have better things to do today. You cook breakfast. I'll run over there and see what I can find."

"But—" She followed him to the door, tagging along on his heels, hoping he might change his mind when he noticed her persistence. "I could help."

He grasped her arms and stopped her from charging out the door in front of him. "You *can* help. You're the Budget Lady, right? Trust me, you've written books on cooking, too, and I'm looking forward to rushing right back here and sampling something delicious."

He opened the door just wide enough to slip through and closed it firmly behind him. Dallas stamped her bare foot, then regretted it as pain shot up the same leg the stringer had yanked on. His truck roared to life, then pulled away quickly, leaving her with an unexplained, hollow feeling in her chest.

She was left in an empty jail, with ham and eggs and potatoes and an antique, wood-burning stove. If Jackson could jump into a raging river for her, the least she could do was cook him a meal. But how? She racked her brain, but could find nothing remotely helpful except that microwave ovens had been in existence for years, and she didn't see one around anywhere. She adopted a very businesslike attitude, walked over to the stove as if daring it to defy her, and tested it with her fingertip the same way she'd seen Martha do.

It didn't help. She hadn't a clue whether burning her index finger meant the stove was too hot, hot enough, or almost hot enough. Jackson was supposed to have brought more wood in with him, according to Martha's orders, but he either hadn't heard her or had neglected to do so.

She found small pieces of split wood in a metal trash can around the corner of the building under the eave, where she could walk without getting much mud on her bare feet. On her way back in with an armload of wood, she held her feet under the roof runoff to rinse them clean. The weather or the mud, or both, got her mind off Jackson and back in that same rut she'd been in when she'd been staring out the window earlier. She chalked the moody change up to rainy days.

She burned her thumb and another finger opening the door on the stove before she realized she needed to use a towel. She threw in a couple chunks of wood. If she'd written a book on cooking, she doubted it covered antique appliances. She wondered if her publisher would be interested in such a book, but then how many of these old stoves could still be in use?

The first few pieces of wood caught nicely. She didn't want the fire to go out when the potatoes were half-done, so she threw in the rest and shut the door.

She searched around the stove and through Jackson's desk, looking for a potato peeler and a knife. She got distracted by the framed photographs on his desk. Two parents and four brothers, from the looks of them. The boys all had the same dark hair and dark eyes, but she could easily place Jackson as the eldest. His mother was short and stocky; clearly Jackson had gotten the breadth of his chest and shoulders from her. His father was tall and rangy; his contribution was evident in Jackson's six-foot frame. He'd inherited the best of both, obviously.

She remembered what she was supposed to be doing when her hand landed on a knife in the second drawer. She scrubbed the potatoes in the bathroom sink and elected not to try peeling them with a knife; she already had enough cuts on her fingers. Once they were sliced thinly in the only skillet she could find, a big, black, cast-iron one, she set the ham slice on top of them.

"Not so bad, if I do say so myself." Maybe she *had* written a cookbook.

She'd been so engrossed with the potatoes that she hadn't heard the front door open, and she jumped when it banged shut.

"Did you find a book?" she asked as she whirled around.

A very old man, thin as a rail, hesitated near the door, looking just as surprised to see her as she was to see him. Then, whipping his baseball cap off his head and smoothing his sparse white hair with bony fingers, he limped toward her in a friendly enough fashion. A wet, German shepherd pup looked miserable huddled under his arm, cradled against the slicker that dripped a dark, wet trail across the wooden floor.

"Howdy, ma'am." He studied her scarecrow outfit with an openly curious expression, as if he knew she wasn't from around there, but couldn't imagine why she'd be dressed in such a fashion. "Name's Jasper."

"Hello."

"I was lookin' fer the sheriff."

The puppy whimpered, and Dallas felt herself drawn from the stove to meet them in the middle of the room. Her hands reached out, as if they had a life of their own, to take the pup. "Is he yours?"

"Naw." He seemed more than pleased to pawn the dog off on her. "He found me last night, by the river. I was jest comin' to ask the sheriff where we're puttin' the live ones."

The puppy sniffed Dallas's fingers, and drops of water flew off his tail as he wagged it in response to his first impression of her.

"Gosh, he's a wet one, isn't he?" Dallas hadn't ever been in a jail before, at least not that she knew of. She didn't know whether to offer to take a message or have the old man sit and wait.

"You best be gettin' a towel afore he gets you soaked."

With a wave of his hand, he urged her to go find one. "I'll jest be lookin' around...er...waitin' around out here. Yeah, that's it. I'll be waitin' fer the sheriff. Don't you never mind 'bout me."

The only towel was the one by the stove, and she didn't hesitate to sit on the floor and rub the pup dry with it. She paid little attention to Jasper nosing around as the pup turned playful, grabbing the towel in his sharp little teeth as if he—at about twenty pounds—could actually wrestle it away from her. She played tug-of-war with him for a little while, knowing it would get his body heat up, and then, when he plopped down on his tummy, she picked him up. He cuddled close into her flannel shirt and yawned.

"I think I'll be gettin' along now," Jasper said as he opened the front door.

She rose to her feet, surprised to find she had forgotten all about the old man, and asked, "Does he have a name?"

"I been callin' 'im Sonnet."

"Sonnet?" She wasn't sure she heard Jasper correctly through his Ozark drawl.

"You know, like Shakespeare's sonnets? But you can call 'im anything you want, I s'pose."

"Sonnet, huh?" She gave the shepherd pup a kiss on top of its furry head.

With a renewed burst of energy, he jumped up and licked her chin just as the wind blew the door out of Jasper's grasp.

It slammed hard against the inside wall, cracking like a sharp clap of thunder. The smell of rain and mud rushed in. The pup licked her chin again, and Dallas found herself in a world she didn't recognize.

She stared down into a tan-and-white beagle face from long ago. Its fur was soaked and muddy. Its ears hung with dismay. Its dark brown eyes were wide and its little body trembled with cold and fear.

In a trancelike state, Dallas squeezed her eyes shut tight, then opened them slowly. Mud covered everything as rain fell all around her, lit only by flashing red lights on top of red fire trucks. She stood as still as a statue, staring at a narrow street which ran under her feet and ended right before her eyes, smothered by a thick layer of gooey muck. Everywhere around her, people ran back and forth, carrying furniture, clothing, and small children.

But there were no houses. Just rain and mud.

And, because of them, she didn't see the fire.

Chapter Five

Jackson parked in front of the red brick, white-shuttered library, pleased to see Millie's blue station wagon in its customary space. There were no other cars there, but he wasn't surprised. People had a lot on their minds these days.

He bounded up the concrete steps, skipping every other one. He wanted to get back to Dallas and breakfast as soon as possible and in that order. He'd already spent the night wrapped around her, sharing no more than what was proper on such short acquaintance.

It was fortunate he hadn't seen the red teddy before he crawled into bed beside her. Knowing he'd been spooned up against a woman who wore such sexy lingerie would have kept him awake and aching all night.

Now he looked forward to sampling a meal made by her own hands, right after he checked out one of her books.

The door was unlocked, but the library was dimly lit and had a vacant feel as he stepped across the threshold.

"Millie?" His call was no more than a loud whisper, thanks, no doubt, to years of conditioning as a child about being quiet in the library. He walked soft-footed past the checkout desk and into the first of the library's two rooms, then put a little more force behind his voice. "Millie?"

In the adjacent room, he heard a book hit the floor, followed by a muttered curse. The normally sedate and composed Millie barreled around the corner, taking Jackson by surprise with her long, red hair flying free from its usual barrette. Her conservative skirt-and-blouse attire had been replaced by snug jeans and a painted T-shirt, and he wondered why Roman couldn't fall for her instead of Julie McKane.

"Oh!" Millie skidded to an abrupt stop. She jabbed a lock of hair behind one ear, balancing a stack of books against her chest as she did so. "I didn't expect anyone to be standing there."

"Sorry if I startled you. I called out." He grinned sheepishly. "I guess I wasn't very loud."

A smile tugged at the corners of her mouth as she took a close look at his face. "You've either been pulling an ungrateful bobcat out of the river, or else you're here to check out a book on shaving techniques."

"Only if it covers useless old mirrors."

"Sorry. Hey, I hear the wedding's back on."

She smiled when she mentioned it, so he didn't suppose there'd be any chance of getting her interested in his little brother. Maybe she'd like Harrison. Then Jackson wouldn't have to risk another brother falling for a McKane.

"How'd you hear that already?"

"On the CB on my way over here," she said with an of-course tone.

"Terrific," he muttered.

"It's about time for this feud nonsense to be over. Why, the other day, I thought your mother and Julie's were going to come to blows over some silly little thing in the market. I'm glad to see you gave in."

"I didn't *give*—" He took a deep, cleansing breath and decided to stick to the business at hand. "Never mind. I'm looking for a book."

"Uh-oh."

He didn't like the sound of that. "Computer down again?"

"Not exactly." She set her stack of books on the nearest table, flipped on the overhead lights, and waved in the general direction of the bookshelves.

They were all bare. It was eerie to look right through rows of empty shelves and see the far wall, especially when he'd never wanted a book so much in his life as he did now.

"I'm going to assume these weren't all stolen," he said.

"The mayor told me to move them all in case the river got this high." She laughed at Jackson's surprised look.

"Did you remind him you're on a hill here?"

She rolled her eyes. "I even offered to build an ark, but he insisted."

"So where are they?" He raked his fingers through his hair, hoping that Millie had some plan of organization, dreading the answer before he heard it.

"All over the county. I stood outside and handed boxes of books to anybody driving past that lived on high ground. All I have left are the romance novels."

"You need me to take a box?"

"Goodness no!" she cried protectively. "I'm leaving them on the shelves and the key under the mat."

"But the mayor—"

"The mayor has no idea what kind of uprising he'll have on his hands if the ladies can't get good books to read."

He sighed. "And all I wanted was a copy of a Budget Lady book. You wouldn't happen to know her real name, would you?"

"'Fraid not." Millie perked right up and, like a loyal Budget Lady fan, asked, "Is it true she's over at the jail?"

He nodded, not surprised word had spread already. News of the Budget Lady in Green Valley was at least as big as the news about a Ridgefield-McKane wedding. Maybe bigger.

"Did you know she's Thelia's granddaughter?" Millie asked.

Jackson imagined he looked somewhat confused. Besides not knowing who the devil Thelia was, he had a sudden hole in the pit of his stomach just thinking that Dallas might be leaving soon.

He wanted her to remember who she was. He wanted her to be reunited with her grandmother. But with that realization, the possibility of her leaving hit him harder than he'd expected. That, of course, was because he'd purposely not thought about it in the first place. He'd been very good about, too, and now he was paying for it.

"Come on, Jackson, you know Thelia...of 'Thelia's Tips.' She's a household name."

He pulled a notebook out of his breast pocket, along with a pen. "Great." He didn't sound excited, even to himself. "How do I get ahold of her?"

"Oh."

He noticed it wasn't a very hopeful sounding "Oh."

"I'm afraid she's been dead for years."

He stabbed the pen at his pocket, missed, and had to try again.

"I'm on my way home," Millie continued. "I'll get on the CB and ask around. If I hear anything, I'll let you know."

He hoped she didn't hear any more about a wedding. "Thanks, Millie."

He drove back to the jail, thinking about how Dallas would have a delicious meal waiting for him and how he'd have no book for her. He was sorry now that he'd left her there alone, waiting, probably getting her hopes up by the minute. Her green eyes would be all lit up with eagerness to read her biography. He never liked being the bearer of bad news and he was particularly hating it today.

He toyed with different ways of telling her. Beat around the bush? Give her hope that Millie was checking? Straight out with no sugarcoating? He was practically on top of the jail when he found he had a much bigger problem on his hands.

Smoke poured out of the jail's side window. Dark smoke, curling up into the treetops, obscuring the leaves. He sped up to the steps, brought the truck to a skidding halt, and threw open his door. He rammed the lever into Park, but didn't bother with any formalities such as removing the keys or closing the door behind him.

He had to get to Dallas before it was too late. He should have known better than to leave her alone. He shouldn't have expected her to know how to cook on an unfamiliar stove.

He burst through the front door. "Dallas!"

He crouched over and, through a haze of smoke, saw her sitting in his desk chair. She cradled something to her chest, rocking back and forth. Was that humming he heard? Whatever she was holding wiggled and whimpered, and he heard her soothe it. Then she started coughing.

He rushed to her side. When he saw she was holding a puppy, he took it from her, set it on the floor, and reached down to scoop her into his arms. He'd carry her out to fresh air, then come back and tend to the smoke.

"No!" she screeched, sounding more like a young girl than the woman he knew. "Where's my doggie?"

"Easy," he murmured, trying to get his arms around her writhing body.

She squirmed like a child, too, all rubber-bodied with no fear of falling as she thrashed and nearly slipped out of his grasp.

"Dallas, let me get you out of—"

"Here, Penny! Here, Penny!"

Her strength surprised him, though it shouldn't have. He remembered how strong she'd been when he'd pulled her from the river. She coughed again, pulling in more smoky air.

"Let me get you outside."

"Penny!" Her screech nearly split his eardrum.

"Who the hell's Penny?"

"My doggie."

"She'll follow us."

His explanation went unheeded as she grabbed the pup and dragged it up under her chin. He scooped them both up, wondering how the hell she'd gotten that attached to anything in the last half hour. And wishing it was he that she cared so much about.

He carried them to the open door. The air inside the jail had cleared considerably with the added ventilation. He crouched on the threshold, leaning against the doorjamb, filling his lungs with fresh air before going back inside, holding Dallas on his makeshift lap. She was none the worse for wear, except that she seemed to have gained a damp, smelly dog. She wasn't on fire. He didn't see any flames anywhere. With the urgency momentarily gone, he found himself contemplating a nice kiss from her for running to her rescue, even if it was somewhat premature. He could see it now . . .

He would set her on her feet, but hold her gently within the circle of his arms. She'd look up at him, her green eyes wide and beautiful behind all those dark lashes. She'd reach up and pull his head down until their lips met—

"Where's all that smoke coming from?" she asked as if she'd just noticed it, no longer sounding childish.

He cradled her protectively against his chest as he surveyed the room. It was just a building. Dallas was safe.

"My guess would be the stove."

She winced. "Ohhh. Breakfast."

If he couldn't have breakfast, he sure hoped he was going to get that kiss. The puppy wriggled free, jumped up, and licked him full on the mouth.

He tumbled them both onto the floor.

Dallas was shocked. One minute she'd been huddled over in the rain, cradling Penny, the beagle she'd raised from a pup, and crying for...

She thought hard, but the more effort she put into remembering whom she'd been crying for, the deeper the information seemed to hide. It lurked just around the corner, teasing her into trying to follow, but eluding her all the same.

And the next minute, Jackson had scooped her into his arms. She'd felt comforted, until he'd ripped her only connection with her past out of her arms and dropped it onto the floor. Now they were both there. Only it wasn't Penny, it was Sonnet. And it wasn't raining on her; she was indoors.

"Jackson?"

He grabbed the towel lying on the floor first, then the skillet and rushed out the back door, leaving it wide open. A cold draft blew through the building, clearing the smoke and chilling her. She missed his arms around her, holding her, soothing her. She missed the deep rumble of his voice coming from his chest, letting her know he was there to rescue her. But did he have to dump her on the floor?

It was just as well. How could she feel so strongly about him when she didn't even know who she was? Whether she was married or attached? They'd just met, for heaven's sake. He runs to her rescue, and she drools over him like some lovesick schoolgirl?

She realized there was more coming into play here than worrying over whether she was married. She didn't feel married. But she looked at Jackson now and felt an overwhelming urge to run in the opposite direction. And she didn't understand why.

JACKSON THREW the burnt food out the back door. It was too far gone for human consumption. The animals were welcome to it. With the floodwaters moving a lot of them out of their homes and feeding grounds, it was possible they'd carry it off, and it would do something some good. He scraped the cast-iron skillet clean, then took a look at the stove. He vented it so it could cool down some before he tried cooking on it again. Other than that, everything looked fine.

"What happened?" he asked as he sat on the floor beside her.

She shook her head absently for a moment, and he could see she was very confused about something.

"How long were you gone?" she asked.

"About half an hour."

She sighed and stared at the puppy sniffing around in the mud outside. "Just after you left, a man came by with Sonnet. He said he found him down by the river."

"Sonnet?"

"Yeah, some skinny old guy in a slicker and a baseball cap."

That description fit several old men in Green Valley. "Sonnet, huh?"

She smiled then. "Like Shakespeare's sonnets, he said."

"Mm-hmm. That'd have to be Jasper."

"He doesn't look the sort to read Shakespeare."

"Does he look like a moonshiner?"

"How would I know?"

"Well, he is. And unless he was under arrest, the last place I'd expect to find Jasper is in my jail. What did he want?"

Her smile disappeared, along with the light in her eyes. He leaned closer, letting his arm brush against her shoulder for whatever measure of comfort it would bring.

"I'm not sure. I think he was looking for a place to leave the puppy, but then . . ." She seemed to be trying to remember something. "I think I remember him saying he was going to look around for something."

He glanced around his jail. The guns were still under lock and key. That was no surprise, since rifles were more common than money in his county. If Jasper had been looking for something, Jackson had no idea what it was.

Dallas turned toward him then, and he was pleased to see a glimmer of life back in her eyes. "You want me to try making breakfast again?"

He patted her arm. It was supposed to be a comforting gesture. Instead, he let his hand linger longer and longer on her sleeve, then skim lower until he was holding her hand in his. He squeezed it gently. He laughed quietly, whether because the idea of her cooking seemed funny or because he was happy to be touching her, he wasn't prepared to analyze. He just went with the moment and thanked his lucky stars that he got it.

"Maybe some other time," he declined. "When I can keep an eye on you."

Sonnet wandered back into the jail, soaking wet, his tail drooping. He headed straight for Dallas.

She felt a connection to this pup that she couldn't explain. He'd licked her, and she'd remembered some of her past. Obviously there'd been a dog she'd been very close to—a beagle named Penny—though she couldn't remember how long ago. She hoped, after spending a little more time with Sonnet, she'd remember even more.

She didn't mind him being wet, but she wasn't thrilled with the muddy paws. She held him at arm's length and headed for the bathroom sink while Jackson saw to breakfast. When she was done in there, she carried him out near the stove and started drying him with the towel again.

"What the heck are you doing?" he demanded.

"I don't want him to catch cold."

"If I wasn't sure you were a city woman before, I sure as hell am now."

"You're just now figuring that out?" She smiled at his obtuseness; talk about the proverbial ostrich! She'd known she wasn't a country girl in the first hour after he'd rescued her.

"Farm dogs live outdoors," he said.

"He's not a farm dog."

"The hell he's not."

"How could you possibly know that?"

"Easy. Nobody in this county would keep anything that size in the house."

"He's just a puppy."

"He's going to get as big as a horse."

"He's soaking wet."

"That usually happens when it's raining."

She cuddled the fluffed-and-dried pup against her chest and stood up, daring Jackson to try to win this argument. She needed Sonnet to stay with her. She needed to comfort him as well as be comforted by his presence, by the hope that he'd somehow trigger her memory again.

"Food's ready. Put him out."

She peered into the skillet. "Looks like there's enough there to share with him."

He placed the spatula so precisely on the edge of the skillet that Dallas knew he was stalling, debating how to get his way with the least amount of fuss. When he turned, she saw a steely look in his eyes, a square, determined clench in his jaw.

"I have never cooked for a dog," he said slowly, obviously trying to control his temper. "I never will cook for a dog."

She maintained a calm, rational air. "He's got to eat."

"I'll find him a nice home where they have dog food."

"No!" She must have said it with more conviction than she knew, because Jackson stopped suddenly and stood very still. "I... I mean, I'd like to keep him."

"No." He took a step toward her.

She moved back one step. "Perhaps I didn't phrase that quite right."

His eyebrows rose in a questioning arch, suggesting that he agreed with her on that one. "Perhaps not."

"I should have said that I *am* going to keep him."

"Is that so?" He advanced again, slowly.

"Yes. Yes, that's so." She wrapped her arms tighter around the pup, as if that would stop Jackson from taking him. He was big enough to do anything he wanted. If she was going to hang on to Sonnet, she'd have to do something more than this.

"Put him out so we can eat."

"I'm not hungry." Her head clunked into the iron bar on the holding cell she came up short on space.

"You put him out or I will." He reached for the pup.

She had no choice really. She darted into the cell, slamming the steel door behind her with a clang.

THE FIRST THING that went through Jackson's mind was *Damn, she does get cranky when she's hungry.*

The second, for which he was much more grateful, was that he may have lost the battle, but he'd won the war. For now, anyway, she wasn't thinking about Ridgefield-McKane wedding plans, the mere thought of which made him shudder. He felt a little safer on that score for the moment.

He left her sitting in the cell, looking like a waif sent to the corner for punishment. One part of him wanted to go to her, take her in his arms, hold her, tell her it would be all right.

Instead, he took his time, wavering between cooling off over her insurrection and being grateful she'd found something more important to think about, while he set the desk for their meal. Two mugs of coffee, paper napkins, old utensils with red plastic handles, paper plates—all the comforts of home. A salt shaker and a jar of humidity-caked sugar, and they were ready.

"You can come out now," he said.

She sat cross-legged on the cot, her back against the cinder block wall, Sonnet snoozing on her lap. "Do you give up?"

He meandered over to the cell door. "This isn't about giving up."

"Then I'm not coming out."

He wanted to open the door, run in and kiss the pout off her lips. He had all he could do not to smile. "You need to eat."

"So does he."

Her hand smoothed the puppy's fur, running over it lovingly, tenderly. Jackson thought he might like some of that attention for himself, but he sure wasn't going to get it this way.

"When we're done, I'll find him some food," he promised.

Her scowl was quickly replaced with a hopeful look. "I can cook him an egg and some potatoes."

"I don't think I should let you near the stove again."

Her cheek dimpled with a smile. "Gosh, if I'm a city girl, I should probably view that as very good news."

He reached for the steel door as he heard a truck pull up out front. The last thing he needed was for Martha to find Dallas in the cell. She'd think he'd locked her in there until she agreed not to help with the wedding. She'd never feed him again.

"Don't open that door if you're thinking of putting him outside."

He hesitated briefly, but it was just long enough for her to spring off the cot, grab a bar on the door with one hand and a stationary bar with the other, brace her feet against an upright, and hold tight. He was amused that she considered herself any kind of challenge for him. He wasn't amused to think he could get caught by Martha any second now.

"Dallas," he warned with a growl in his voice that even he hadn't ever heard before, which was no surprise. To the best of his recollection, no one had ever defied him in such a blatant manner. Everyone in Green Valley had more sense.

The front door of the jail opened, then shut with a bang. Jackson closed his eyes and prayed it wasn't Martha. Anybody but Martha.

"What the hell?" It was Roman.

Thank you, God.

"What's she doing in there?" Roman's tan-and-brown uniform matched Jackson's, except that it was slightly crumpled, and he'd rolled his unbuttoned sleeves up his forearms. Over his shoulder he carried a black, rigid, medium-size bag which bounced against his hip as he crossed the room.

Jackson would have reprimanded his brother for taking liberties with the dress code again, except that he was just so darn grateful it was Roman who'd come in. He pulled the cell door open, swinging Dallas outward with it, not even noticing that she no longer put up any resistance.

"Julie said—"

"And just what did Julie say *this time?*" Jackson demanded as he wheeled on his younger brother.

Roman advanced on his taller, broader brother as if he felt evenly matched. "I couldn't catch it all," he said through gritted teeth. "It was difficult to understand her through all her tears."

Jackson stood his ground as Roman squared off in front of him. He'd never seen his brother quite so angry, and he idly wondered if they might end up in a wrestling match on the floor.

"What the hell did you yell at her for, Jackson?"

"I never yelled," he answered in a calm tone, hoping to placate Roman.

"She says you did."

"Dallas was right here. She'll tell you. Dallas?" He was so sure she'd back him up that he didn't even look at her to see what kind of mood she was in.

Roman glanced over Jackson's shoulder at the woman Julie had told him about. The moment stretched out as he observed her. Concern edged into his voice. "Hey, is she all right?"

Jackson spun on his heel to see what had Roman concerned. "Oh, hell."

DALLAS DIDN'T HEAR any of their conversation. She'd gotten a funny feeling—one she was beginning to recognize— as soon as Jackson had stepped out of her way and she'd gotten a look at the newcomer.

He was a smaller, more compact version of Jackson. Also more relaxed as far as the uniform went, with his sleeves rolled up and creases that didn't look as if they would shatter if he sat down. He toted a black bag, which he let drop to the floor as he squared off in front of Jackson.

Her grip on the bars loosened, and she slid to the floor. The puppy, who'd been awakened by all the ruckus and was ready to play, tugged on the ties on the front of her flannel shirt.

She had difficulty seeing where she was this time—she didn't know if it was because of pouring rain or a fuzzy memory—but she could make out two small girls. They were playing with Penny the beagle, laughing, giggling, tumbling over and over. She couldn't tell exactly where they were, either. Everything was faded, nearly black and white. She knew she wasn't either of the girls, but that she was very close to them. And that she didn't feel like playing or laughing.

She squeezed her eyes closed tighter, trying to focus harder, to bring the picture in closer. Again she failed, but this time she felt all her hair stand on end, prickling her skin on the back of her neck, on her arms and legs. Fear of success? Or fear of failure?

A crack of thunder sounded nearby. She clapped her hands over her ears.

"Dallas?"

Someone tugged at her hands.

"Jackson, what's the matter with her?"

Arms encircled her. She felt a strong, hard chest. She was warm and dry.

"Shh, it's okay," he crooned. "You're safe now. Nothing can hurt you. You're safe here with me."

He rocked her until the picture of the two small girls and Penny was replaced by the stark reality of the cinder block jail and the bare wood floor on which she was sitting.

"Oh, my God," she whispered faintly.

"What is it? Did you remember something?"

She trembled in his arms. Her hand shook as she reached up to feel a teardrop run down her cheek. Jackson brushed her hand away, then, with the pad of his thumb, he erased the damp trail.

"Tell me before you forget, darlin'."

She heard the pain in his voice and knew he was suffering along with her. And he didn't even know how wrong it was for him to call her that. He wouldn't know until she told him. She didn't want to say the words.

She had no choice. "Jackson..." Her voice caught on a sob.

"What is it? What do you remember?"

"I've got two children."

Where, she had no idea.

Chapter Six

Jackson didn't mind the idea of Dallas having two children. Little girls were cute and cuddly and sweet. He was sure any little girls Dallas had would be, anyway. He wondered if they had dark, reddish brown hair, as she did. Of course they wouldn't have any other eye color than her emerald green.

It occurred to him that she could have boys. But when he pictured them, they possessed his dark eyes and dark hair, and, as his mother said, the mischievous Ridgefield smile that could charm a snake.

What he did mind was the thought that where there were children, there might be a husband. Some other man holding her, caressing her, coming home at night and sharing the family with her—those were not appealing pictures. They'd have supper together. She'd encourage the little girls to show their father, who remained a ghostly image in Jackson's mind, their artwork. They'd bathe them and put them to bed together.

He was torturing himself, he knew. He shouldn't want someone else's wife. If his mother's religion hadn't taught him right from wrong, growing up with a father who was a judge certainly had. But damn it, he did want her. Badly.

"Jackson, are you all right?"

"Huh? Oh . . . Roman. Yeah, I'm fine."

"You don't look fine."

"Well, I am." He'd have to do better than growl at his brother if he expected to be believed.

"If you were fine, we'd still be arguing." Roman gave up and kicked the black bag out of his way, sending it sliding across the hardwood floor with a noisy scrape. He strode to the front door. "I'll be back when you're more in the mood."

"Roman?"

"Yeah?"

"I've got some work to finish up here, then I'll need you to take over. Say, late this afternoon?" Jackson suggested.

Roman retraced his steps, surprise clearly written on his face as he looked down at Jackson, still sitting on the floor with his arms around Dallas. "You're leaving me in charge?"

"That's right."

His eyebrows narrowed as suspicion warred with eagerness. "You always leave Harrison in charge."

"And you always complain about it."

"If you think this'll make up for what you did to Julie—"

"This has nothing to do with Julie," Jackson cut him off before he got going again. He didn't want to fight now. He wanted to get off the cold floor and hold Dallas in his lap in the chair until she felt better. He wanted to be alone with her. "You want the responsibility or not?"

"Hell, yes."

"Good." He watched Roman hesitate before he turned to leave, obviously unsure whether this was for real. He'd badgered Jackson for the opportunity to prove himself a capable deputy often enough. "And button up your sleeves before you come back."

Roman had his sleeves unrolled and buttoned before he was halfway to the front door. Without missing a step, he glanced at the smoky walls and said, "Nice color. Very original the way you did some areas darker than others."

Jackson ignored his laughter, which managed to linger even after the door closed behind him. He slipped an arm beneath Dallas and started to rise, lifting her off the floor, but she'd have none of it.

"I'm fine," she said, pushing away from him. "Did you get the book?"

He was big and strong enough to stop her, but he didn't. He wanted to give her some sense of control over her life right now, as this predicament could be nothing but difficult for her. No name, no past, no clothes—he didn't know if he would handle it as well as she'd been doing so far.

"Sorry. They don't have any right now." He watched her scoop up the puppy as he'd wanted to do with her. She cradled it against her chest, as he'd been doing with her. "I thought you might want me to hold you a little while longer."

She rose to her feet and took a step toward the lone cot in the cell.

"At least come out and eat." When she didn't comply, he gently took her hand in his and led her out of the cell. She followed him to his desk without resistance. "You go ahead. I'm going to call the library over in Clark County."

She nodded vacantly, and he smeared a piece of hard, dry toast with jelly and put it in her hand to get her started. The breakfast had turned cold, but it was still food, and he didn't think she'd notice, anyway. He kept a watchful eye on her as he dialed the phone. If she broke down and started crying, he'd hold her no matter what she wanted. The puppy ate more of the toast than she did, but she was starting to smile again, so he said nothing. He knew if he did, it would come out sounding as if he were jealous, which he wasn't about to admit. When he couldn't get through to the Clark County Library, he hung up.

"What's wrong?" she asked.

"My best guess would be that the phone lines are down between here and there."

"How long before they fix them?"

He grinned as the puppy swiped another bite of her toast, then wondered what had come over him that he would find that amusing. He'd been raised to know that dogs belonged outdoors where they could guard the animals, not indoors sharing breakfast, and especially not the same piece of bread.

"Let me put it this way," he answered. "I can walk there faster than we get repairs out here. Roman'll be here later. We'll drive over then."

"We?" Hope lit up her eyes again.

"Sure. You don't think I'd leave you here again, do you?"

A smile teased the corner of her lips as she gave him her most innocent look. "You wouldn't be afraid I'd burn down your jail while you were gone, would you?"

ROMAN ARRIVED at the jail late that afternoon with Julie in tow. Gone were the tears she'd exhibited when she'd fled earlier that day. They'd been replaced by a firm set to her jaw that boded trouble for Jackson if he so much as frowned at her.

"You don't have to pick on me. I'm not staying," she said, her chin in the air. "I just wanted to bring Dallas some duck shoes and tell her I'm on my way over to Madame Celeste's to consult with her about the best time for the wedding."

Jackson bit his tongue to keep quiet.

"Who's Madame Celeste?" Dallas asked.

"She's the most wonderful woman!" Julie's face lit up. "She knows all sorts of things, like the best time to move, or when to start a new job. And the best time to get married."

Jackson glanced at Roman to see how this new development sat with him. Madame Celeste, who billed herself as a psychic astrologer, was the most controversial character in Green Valley. A hundred years ago, a woman such as she would have been considered nothing more than an opportunistic gypsy and run out of town. But she'd latched on to the New Age terminology and used it to her advantage. The Ridgefields had never put store in such nonsense, but Roman seemed quite unruffled by Julie's interest. If he wasn't careful, his younger brother would turn into a McKane right before his eyes. This wedding was just wrong, pure and simple.

And Dallas? Jackson was pleased to see hesitation on her face—as if she had more sense—but it quickly disappeared. He may have even imagined it in the hopes that she wasn't taken in by such chicanery.

"What do you want me to do?" Roman asked him, effectively ending his eavesdropping on the women's conversation.

"Jasper brought a puppy by that he said he found at the river. I want you and Harrison to take the chopper in that direction and see if you can locate the still from the air."

"Uh-uh. There's no way in hell I'm going up with that kamikaze. Besides, I already found what's left of their still. Just a fifty-five-gallon drum and a lot of broken jars."

"How about the coil?"

Roman shook his head. "It could've been washed down—"

"How about jar lids?"

Roman vented his frustration in a long, drawn-out sigh that said they'd covered this ground before. "You're a fanatic."

"Yeah, well, you're not the one who'll be standing in front of the judge looking stupid. He doesn't cut me any slack just because he's our father, you know."

"I'm still not going up with Harrison."

"Oh, hell, Roman, he hasn't killed anybody yet."

Jackson was ready to take Dallas and leave, but she was taking her time getting the duck shoes on. They were too large, he could tell that at a glance, but they'd have to do until something better came along.

Elvin Brooks opened the door and hesitated on the threshold. After a long moment, he leaned forward and shuffled his way across the floor. Jackson idly wondered how many pairs of shoes the man wore out each year.

He zeroed in on Jackson and blurted out, "Sheriff, someone's been snatching my chickens."

Jackson supposed everything Brooks did took him so long that he'd dispensed with all the social niceties years ago. "Now, Mr. Brooks, you know I can't come out to your place and sit there all night just to catch a varmint."

"Ain't no four-legged varmint."

"Well, you tell Roman all about it, then. He's in charge."

"You're the sheriff."

"And I've got business in Clark County. Roman's my deputy. He'll take care of you."

Brooks scowled in Roman's direction and made no effort to lower his voice. "He ain't even dry behind the ears."

Dry or not, Jackson left the two of them to argue it out. He took Dallas by the hand and fled the jail for the first time since he'd been elected, wondering what had come over him, knowing it was Dallas but now wanting to admit it. He even left Julie behind instead of waiting around to make sure she went on her way; she was a distracting influence on Roman.

"THERE HE GOES," Jasper whispered to Elmer and Otis.

The three skinny old men were crowded into a shadowy corner on a porch across the street. They weren't related, but age had turned them into carbon copies of each other, with their sparse white hair and sun-wrinkled skin above denim overalls and plaid flannel shirts. The overhang protected them from the late afternoon rain as well as Jackson's observant eye.

"What'd I tell you?"

"She's be-yutiful." Elmer stepped forward for a closer look, only to be yanked back into hiding by the other two grabbing at his shoulder straps.

"What're you tryin' to do? Get us caught?" Jasper cried.

They watched in silence while Jackson held the truck door for Dallas, and then the three of them shrank back even farther into the recesses as the sheriff drove by.

"I reckon if they're leavin' together, we can spread out and find us some jars without much worry," Jasper said.

"What about the other two? Harrison and Roman?" Elmer asked.

Jasper shook his head. He'd known Elmer and Otis his whole life, but he couldn't say they were the brightest two souls in the world.

"And he didn't take her in the direction of his cabin," Otis informed them. "No tellin' when he'll be back."

Jasper ran a hand over his whiskered chin, refusing to admit that their questions made him think the situation through further. "All right, tell you what we'll do. I checked the jail fer jars and didn't find none. We need to check ever'where else, but it'll look a mite suspicious if we spend a lot of time in town all of a sudden like."

"Why? Ever'body knows our still 'washed away.'"

"Elmer, you done drunk too much of your own 'shine. The sheriff'll know we're lookin' fer jars and such unless we got another excuse."

"Oh." He ran his thumbs up and down inside the bib of his overalls. "Like what?"

Jasper continued to rasp his hand over the stubble on his chin for a moment. "Like strays," he said with sudden insight.

"Huh?"

"I already left Sonnet at the jail and looked fer jars there. There's plentya strays around with the river pushin' people outta their homes. We'll keep bringin' 'em inta town, dumpin' 'em on the sheriff, and lookin' fer jars while we're here. He'll be too dang busy to care what we're up to." He chuckled at how easy it would be to make a Ridgefield's life difficult.

"I dunno, Jasper. Sounds iffy to me."

"Oh, Elmer, if he throws us in jail at our age, all we gotta do is fake chest pains. Whatta we got ta lose?"

"A drum of prime 'shine, that's what."

"THERE'S THE MAN that dropped the puppy off," Dallas said as they drove down the street.

"Jasper? Yeah, I saw him."

"I think he said he was looking for you."

"Doesn't look like he's looking too hard right now. As a matter of fact," he said as he glanced in the rearview mirror, "I'd say he's more interested in not finding me than finding me."

"Why?"

"Because he's up to no good."

With sudden insight, Dallas asked, "Is he a McKane?"

"That's got nothing to do with it."

"Is he?"

"As a matter of fact, no. Not directly, anyway."

They left Green Valley behind them and headed north on a winding, asphalt road that carried them up into the surrounding hills, away from the river. Houses were scattered and few, and generally accompanied by rain-soaked cattle and an occasional mud-caked horse. An hour later, they were back down in a valley, not too far from the river.

"We're in Clark County now. It won't be much longer."

Dallas studied the backwater paralleling the right side of the road, lapping at the asphalt restriction just five feet away, threatening to inundate it. She'd disliked the rain during the day when she'd been looking out the window of the jail. It made her feel small and inconsequential, at the mercy of a larger, unknown force. Those feelings increased tenfold as more rain clouds moved in and the sky grew darker, making it impossible to tell whether the sun had set yet.

"Will we be able to get back?"

"Yeah, this road won't flood." He sounded knowledgeable, but Dallas wasn't reassured. He must have been able to tell, because he added in a softer tone, "If it does, we'll just go around. There's nothing to worry about."

"I hate rain." She scootched down and rested her head on the back of the seat. Slowly she became more aware of his eyes on her inside the shadowy confines of the truck, and less aware of the weather.

"Did you just decide that, or are you remembering it?"

She shrugged. "I'm not sure. I just know I hate rain. It makes me feel vulnerable."

"Like . . . ?" he prompted.

"I don't know."

Jackson turned off the narrow road and down a tree-lined side street. The nose of the truck dipped as he went down a hill, straightened out as he drove through standing water, then rose again as he pulled to a stop on an incline.

"Here we are. High and dry."

Dallas looked through the windshield to see that the library was, indeed, high and dry. She couldn't say much for the parking lot and street, but the building itself sat at the head of a dozen concrete steps. It was brick, it was big, and being inside it would be a far sight better than driving around in the rain in a truck.

"Here." Jackson pulled a jacket out from behind the seat and offered it to her.

She held it over her head and shoulders as they ran through the rain together. He put a protective hand on her arm and left it there as they dashed up the steps to the front door.

The feel of his fingers through Dallas's shirt made her forget there was something about rain she hated. Suddenly all she was aware of was him, his strong fingers, his warm hand, his comforting presence. She was ready to barrel through the door in front of him, but both were brought up short as they found it locked.

"They're closed?" she asked with dread.

He peered through the glass. "I think I see the librarian." He knocked on the door to get her attention.

The overhang protected them from the rain, but the breeze was cold and damp. Dallas shivered, and Jackson slipped his arm around her, pulling her close beside him to share his warmth.

"Does she hear you?"

"Not yet." He hesitated a moment, during which Dallas figured what the heck and huddled even closer. He knocked again. "Here she comes."

The librarian proceeded slowly, studying them carefully through the glass as she approached. Dallas didn't mind the delay, because when the door opened, she'd have to step away from Jackson—something she was in no hurry to do—and remember what it was they'd come here for.

The middle-aged librarian seemed satisfied to see Jackson's uniform and unlocked the door, holding it open wide. Half-glasses hung over her ample chest, dangling there by a chain which disappeared beneath the collar of her white blouse.

"I'm sorry, Sheriff," she said with an apologetic smile. "We've had so much trouble with looters the past week that I lock this whenever I'm here alone."

"That sounds like a good idea."

"I hope you locked your truck. They're taking anything that isn't nailed down."

"Yes, it's locked." He looked around and pointed out an oak coat tree to Dallas. "You can hang the jacket over there."

She would have preferred to drape it over her shoulders and keep it with her, like a prize, but it was too wet. Reluctantly, she parted with it.

"Do you need some help, Sheriff?"

Dallas gave the woman credit for not batting her eyes at her scarecrow outfit; it was more than she could have done if a woman, dressed as she was, suddenly ran up to the front door of the library at the end of the afternoon. But then, as she watched the librarian longer, she realized her politeness didn't come from practice so much as from the fact that she had her undivided attention pinned on Jackson. He flashed her a smile that Dallas was sure would produce the required books within seconds, in spite of her sensible shoes and heavy stockings.

"We're looking for some of the Budget Lady's books," he explained.

"The Budget Lady?" Her eyebrows arched as if she'd never heard of her. Dallas felt her stomach plummet.

"Yeah, you know. *How to Redecorate from Top to Bottom . . . on a Budget* and *Birthday Bashes . . . on a Budget.*"

Dallas was more than a little surprised to find out he actually knew some of her titles verbatim. She wondered if he was a closet *Budget* reader.

"Oh, yes, I believe I've heard of those. I don't know if we have copies, though. Now, let's see." She stepped behind the counter, slipped her glasses onto her nose, punched some buttons on the keyboard a few times, then slipped the glasses back off again, "I'm sorry."

Dallas groaned. "You mean you don't have any?"

She glanced at Dallas as if surprised that Jackson had company. "No, my dear." She smiled, but it was aimed at Jackson. "I'm afraid the computer's down. I don't know if we own any or not."

"Could we just look?" Dallas asked.

"We've moved a lot of books around due to the flood." The librarian pulled her shoulders back as if offended by the suggestion. "It would be silly to look through everything unless we knew there was a copy."

"How about the card file?" Jackson suggested.

"Well . . ."

Dallas would have liked a whole lot more enthusiasm here. Her real name, at least, might be in the card file.

"It's hopelessly out-of-date since we went to the computer."

"Do you happen to know the author's name?" Dallas asked.

"No, I can't say I do."

Dallas wasn't sure if her shiver was due to the cold or impending disappointment. Whichever, Jackson slipped his arm around her again, rubbing his hand over her sleeve to warm her. It worked well as she felt heat rush through her entire body.

The librarian's lips pinched into a thin line. "Why don't I get you two started on the card file?"

She led them along a hall that bifurcated the building from front to back, then through a small back room with waist-high windows and two vending machines, one for sodas, and one for candy and crackers. They followed her down a set of narrow cellar steps, topped with a rickety handrail.

Jackson descended in front of Dallas, holding his hand out for her to grasp, placing it on his shoulder and holding it there as they felt their way down. At the bottom, the librarian pulled a chain and turned on one, lone, bare light bulb which did little to illuminate their surroundings.

The ceiling was low enough to make Jackson stoop. The walls were cinder block, stacked above and around natural rock formations, as if the cellar had been carved out of stone.

The librarian pointed out the wooden card cabinet standing against a rough wall. It was old, dark, had a dozen drawers, and looked as if it hadn't been touched in a decade. Dallas blew on it, only to find it wasn't dusty, it was mildewed.

"I hope you can find what you're looking for. Like I said, we haven't used the cards since we switched to the computer three years ago." The librarian didn't wait for a response, just retraced her steps up the stairs with more speed than Dallas would have thought possible.

They were alone in a cellar that reminded her of a dark, damp cave. "I hope there's no bats down here," she muttered.

"She certainly was in a hurry to leave."

"She left the door open, didn't she?"

"I'm sure she did," Jackson replied.

Dallas peeked up the stairs to check anyway, not willing to take a chance on the woman wanting to keep a specimen like Jackson locked up in her cellar. A couple scenes from *Misery* came to mind.

"You look under *B* for *Budget Lady* and *Birthday Bashes*," he suggested. "I'll look under *H* for *How to*. Maybe we'll get lucky."

The bare bulb cast little light for them to see by. Somewhere, back in the darkness, a *drip...drip...drip* kept them company. Jackson stooped over, his head practically in the drawer. Dallas was crowded next to him, her arm brushing against his, their hips close enough for her to feel his body heat.

"Find something?" he asked when her hands quit moving over the cards.

"Um...no. I thought I did, but it was nothing. Birthday, birthday," she said under her breath, more to remind herself to keep looking than anything else.

"I should have brought a flashlight down here."

She squealed when she found it. *"Birthday Bashes...on a Budget,* right?" She turned toward him for confirmation, and found herself staring hopefully into eyes that were so dilated, they were almost black.

"That's it."

She pulled the card out and held it against her chest.

"What's the author's name?" he asked, and she noticed he didn't say *your* name.

She took a deep breath, knowing he was right to be cautious. So two women thought she looked like the picture of a woman on the back cover of a book they'd pored over for wedding advice. How often could they have seen it? How closely would they have looked?

"I'm afraid to look."

"Give it to me, then."

She clutched it tighter. "Okay, I'll look." She closed her eyes tightly, took a deep breath, then opened them again.

Jackson held his place in the *H* drawer with his hand as he moved around behind her where he could read over her shoulder. The physical result was that he had her pinned between him and the cabinet. The emotional result, however, was that she felt both safe and dangerous at the same time.

"Radcliffe, D.," she read.

"D?"

"Oh, no fair," she muttered.

"Here, let me see." He took the card from her, then handed it back. "Sound familiar?"

"Oh, sure. People call me *D* all the time," she grumbled.

His chuckle was low and sexy enough to make her feel silly over her disappointment. "I'll keep looking in the *H*'s. How's the Radcliffe part sound?"

She shrugged her shoulders, wondering why she didn't feel more connected to it. "I don't know. Do you think it could be a married name?"

He kept sorting through the cards. "I'll see if there's a full name on any cards I find. Why don't you go into the Author cards and see what you can turn up?"

She bent down, searching through the drawers until she found the author cards. Being low in the cabinet, she found herself hovering in the vicinity of a very sturdy masculine thigh.

"Same thing," he announced a moment later. "Radcliffe, D. Sorry."

"Well, I guess I can still go by Dallas a while longer. Oh, here we go."

Jackson hunkered down beside her.

"Radcliffe, D.," she read aloud. A quick glance told her this was the author of the *Budget* books, which she already knew.

"Radcliffe, Diana," Jackson read as he thumbed his way farther into the drawer. "According to this, it's a book of photographs."

"On what?"

" 'An award-winning, uplifting photographic account of human resilience in the face of natural disasters.' You know, mud slides, earthquakes, that sort of thing."

"Diana, huh?"

"Sound good?"

His breath was warm on her cheek, too near her ear, and she forgot she was supposed to be thinking about names, not games.

"Uh...no, not really. I hate rain, and I'm not wild about this flood you're having. Why would I go anywhere near an earthquake?"

"Let's go look for D. Radcliffe's picture, then." Jackson straightened up, holding his hand down to assist her, forgetting the low ceiling and bumping his head as he did so. Reflexly, he ducked again and put a hand to his head.

"Are you all right?" She reached out instinctively and rubbed the top of his head.

It was an innocent mistake. Her fingers threaded through his thick hair in a gesture that did more to get her blood racing than to ease his momentary pain. With Jackson stooped over as he was, his face was close to her level. His breath was warm on her cheek at first, then, as he tilted his head and moved closer, it was warm on her lips.

"I don't think so," he answered quietly.

She'd forgotten what she'd asked that had gotten that response from him.

"Maybe if you rub it a little more, it'll quit hurting," he said.

That really made her wonder what she'd asked. She didn't care. His lips hovered bare millimeters from hers, and her hand slid down to the back of his neck. It would be so simple to apply just the slightest pressure, to let him know that she wanted to taste what she could almost feel, to tug him closer.

"Jackson..."

"Shh," he whispered. "We're in a library, remember? No talking allowed."

His lips covered hers in a stream of gentle kisses that blazed a sensuous trail from her mouth to her ear. By the time he got back to her mouth again, there was nothing gentle left. He devoured her in a hungry kiss that left no room for thinking or breathing.

Her hands weren't pinned between them this time, not like their first kiss in the bedroom of the jail. She had free roam of his strong neck, his broad back, his thick hair. She had no control over her hands, and that seemed to please Jackson just fine.

He engulfed her in a hug that pressed her intimately against his body. He was aroused, ready for her, and she pictured them naked beneath the stairs in a heated frenzy.

The librarian's voice cut like an ice pick into Dallas's deliciously sensual thoughts. "Did you find what you were looking for?" she asked from the top of the stairs.

Jackson recovered first. "Yes, I think so," he replied.

His eyes were locked with Dallas's, conveying a much deeper message to her. Or did she imagine it just because he had her all hot? He raked his fingers through his hair to straighten it, then did the same to hers. The feel of his hands twining through her waves did nothing to cool her down.

"Ready?" he whispered.

She followed him in a self-conscious daze, sure that th
librarian met them at the top with a knowing look on he
face. Jackson acted natural, though, as they followed he
back to the front of the building.

The windows by the door were bathed in black now. Dal
las's thoughts of what she'd shared with Jackson were re
placed with a sudden feeling of dread as a bolt of lightnin
illuminated the trees, which were bent over in the face of
strong wind. The thunderclap followed within a second
cracking so loudly that it made her jump. The lights flick
ered momentarily.

"A storm blew up while you were in the cellar," the l
brarian said, as if they couldn't tell for themselves.

Dallas turned away from the rain pelting the windows an
followed Jackson and the librarian into the main room
There was a couch, a coffee table, several chairs, and ro
after row of empty bookshelves.

"Oh no, not you, too," Jackson said with a groan.

"No books?" Dallas queried with a squeak.

"We moved them all upstairs," the librarian replied as sh
kept on walking, clearly expecting them to follow. "W
didn't want to take a chance on how high the river woul
go."

They followed her to a wide staircase, where she stoppe

"It'll be a bit cramped up there, and I can't promise
logical sequence of Dewey decimal numbers, but I'm su
you'll do fine." She tittered. "It's not like we're a big ci
library, after all." She pushed a switch on the wall, fillin
the second story with a welcoming light that spilled onto t
landing.

Dallas started up the stairs, figuring anything was bett
than the drippy cellar.

"You'll be sure the door's locked behind you when yo
leave, won't you, Sheriff?"

"Of course."

Dallas was halfway up the stairs when she felt him take her hand in his, very aware that they were now assured of being alone together. Anticipation warred with caution. They might be ten minutes away from finding out she was a married woman. What had she been thinking down in the cellar? The answer was obvious—she hadn't been thinking at all. She'd been feeling, reacting, responding. Definitely responding. Maybe even instigating.

She gave his hand a quick squeeze, as much to reassure herself as him that she wasn't angry over what had happened, just reserved, and then she pulled free from his grasp. He let her go, but followed closely, as if he hadn't even noticed.

This was a main part of the library, with full bookshelves for everyday use. And on the windowsills, the table, the chairs and the floor were stacks of relocated books. They were stacked neatly and, as the librarian had indicated, not in a totally random order. It was obvious the ten-minute theory was going to be blown to bits. One pile blocked another, and it took them an hour to weed through to the right batch.

Dallas was lying on the floor, twisted around one mound of books to read the spines on another behind it, when she saw *101 Things to Do on a Rainy Day... on a Budget*. She forgot the storm. She forgot the flickering lights.

"I found one!"

She felt Jackson's presence as he crawled closer. His hand burned on her hip as he craned his neck and tried to see the book.

"Just one?"

"That's all I can see right now."

"Can you get it out?"

"We'll have to move everything on top of it first."

"Okay." He got to his feet and started shuffling books putting them on any surface that would hold them. "Let m know when you can pull it out."

A few more handfuls, and she had the book in her grip She held it up for him to take so she could unwedge herself and she was more than happy to feel his hands grasp he waist and help her off the floor.

"Does it have a photo and a biography?" she asked ea gerly.

He held the book against his chest, much as she had don with the card earlier.

"What?" she asked impatiently.

"Are you sure you can handle this? I mean, what if Mu tha and Julie were wrong, and the author is some fifty-yea old lady?"

"They couldn't be that far off." She made a grab for th book, and he released it.

The lights flickered. She opened the book and saw a pho tograph of herself staring back at her, though it looked a he of a lot better than she did in the mirror at the jail.

"It's me," she whispered.

As she started to read, the lights flickered again, then wei out completely.

Chapter Seven

"I don't believe this!" Dallas shrieked as the library plunged into darkness.

"Gee, you'd think a place like this would pay its electric bill, wouldn't you?" Jackson chuckled as she hit him with the book. Her aim in the dark had been pretty fair, hitting him square in the chest. He massaged the spot absently. "See if I try to make you feel better again."

"Find a different way," she snapped.

"What would you suggest?"

"Jackson, you're really irritating me."

He surmised that he best let up on the humor until her mood changed, which would probably be about the same time he found a flashlight. In the meantime, he was quite content to be closed up in a dark room with her. She hovered near him, trying to maintain contact without really touching. He remedied that quickly by reaching for her hand.

"Hey, watch it," she said on a low breath, and he knew she wasn't angry.

"I'd like to."

"Ha ha."

"Give me your hand."

"Is that what you were looking for?"

"Yes."

"Hands are usually lower. You know, on the end of an arm."

"I was reaching for your arm."

"Well, you missed."

"What did I get?"

"Never mind."

He knew, though. What man wouldn't know a breast when he felt one? And he wanted to feel one again.

When her hand landed on his chest, he took it in his and held it close to his heart. "In the interest of safety, I suggest we sit on the floor."

"Interesting. You never impressed me as a safety-oriented kind of guy."

"What do you mean?"

"Jackson, you jumped in a river to save me."

"It was the smartest thing I ever did." He knew that, without a doubt.

"But not the safest."

"True. What would you rather do?" He sensed her hesitation and wondered if she was thinking along the same lines as he. They were alone, two people physically attracted to each other, in a relatively comfortable building. It was dark. They had hours before the sun came up and the librarian returned.

"I'd rather find a light and read this biography. I saw the picture. I'm sure it's me."

"Boy, a sheriff's job is never done. I don't think I'm going to run for reelection next year." He said it with jest, but, deep inside, he was afraid he wasn't cut out for the job any more. Not until he resolved this issue of wanting to steal another man's possible wife. It was the *possible* part that allowed him to justify his feelings for her.

She was shaking his hand, and he realized his mind had wandered. "Jackson, are you listening to me?"

"Sorry. What?"

"Do you carry a flashlight in your truck?"

"Sure."

"Well," she said with a sigh that spoke of decreasing patience, "do you think we might go get it?"

"It's raining," he said with great logic.

"Ow!"

"What?"

"I stubbed my toe."

"You mean you kicked the bookshelf instead of my shin."

"Let me try again."

"You're quite physical, aren't you?" Anticipation filled him.

"I wouldn't know. I don't even know who I am. Yet," she emphasized pointedly. "Where are you going?"

"To the truck."

He tugged her along behind him as he felt his way over and around stacks of books to the upper landing. She stumbled along behind him at first, then got into the rhythm of his step when they were clear of all the obstructions.

"Boy, you'd think there'd be some moonlight," she muttered.

"You don't get out in storms much, do you?"

"You're a real funny guy, Jackson. How'd I miss that before?"

"Simple. When the lights are on, you're too busy ogling my body."

"*Ogling?*"

"You heard me."

"I heard you. I just can't believe you said it."

A flash of lightning clued Jackson into the whereabouts of the first step going down. He grabbed the rail with one hand. "Here, let me help you. Put your arm around me."

"Huh?"

He didn't give her time to think about it. He slid her arm around his waist, wrapped his around her body, and moved forward. "Step down here."

He could have put her hand on the rail and let her find her own way behind him, but it wouldn't have been nearly so interesting. She clutched him tightly, her fingers digging into the skin on his side until she found the first step, then the second.

"How many are there?"

"I expect we'll find that out when we get to the bottom."

"Is this how you run your sheriff's department? By the seat of the pants?"

"It's worked so far."

She fumbled on a step, and he tightened his grip, his fingers erring in the vicinity of the outer curve of a well-rounded breast. He said a silent "thank you" to Martha and Julie for not bringing Dallas a bra. Not that he thought she'd choose to wear something so tame in comparison to her red teddy. And, thinking of lingerie, it dawned on him that she wasn't wearing any underpants, either.

"Careful," she cautioned as he nearly missed a step. "If you fall, we both go."

"Sorry. My mind was on something else."

"What?"

"Never mind."

They were nearly to the bottom of the long staircase, so they wouldn't have far to fall. He thought of how her body would feel beneath, then on top, then under his again as they tumbled. Her arms and legs would probably be wrapped around him. It was almost enough to make a man forget how to walk.

"Thank God that's over," she said when they both reached for another step and found themselves on level floor.

But Jackson kept his arm around her, and he noticed she wasn't quick to release him, either. They felt their way through the library, each with their free arm out in front of their bodies, Dallas still clutching the book in her hand. Lightning flashed again, aiding them in their search for the front door.

"I never thought I'd be glad to see lightning," she said with a nervous giggle.

He was glad she found some humor in their situation. "What?"

"You know that old saying about every cloud having a silver lining? I never took it so literally before."

Neither had he, but, as he pressed her close against his side, molding her to his rib cage, he began to. Their kiss in the cellar had happened quickly and innocently enough. He wanted to take her right now, turn her in his arms, and kiss her again, feel her lips moving beneath his, tasting him back. But he knew she had something more pressing on her mind right now, so he took his silver lining and contented himself to hold her against his side.

Another flash of lightning, and they could both see that nothing stood between them and the front door. No shelves, no stacks of displaced books, no reason to hold on to each other.

They didn't let go. When they reached the jacket he'd loaned her, still hanging on the oak coat tree, Jackson helped her drape it over her head even as he maintained his hold on her. He opened the front door to reveal a pouring rain. The kind that old timers called "cats and dogs."

"The book'll get wet," she said.

"Put it under your shirt."

She giggled again. "There's room enough, that's for sure."

He thought she'd filled it out rather nicely, but, as lightning flashed again, he watched the book disappear down the front of her shirt. "Need any help?"

"No, thanks."

"Just asking."

"Mm-hmm."

So she didn't believe him. Did he care? She hadn't pulled away from him yet, giving him all sorts of delicious ideas about where the book had come to rest. Damn lucky book.

"It's raining so hard, I can't even see the truck," she said with dismay. "Maybe we'd better wait."

"Won't help any. We can't see the truck because it's not there."

It was a brief moment before she spoke, and he knew it was from surprise.

"It didn't wash away, did it?" He felt her shiver beneath his arm at the thought.

"I think looters are more likely to blame."

"How far are they going to get in a sheriff's truck?"

"Tonight? Wherever they want would be my guess."

They stood on the porch at the head of the dozen concrete steps, watching in silence as rain poured off the roof in buckets all around them.

As much as she hated rainstorms, Dallas somehow felt safe with this strong, solid man beside her. He kept his arm around her, warming her even as a cold, damp breeze threatened to chill her to the bone. She quit wondering why she hated rain and wondered instead whether the shiver she felt race up her spine had to do with getting closer to him, or not getting close enough.

"We'd better get inside," he said after a long moment, during which she absorbed all she could from his presence without actually turning into his embrace.

He drew away from her as she felt around in the entry for the coat tree and hung the jacket up again. The book inside her shirt was weighty, but she left it there to keep her hands free for now.

"I'm going to look for a place to get comfortable," he said.

"I'm going to look under the counter for a flashlight," she said.

"Okay. Meet you back here."

She could hear a grin in his voice, as if they were each viewing this as some kind of a mission impossible. "Right."

She found the circulation desk without any problem—she ran right into it. Lightning flashes came often, but were no help as the underside of the counter faced away from the windows. She ran across a phone and picked it up, only to find it dead. She felt along the shelves and in the drawers without luck.

"Jackson?"

When she got no reply, she struck out on her own.

IF JACKSON REMEMBERED right, and he hoped he did, there was a couch in the next room—only one. There were chairs, but he sure as heck wasn't going to try to sleep in one of those. He wanted to share the couch. The fact that it was even narrower than the twin bed they'd shared in the jail was only icing on the cake. He went back for her, in case she was having trouble finding her way.

"I found us a place to sleep."

When he received no response, he paused and listened. He heard banging coming from the back of the building. A loose shutter in the wind? A tree branch? A muttered curse, followed by more banging, gave him his answer.

He set out down the long hall that led to the back of the building, the same way they'd gone to reach the cellar. With his arms outstretched, he could trace the walls on either side of him with his hands, and he went forward without hesitation.

He'd never expected a flash of lightning to reveal her in all her fury. She was a glorious sight, with one leg up in the air, cocked back and ready to let loose, her hair flying as her foot shot forward, her arms out to the sides for balance. He nearly forgot it was his job to stop her, but not quite. Old habits were hard to break.

"What the hell are you doing?"

She jumped, but she still managed to place another well-aimed kick to the front of the nearer vending machine. "I'm hungry and thirsty."

"Oh, I see. You're cranky again."

She paused long enough to catch her breath and ask, "Do you have any change?"

"Wouldn't help. They have electric components, and we're fresh out of electricity."

She shrieked a good imitation of a movie-inspired karate yell as she kicked it again.

"I see your leg's feeling much better."

"Some help you are."

"Dallas, I have to tell you you're in danger of being arrested for destruction of private property."

"Good, then you can take me to the nearest jail and feed me."

"Those machines are built to stand up to some pretty rambunctious teenagers, you know. And even if you did manage to break in and get something, you'd be stealing."

"I'll mail 'em a check when I get home." She kicked it again. "Besides, it's not stealing if it's for survival."

He chuckled then. "I guess it's a safe bet you're not a lawyer."

"Give me your gun."

"No."

"Come on, Jackson. I'll pay for the damage."

"How do you know you can afford it?"

"I write books. How poor can I be?"

"Come on, I found us a place to sleep."

She let out a long-suffering sigh. "Where?"

"There's a couch in the other room."

A couch? As in *one?* For the both of them? The mere thought of it distracted Dallas from the impossible vending machines. She'd need an axe to break into them and she didn't have one, so she followed him to see what he had planned for their second night. Thoroughly distracted, she ran smack into his backside in the hallway.

"Sorry," she mumbled, laying a hand on his broad back and leaving it there so they wouldn't collide again.

His heart beat steadily, pulsating through his back and into her palm. She felt the play of his muscles, bunching and releasing with every swing of his arm, under her fingertips. One couch would be very dangerous indeed.

"Is it getting colder in here?" Silently she rebuked herself for such an inane question, as if discussing the temperature was any better than discussing the weather.

"The furnace won't work without electricity."

"Oh."

"It's going to get progressively colder all night." So he was as inane as she.

It was better than discussing what was really on her mind. Was he trying to rationalize sharing a couch? She remembered waking up in the jail in the same bed with him. He'd been all warm and toasty, and she'd felt cocooned and safe, right up until she'd kicked him out of it.

And she recalled the kiss he'd collected from her shortly thereafter, the one he'd said he'd already paid for. She was tempted to push him off the couch, once they got there, just to see if she got the same reward. One along the lines of the kiss in the cellar today.

"Here we are," he said. He took her hand off his back and placed it on top of the couch, orienting her. "You want the front or back?"

She bumped into him quite unintentionally, but the effect was no less pleasurable just the same. She noted that there was nothing soft about the man where they'd just connected.

"Hmm," he said, as his hands found her arms, slid up to her collarbone, and dipped inside her shirt right above the first button she'd buttoned. "You'll sleep a whole lot better without this."

His fingers were cool on the skin beneath her shirt. She felt his knuckles against her sternum and absently wondered why he was using the back of his hand to caress her. Her brain told her to step backward—fast. Her knees locked to keep from going mushy and collapsing on the spot. Her breasts tingled, not with the feel of his hand, but with the thought of his hand as he slid the book from its nest inside her shirt.

She expected to hear his breathing escalate, to hear him clear his throat or have a catch in his speech.

"There, isn't that better?" he asked smoothly.

She wanted to shout "No!" She wanted to know why he wasn't as affected as she, but the power of speech eluded her for the moment. And he wanted her to curl up on the couch with him? She'd be useless. She'd make a fool of herself if he touched her again and she melted in a puddle at his cool feet.

He stretched out on the couch, on his side, reached up and tugged on her hand. With a sudden burst of willpower, she gently pulled free and arranged herself at the opposite end. It wasn't an overly long couch. Their thighs touched in the middle, building a heat between them that had nothing to do with sharing and everything to do with chemistry.

"Do you mind taking off those clodhoppers?"

She could hear the smile in his voice. So, he was amused by her choice of sleeping arrangements. She kicked off the duck shoes, hearing them hit the floor with two distinct, heavy rubber thuds. His stockinged feet cozied up against her back. One toed its way beneath her arm, like an animal seeking shelter.

"Do you mind?" she asked. She didn't think it was shelter he was seeking.

"My feet are cold. Aren't yours?"

He *had* to ask. He *had* to plant that suggestion in her mind. Within minutes, she was cold everywhere but where their bodies touched. With a deep, melodramatic sigh designed to make him think she wanted no intimate contact whatsoever with him, she sat up, turned around, and lay back down in front of him, spoon fashion.

His arm wound around in front of her, the weight of it heavy across her breasts. His breath gently whispered through her hair, tickling her ear. A little voice, not his, told her just to turn around in his arms and kiss him and get it over with. Let whatever was going to happen just happen.

An unbeckoned, unwelcome, inexplicable chilly feeling of dread suffused her whole body at the very thought. She didn't know where it had come from, but it wasn't unlike the feeling she got from the rainstorm. She couldn't make that first move. She wasn't sure she could make any.

"What's wrong?" he whispered.

"You're jabbing me," she said without thinking, then wondered exactly what was poking into her behind. The answer could be embarrassing. Her cheeks grew hot. She hoped he wouldn't answer.

"I've got keys in my pockets."

"It's your gun belt, too."

He crawled over her. She felt instantly cold and hot at the same time, cold where he'd been and hot where he was feeling his way over her. She heard keys jangle as he dropped them onto the coffee table with a clatter, followed by several coins. The gun belt made a dull thud.

"I think that's everything."

She jumped up before he crawled over her again, and she thought she heard him chuckle as he lay back down. She sat, and it was the last thing she initiated. His hands were on her arms, turning her the opposite way of what she had been before, so that she lay with him face-to-face. And chest-to-chest, she thought, trying to keep space between them, but unable to do it.

His arm behind her back pulled her closer. He opened his thighs, making room for one of hers between his as he reached down, hooked a hand behind her knee, and draped her top leg over his. "How's that?"

Finally there was a catch in his breathing that clued her in to how she was affecting him. The dread she'd felt before began to dissipate slowly, as if his body heat vaporized it for her, sent it up in steam, hopefully never to be seen again.

When he touched her cheek with work-roughened fingertips, she felt only tenderness in his caress. When his hand tunneled beneath her hair and slipped behind her neck, she felt only longing. And, when he tilted his raised head and lowered his lips to meet hers, she felt as if she'd entered a whole new world. One she never knew existed. One where she wanted to stay forever.

She returned his kisses with a growing heat that matched his as he coaxed her lips apart and traced them slowly with his tongue. The moisture turned instantly cool in the chilly room, but it was quickly replaced with the rising temperature between them. She felt him grow hard against her thigh, and this time there was no doubt as to what was poking her.

"Dallas," he said in a breathless murmur.

She could barely focus enough to answer with a "Hmm?"

"This was just supposed to be a good-night kiss." His voice was ragged.

"It's good, all right." The cold spot deep within her hadn't quite been extinguished, after all. She pushed it down, resolutely. She didn't want to deal with it now. When she was in his arms like this, she didn't want to deal with it ever.

He chuckled. His palm was warm against her cheek as he kissed her closed eyelids. "We should get some sleep now."

"Tell that to my body."

"Yeah." He eased his hips back, putting some space, a mere inch, between his erection and her body. "Mine, too."

An inch wasn't enough. It was far too much. She'd never be able to think straight again. But he was right, and she knew it. Was a good-night kiss all it was meant to be?

"This isn't the right time or place," he whispered.

Or had she imagined hearing it? Out of hope? Whichever, it was true. There would be a right time and place, somewhere, someday. She hoped. And she didn't think it depended on either of them as much as it did on her past.

JACKSON PULLED HER CLOSER and felt her heartbeat against his chest. She had on far too many clothes. They both did.

Their shirts disappeared immediately, melting away into nothingness, which is exactly where they should be for what he had in mind. Her breasts were cool against his bare chest as he peeled off red lace, her nipples hard and beaded. He reached down to take one firm mound in his palm, to tease it with his fingertips and make her nipple pucker more.

Her breathing escalated, hot and moist on his cheek, in his ear. Was that a whimper? Of excitement? Of longing for more? Or was he going too fast for her? He slowed his pace, caressing the smooth skin over her flat stomach to reassure her that he had control of his emotions, that he wouldn't get carried away like a lovesick teenage boy.

He trailed kisses from one corner of her lips to the other, up to her softly closed eyelids, down the delicate arch of her throat. She tasted of spring, of wanting to learn him as much as he wanted to learn her. To please her.

He shifted his weight, easing himself on top of her, easing his knee between her thighs, letting his own thigh come to rest against the most intimate part of her. He expected a soft moan; he got nothing. Not even hot skin.

He didn't understand; the confusion made him feel as if his brain had been fogged. Had she pulled away?

He reached for her again, to pull her close again. Nothing. Frustrated, he tried to think where she could be. He tried to wake up and go find her. A heavy weight on him kept him from moving.

Sleep. He needed more sleep. He'd been overworked for days, kept alive on caffeine, with an overpowering need to help others. He was the sheriff; it was his duty. But, more than that, it was the way he lived.

The librarian had complained about looters. It was his duty to catch them. Then he remembered he was in a different county; it was some other sheriff's responsibility. Unless, of course, he ran across them red-handed. All though, he thought with a broad smile, even as he slept fitfully, he might owe them a small debt of gratitude. If it hadn't been for them stealing his truck, he wouldn't be cuddled on this narrow couch with Dallas. Maybe a large debt of gratitude.

He jumped awake with a jolt, eyes wide, then narrow as he glanced around the room. A dim gray light filtered through the library windows; dawn. Another day of rain in Missouri from the looks of things.

He'd been hot next to Dallas, ready to strip off the rest of their clothes and make love to her. When he realized he was alone on the couch, he grew chilly in spite of being fully clothed. The cushion in front of him was cool to the touch, he discovered as he lay his hand on it, as if she'd been gone for a while.

An uneasy feeling crept up the back of his neck as he wondered what had jolted him awake.

Gunshots. Two of them, in quick succession, sounded from another part of the library. Jackson was on his feet in a flash.

Chapter Eight

Where was Dallas?

And who the hell was shooting at her in a library at dawn?

Jackson reached automatically for his gun belt on the coffee table, snatching it up as he left the couch in a dead run. Too light, he realized as its weight, or lack thereof, registered in his brain. His hand landed on the holster knowing it was empty without looking, but compelled to do so anyway.

Was he still dreaming? He didn't think so. He wanted to call out Dallas's name, hear her answer him, hear a reasonable explanation as to why she and his revolver were both gone.

Instead he kept silent for the moment, listening for sound of a struggle. Was it possible she'd heard looters and gone looking for them, taking his weapon along for protection? That didn't sound like the Dallas he knew, or as much about her as anyone could know at this point. But perhaps she'd regained her memory. Perhaps she was familiar with gun and perpetrators.

Then again, he could be the one getting shot at if he sneaked up on her.

He heard noises from the back of the building, near the cellar door. It sounded as if glass were breaking, large pieces of it striking the hardwood floor. A break-in through a rear window? He wished he knew where the hell Dallas was, and if she was a trigger-happy sort.

Bending low, peeking around corners before he stuck his head out so he wouldn't get it shot off, he carefully crept through the library. There was just enough early morning light filtering through the windows to keep him from bumping into the walls as he made his way to the back hall.

He heard the unmistakable *pffss* of a pop-top on a soda can. As he peered around the last corner, he discovered Dallas sitting on a wide, marble windowsill, framed by the gray dawn, her head tipped back, a can to her lips, her Adam's apple bobbing as she swallowed what must have been half its contents.

"What the hell did you do?" he demanded, straightening up for the three long strides which put him near her knees.

She jumped, obviously startled by his abrupt appearance. The last gulp of soda went down wrong, and she choked and gasped until she could catch her breath. By then he'd snatched his revolver from the windowsill where it lay next to an open package of cheese crackers with peanut butter. He slid it back into the holster and buckled the belt securely around his waist. See if he took it off *next* time they slept together.

Now there was a thought that distracted him and took the edge off his anger. He couldn't help himself, he clapped her on the back, trying to help her past her choking spell. When she finally regained her breath, she looked up at him with a smile he felt sure was meant to win him over.

"I was hungry. Remember, I get cranky when I get hungry."

"*This* is cranky?"

"No, *this* is satisfied, now that I've had some food." She pointed at the bullet-ridden vending machines, the protective glass on the front of both of them blown away. "*That's* cranky."

He raked his fingers through his hair, smoothing it out after a night on a skinny couch with a woman he wanted to make love to, not throttle. "Damn, woman," he said with a healthy respect which men normally reserve for larger, more dangerous animals. "Remind me to feed you regularly."

She held up a peanut-butter cracker. "I'll share."

She could see the indecision written on his face in spite of the dim light filtering through the dirty window behind her. Holding out a cracker, all she could think about was his last word. *Regularly.* As in, she'd be around for a while? Because he wanted her to stay? Or because he was stuck with her?

She'd like to stay. But, at the same time, she wanted to go get the *Budget* book, read her biography now that there was enough light and she wasn't starving anymore, and go find her own family, if she had one.

Apparently Jackson felt the need to lecture her, because his voice lowered to a growl. "Don't you know guns are dangerous if you don't know what you're doing?"

She attempted to throw him off guard with a teasing smile. "I'm a quick learner." When he didn't take the cracker, she held out the soda can instead. "You can have some of mine, or I can get you your own."

"No!" he said too quickly, his hand flying protectively to his revolver as if he were afraid she'd wrestle him for it.

"Relax. The glass is already broken. I can just reach in and grab one for you." She started to scoot off the windowsill.

He quickly blocked her way, putting his body directly in front of her knees. "Never mind."

She knew he needed to eat. She continued to munch and drink, munch and drink, trying to break down his defenses. His stomach growled in protest at being ignored, loud enough for both of them to hear it.

"I've never broken the law before," he mused aloud.

She sensed his indecision, the first chink in his perfect armor that she'd been aware of since they'd met. "I told you last night, this is survival. It's just a little bend."

"I've never bent the law before, either."

"Never?"

"Never."

"No speeding tickets when you were sixteen?"

"Not one."

"Lucky, huh?"

"Luck had nothing to do with it."

"No underage drinking before you were twenty-one? A little beer at a party, perhaps?"

"Dallas, my father's the judge. How would that look?"

"The judge? Well, hell, Jackson, if you get arrested for this, he can get you off."

He sighed. If he thought she'd missed the whole point, an impish tug at the corner of her lips told him otherwise. "I guess I could write a note explaining the circumstances."

"If you feel you must."

His glare looked official and well-practiced, as if it had been taught in a special sheriff's course on law and order. "You can sign it, promising to pay damages, and I'll witness it."

"Yes, sir." She gave him a mock salute.

"And don't let this get to be a habit."

Her response was a sigh that surpassed his own of a moment ago. It clearly said she didn't know how to deal with a man like him. All he knew was that he'd like her to try.

NOT ONLY WAS Jackson's truck gone, they noted as they stood at the front door, but the parking lot below them was flooded. The library was completely surrounded by water.

"You're sure it didn't float away?" Dallas asked.

"Not in twelve inches of water."

"Great. The phone's dead. I doubt the librarian's coming back this morning when she sees the moat. How do we get out of here?"

"Wade."

"You'll come back for me, of course."

"I could carry you on my back."

"Maybe next time. I'll read until you get back."

She took off for the main room. It was her intention to find the *Budget* book and read her biography, not straddle his hips and wrap her legs around him for a jaunt across the parking lot. She wasn't afraid of getting *on* him; she was afraid she wouldn't want to get *off*.

The book lay on the coffee table. She sunk onto the edge of the couch and stared at it until Jackson entered the room.

He stood nearby and asked tentatively, "What did it say?"

She shook her head. "I haven't read it yet."

"Why not?" He stepped closer and reached down for the book.

"No!" She snatched it off the table and clutched it to her chest. "I'll do it."

He leaned on a chair across from her.

"Don't stare at me."

He moved away and started to walk out of the room.

"Don't go."

He threw his arms up in the air. "Tell me what you want. I'm not a mind reader, you know."

She shrugged, wishing she knew.

"Just get it over with."

"I might be married," she whispered. She received no response from him and she was afraid to look at him, to read something she might not want to see in his face.

"Just do it."

She picked up the book and opened it to the back cover. It was her picture, all right. She hadn't spent a lot of time looking in the cracked mirror in the jail, but she'd know those eyes staring back at her anywhere.

Diana Radcliffe comes from . . .

"It's Diana," she said.

"Diana?"

"The D, remember? It's for Diana."

"You're sure it's not for 'Delay'?"

"Very funny."

"Read it out loud."

"'Diana Radcliffe comes from a large, admittedly bois- terous family, all progeny of the famous Thelia of Thelia's Tips fame.' Who's that?"

"She writes how to get out stains and stuff. Keep read- ing."

"'She presently lives in Connecticut with her . . .'" Her voice trailed off as she was faced with the next word. Her *husband*.

She glanced over at Jackson then. Even without saying it out loud, she saw the recognition on his face, the resign- ment that he'd have to face the fact. They both would.

"Go on," he encouraged her softly.

But she couldn't. Her vision had blurred with moisture that threatened to run down her cheeks. Happiness? Sad- ness? She wasn't sure. Maybe a little of both. She wanted to know who she was and where she came from. She wanted to know if she had a husband, family, responsibilities. She also wanted to get to know Jackson better. Thank God he'd called a halt on the couch last night.

She jumped up off the cushion as if it had caught on fire beneath her.

"What's the matter?" Jackson surged to his feet, too. He took the book from her numb fingers and continued reading. "'...with her husband, three children, and way too many pets which she accumulated while researching her next book, *A Perfect Pet for Everyone...on a Budget.*'"

He closed the book silently. It slammed in Dallas's ears as if to signal the close of any possible relationship she might have been developing with him.

"Three children," she murmured, her hand absently massaging a circle over her navel, as she tried to imagine soothing a fetus that way. "I wonder why I only remembered two."

Jackson hadn't thought that far. He was having trouble getting past the husband part. He'd known it was a possibility, of course. And he wouldn't wish a divorce on anyone, but, faced with the truth in black and white, he finally admitted to himself that he'd hoped she'd dumped the guy long ago.

Until he could resolve his own deep feelings for Dallas, he knew he'd best put some distance between them, for her sake.

DALLAS HEARD A DEEP, muffled *wup-wup-wup.* "What's that?"

She was alone, slumped down on the couch cushions, the *Budget* book on the coffee table staring back at her.

The last time she'd gone into herself like that, she'd at least remembered something. This time, nothing. No husband lurking in the recesses of her mind. No children, in spite of the fuzzy picture she'd gotten of two of them the day before. No pets, no house in Connecticut, no nothing.

"Dallas?" Jackson called out from the front of the library.

He opened the front door, and she had no trouble recognizing the sound of an approaching helicopter. Rescue! She grabbed the *Budget* book as if it were a lifeline, even though she'd already memorized the bio. She ran to the front door, grabbing the borrowed jacket off the coat tree as she breezed by it.

She noticed Jackson had been busy while she'd been sitting on the couch playing hide-and-seek with her past; in his hand, he held two more *Budget* books, retrieved from the stacks of books upstairs. She didn't hold out any hope that the subsequent bios were any more explanatory than the first one, but she was looking forward to reading things she'd actually written. Maybe there were anecdotes scattered throughout the text, sort of a "This is how my little girl, so and so, did it." So and so sounded coldly impersonal, but it was better than thinking of her daughter as Miss X.

They watched as the helicopter touched down on the highest spot in the parking lot.

"Will they pick us up?" she asked hopefully, yelling over the noise even though Jackson stood right by her shoulder.

"It's Harrison, my brother. He probably found my truck abandoned somewhere and knew we were stranded here."

Upon closer inspection, the helicopter was clearly marked Twain County Sheriff's Department. His father was the judge, she remembered. And *two* of his brothers were deputies. "Remind me not to break any laws in your county."

He grinned and took her hand in his. "Let's go."

They ran down the steps to the helicopter, bending low beneath the blades on their approach. Jackson tossed the books onto the nearest seat, then turned and helped her climb in. His large hands lingered longer on her waist than absolutely necessary, distracting her to the point where she almost dropped the book she was carrying.

The helicopter wasn't the brand-new, state-of-the-art model she'd pictured when she'd first heard it. Instead it was old, repainted and uninsulated. A winch was mounted above the missing cargo door. Luckily, there were enough head-sets to go around.

"Harrison, this is Dallas. Dallas, this is my brother, Harrison."

"The kamikaze pilot?" she asked with raised eyebrows.

"You must have been talking to Roman," Harrison answered with a chuckle that was as deep as Jackson's, but didn't tempt her to melt into a puddle at *his* feet.

If the rain had made her moody from time to time, riding in the helicopter did just the opposite. Her spirits soared as it shook, lifted off the ground, then swooped forward and up above the trees. Cold wind blew through the cargo doorway, but she didn't mind the chill. She sat on the edge of her seat, leaning toward the opening for a better look at the river.

Jackson's arms circled her as he belted her in securely. Then, apparently not trusting her fate to a thin strip of webbing, he slipped his fingers into the waist of her baggy jeans and held on tightly. She could have swatted him away...but she didn't want to. Every time she moved or wiggled, she could feel the backs of his knuckles grazing her skin. Either they gave off a lot of heat for knuckles, or she was just chilled everywhere else from the breeze. She wondered if she'd always been into denial, if that was a charac-teristic that would stay with a person even through amnesia.

"Did you find my truck?" Jackson asked his brother.

"Ditched about twenty miles upriver. I dropped Roman off to bring it back."

"He flew with you?"

"Yep."

"Without me ordering him to?" Jackson chuckled at that, and Dallas was instantly curious as to how two men could sound so much alike, yet only Jackson's voice made her blood race.

Between analyzing his effect on her libido and his fingers burning a hot spot at her waist, she nearly missed seeing the deer stranded below.

"Look!" Without taking her eyes off the deer, she reached back and tugged at Jackson's shirtsleeve with one hand while she pointed out the door with the other.

He leaned closer, his chest pressing against her back as his arm slipped around her shoulders. The weather had chilled her; his nearness warmed her right back up, and it had nothing to do with simple body heat.

"It's a doe," Harrison commented from the controls. "She's stuck out on that island."

She'd apparently taken refuge on a high piece of ground as the river had risen and now was surrounded. It reminded Dallas of how she'd felt when she'd come to two days ago. Scared spitless. And from the way the deer was dashing around, she looked like she was about to take the plunge in the wrong direction.

Dallas reached for the camera she always had around her neck whenever she was on location. When she didn't get it on the first grab, she tried again, then looked down in confusion at her empty hands. She had no camera.

"She's got herself stuck in the mud now," Harrison said, hovering the helicopter nearby.

Dallas glanced out the door, then turned to Jackson. During her confusion over expecting to find a camera around her neck, she hadn't noticed he'd moved away. Now he was bent over behind her seat, rooting through equipment.

"Isn't there someone who can help her?" she asked, more concerned over the doe's welfare than a fleeting memory at the moment. It would come back when it was ready. In the meantime, it was one more puzzle piece she'd hold on to.

"I could work on this a whole lot faster if you'd quit leaning out that door," he said with a low growl.

She kept her eye on the doe as she leaned back, more in her seat now, wishing she could photograph the beautiful, frightened animal. She knew just the angle, just the settings that would be perfect. She could visualize the end product already, in startling clarity, gracing the page of a coffee-table book.

"Jackson..." She turned and found him buckling on a harness, and she promptly forgot whatever she'd been about to ask. "What on earth are you doing?"

"I'm going to see if I can get her over to dry land." He adjusted the fit, pulling it snug.

"You?" Was it possible her heart stopped?

"Isn't that what you suggested?"

The thought of him dangling in a harness below the helicopter, with a pilot at the controls who thought *kamikaze* a humorous description of his flying ability, was a bit much for her to handle just then. She unbuckled her seat belt, wanting to touch him, to talk some sense into him.

"Damn it, Dallas, put that belt back on and leave it on."

She made no move to do so. She knelt on the seat as she felt herself drawn toward him. "I thought you'd radio in a ground crew or something."

His deep, frustrated sigh carried over the headset as he finished the last buckle. "Lie down on the floor."

"What?"

"Lie down on your stomach on the floor. That way I know you won't fall out while you watch me."

"I'm not going to—"

She received sudden insight to his strength as Jackson grabbed her, twirled her around, and flattened her out in a prone position on the floor in front of the seats. He kept his knee on her back as he stuck a black control box on the end of a fat electric cable into the palm of her hand.

"This button hoists the cable up." He put her thumb on it, his on top of hers, and pressed. "This one lowers it." He moved her thumb and demonstrated again. "You stay on the floor like this. You can inch up to the door and watch what I'm doing."

"Terrif—"

"And you can give Harrison directions as to which way to move the chopper."

"Huh?" As soon as the pressure in the middle of her back eased up, she lifted herself up onto one elbow and twisted around to get a better view of him. "Surely you jest."

"He can't see me when I'm down on the cable."

"I don't know if I can do this," she objected. "I write books for a living, remember?"

"Consider it research."

"For a *Budget* book?"

"Call it *Seeing the Countryside . . . on a Budget.*"

"I don't think that'll make the bestseller list."

"Dallas, it doesn't take a rocket scientist to push two buttons. Now, start me down. And see if you can direct Harrison to set me down right next to her. Then, when it looks like I've got a good hold on her, and I'll try to nod my head when that happens, tell him I'm ready to move her over to dry land."

"You've done this before?"

"Wish me luck." He set his headset aside and stepped over the edge.

He *sounded* as if they'd done it before, but she wasn't so preoccupied that she hadn't noticed he'd avoided answering her question altogether.

In half a minute, he was beside the doe. In that same half a minute, Dallas wanted to tell him half a dozen things that plagued her mind, but she had no way to communicate with him without his earphones. Damn the man! She could understand him jumping into a river to rescue another human being, but a stupid deer? Didn't he know how much he meant to her?

. . . lives in Connecticut with her husband . . .

The words flooded into her consciousness from where they'd been hiding. She'd read them all right. They'd been in black and white. But they still didn't sound right. A woman didn't just forget a husband, did she?

"Doesn't he have her yet?" Harrison asked, jarring her into action.

"Oh . . . yeah." She peered over the edge of the doorway and relayed, "He's got a choke hold on her, but she's still stuck."

"I'll try to pull her loose. Which way?"

"To the right," she guessed.

With the added muscle behind the pull, the deer came free.

"Okay. She's struggling a lot."

"I'm going to try to drag them across so he won't have to lift her."

Fortunately the doe was small, tired from being stuck out in the open too long, from fighting the mud, and from lack of food. Jackson held on to the wriggling animal as long as he could, which turned out to be about three feet from shore. Suddenly free, she bounded out of the water and disappeared beneath the trees.

Jackson looked up and saw Dallas leaning her head and shoulders out the door, and he gave himself a mental pat on the back for having the foresight to put her on the floor. Although he was a little surprised she'd stayed there. A woman who would steal his gun and shoot the dickens out of innocent vending machines didn't seem to be the type to take orders too well.

He gave her a thumbs-up to start the winch, then rode the cable up. Half a minute later, he was back inside, and she was on her feet, helping him unbuckle the harness, her hands burning through his river-splattered uniform shirt wherever she touched him.

He didn't need to put on his headset to know what she was thinking. Relief was written all over her face, echoed in the brightness of her green eyes, colored with confusion. It didn't take a mind reader to know she was in deeper than she wanted to be, emotionally, and that there was more between them than sexual attraction. She'd been deeply worried about his safety.

Concern over her uncertainty and predicament warred with an unsurpassed joy that what he felt for her was mutual. And as she certainly had her doubts, knowing she was married and therefore off-limits, so did he. He'd told himself before that he had no business lusting after another man's wife. He told himself again. Reciprocating her feelings would only make the adjustment more difficult for her, and that was something he didn't want to do.

He brushed her hands aside before they weakened his resolve, even though he wanted to take them in his own and reassure her that everything would be okay. He wanted to tug them up to his lips and whisper against the abraded skin over her fingers that he understood, and that they'd find a solution to this somehow.

Instead he slipped his headset on and gave her a simple, "Thanks." For her sake, it was better if he did nothing that would tempt her to do something she'd regret later.

Even that was easier said than done, though, he realized, as he quickly stripped out of his cold, wet shirt and found her staring at his bare chest.

Freud would have had a heyday analyzing the subconscious motivation behind that move.

DALLAS SAT CAREFULLY RIGID in the helicopter seat and tried to clear her mind, hoping that whatever she'd almost remembered about a camera and taking pictures out of a helicopter's cargo door would come back to her. It seemed the harder she tried, the less she accomplished. She focused on the pain in her hip as she stretched into position; better that than on the half-naked man seated beside her.

Oh, she'd seen the twinkle in his eyes when he'd caught her staring at his well-developed pecs and corded biceps. She wondered how the heck she knew the names of the appropriate muscles, but even that thought flew out of her mind when her gaze wandered down to his flat stomach. She willed herself not to think about his abs and how they disappeared beneath his trousers; she'd turn beet red if she followed that train of thought. She prayed for the journey to end quickly, and it had nothing to do with Harrison's questionable reputation as a helicopter pilot.

As they approached the jail, it looked both familiar and inviting through the steadily falling rain, as if it had become home in the short time she'd been there. Considering it was the only place she remembered, it *was* home. She didn't remember life before, but if a jail with a mud-covered sidewalk looked good now, what were the chances she liked her life in Connecticut?

Even without much memory to speak of, she knew that was rationalization, trying to make the best of her situation, trying to justify her growing attraction to Jackson and anything connected to him.

The night's rain had turned the front lawn into a sea of mud from the street, where they landed, to the front steps. The mud was dark and smooth, rippled where it had run downhill, deeper in some spots than others. The trouble was deciding where it was shallowest, and she relied on Jackson to lead the way as Harrison took off again.

It was only a matter of a few feet before one of her too large duck shoes stayed behind when she stepped forward. She hopped on the other foot to keep her balance while she figured out—

"Dallas? Are you okay?"

The voice came from far away, faded and unreal. She didn't connect it to herself at all. Instead she heard a roll of thunder and a man, much larger than she, asking if she was okay, if she knew where her mother was.

"Mommy's missing," she heard herself say in a voice that seemed somehow different. Younger. Frightened.

Strong arms closed around her then, one behind her back, one under her knees as he lifted her effortlessly against his bare chest. "Where's your mommy?" he asked quietly, prompting her.

Rain spattered them both as he held her close. His heartbeat soothed her as it marked time against her ribs. She pushed a sopping ringlet of hair off her forehead and nose.

"My shoe. I lost my shoe."

"I'll get it later. Where's your mommy?"

She glanced around. Night became morning. Thunder receded into a distant helicopter. A uniformed National

Guardsman became Jackson as she was faced with those chocolate brown eyes just inches from her own. "What?"

She could tell from the heat in his eyes that she was back from wherever she'd been, that he knew he shouldn't be holding her in his arms like this, and that he didn't give a damn at the moment. When she noticed she was cradled next to the smooth, bare skin of his chest, she nearly didn't give a damn about anything else, either.

"What else do you remember?" he prompted.

"Oh, I remember losing my shoe in the mud."

He turned her so she could see the duck shoe.

"No, I mean one of my Keds. A small one. And a National Guardsman came and promised he'd help me find my mother." And he'd put a wide-eyed beagle puppy in her arms, one that had puppy kissed her as if he'd just found his best friend.

She wondered what Jackson would do if she turned ever so slightly and kissed his neck, right below his ear, and stole a taste of his skin. Would it be salty? Would he drop her?

"And did he?"

She really needed to concentrate. "Did he what?"

"Help you find your mother?"

She closed her eyes and tried to remember, too hard again, it seemed. "I don't know."

It was easier to inhale Jackson's scent, the fresh smell left behind by his shampoo. It was also so much more rewarding.

Chapter Nine

"You'd better sit here and get warm," Jackson said as he set Dallas on her feet in front of the wood-burning stove.

The shepherd puppy jumped up and down and ran around their legs, trying to get attention, but Dallas only noticed that she already missed being in Jackson's arms. Cold replaced heat where she'd been pressed up against his body on their short, wet trek from the helicopter.

There was wood in the tin bucket beside the stove. She grabbed a faded towel, opened the door, and shoved some in when what she really wanted to do was fake a fainting spell and fall against him. Feeding the fire in the stove wasn't nearly as much fun as feeding the one within her, but it would have to do.

He left her side for only a moment, returning with a wooden chair. He looked over her shoulder to see how much wood she was adding. "Careful." His warning, laced as it was with humor, lost its effectiveness and only served to warm her from the inside out.

"Don't worry. I won't try to burn the place down again." She had the good grace to blush as she remembered how he'd rushed in and scooped her up.

He grinned, then glanced at the cinder block walls as if measuring them up against a fire code. "I'm more worried about getting smoked out while I'm on the radio. Now that we know your name, maybe we can find someone who's been looking for you.''

She sighed audibly as she curled up in the chair, resting her feet on the front edge, her heels tucked in by her behind, her arms wrapped around her shins. She was still stiff and sore from her ordeal in the river, and it felt good to relax.

''What?'' he asked in response to her sigh. His hands came to rest on the back of the chair. His fingers grazed her shoulders with reassurance that she wasn't alone.

''Oh, I was just thinking about the biography.''

''And?'' he prompted when she didn't continue right away.

''It doesn't feel right.''

''Which part?''

She wondered if she imagined the hope in his question. ''Well, you said Thelia's my grandmother. I'm comfortable with that. But a husband and three children?''

Maybe she was comfortable with the grandmother part because she'd had one longer than she'd had a husband. But wouldn't a husband and children be closer? She tried to remember something that would have occurred often in her past and would therefore be etched into her memory, like getting three kids ready for school every morning. It was safer than thinking about Jackson and, in the long run, would be more productive. But, as usual when she put forth the effort, she got nothing.

''It's right there in black and white. It must be true.''

She craned her neck back and studied him. ''Do you believe everything in life is black and white?''

''Absolutely. Black and white, illegal and legal—it's all the same. Gray areas are just an invention to hide absence of truth.''

She may not have been in Green Valley for long, but it was long enough to know he never seemed to have trouble deciding what was right or wrong. With the vending machines, he'd resisted eating what he'd termed "stolen food" until she'd wheedled him into it. With his brother, he'd insisted that he keep his sleeves properly buttoned on his uniform. With the wedding, he'd opposed her helping Martha and Julie plan it because . . . because . . .

"Why are you against me helping Julie plan her wedding?"

"Roman's too young to get married."

She snickered. "Apparently he's not too young to be a father."

"Maybe."

"Maybe?"

He took up pacing, something she hadn't expected to see Jackson do. At least it was off to the side where she could see him without breaking her neck.

"You think it's not his baby?"

"She's a McKane."

"So? You don't believe her because of genetics?"

"You don't understand. Nobody's perfected gray areas like the McKanes."

"So you think, one, she's lying. And two, even if she's not, he's too young?"

"That's right."

She slid off the chair onto her feet.

"Where're you going?"

"To read my books. I promised Julie and Martha I'd help them."

"Even though you know I'm against this wedding?"

"Well, I might not be as sure of everything as you are with your black-and-white theory, but I believe in keeping my word. They asked me to help, and I said I would."

THE BOOK ON kids' birthday parties told her zilch. There were cute little anecdotes, all right, but they didn't include the names of her children.

When she chose between the two remaining books, she reached automatically for the one titled *Studio Quality Family Portraits...on a Budget.* Maybe she could find out how much she knew about cameras and why she'd thought she'd had one with her in the helicopter.

The technical material didn't confuse her. She found herself skimming through shutter settings and lens selection, able to predict what was said, and perusing the chapter on "Positioning the Subjects." It was more interesting at the moment because she had Julie on her mind.

"Hey, Jackson..."

"Hmm?" He didn't even look up from his paperwork. He'd mentioned earlier that it had increased tenfold without battery backup on his computer, then he'd lit an oil lamp and set to work as if he ran into this problem routinely.

"What kind of wedding photo do you think Julie and Roman would like?"

"I really don't care."

"Oh, come on. He's your brother."

He sighed and set his pen down. Dallas wasn't deterred. For a man who believed in right and wrong, black and white, it hadn't seemed to dawn on him yet that he was trying to force a young woman into single motherhood against her wishes.

"Portrait only," he stated unequivocally. "Since she's due to deliver at any moment."

"So?"

"So?" he repeated calmly, as if the answer would occur to her if she gave some more thought to how Julie might like to hide her big, round belly.

"She's not ashamed of being pregnant, Jackson."

His chair scraped across the floor as he shoved it back and got to his feet. The pacing started again.

"I don't get it," Dallas said. "How can you risk your life and hang from a helicopter by a cable to rescue a stupid deer, and then turn around and refuse to help your brother be happy?"

"It's not the same thing."

"You're right," she said pointedly. "It's not."

He obviously missed her point and looked pleased to hear her admit that.

"I'd think your brother would be a hell of a lot more important to you than a dumb doe."

His pacing came to an abrupt halt as he turned on his heel without a word. Though, from the way his lips pressed into a thin line, she thought he had plenty to say. The opportunity was lost, however, as he stormed out the front door and slammed it behind him.

"Can't take the heat, huh?" she muttered.

Here she wanted to be reunited with a family she couldn't remember, and he was willing to risk alienating his brother over a wedding that didn't concern him in the first place. Someone needed to bring him into this decade.

The shallow mud covering the concrete walk didn't deter Jackson's pacing back and forth outdoors.

So it was back to the wedding business, he fumed, and she wasn't going to leave well enough alone. He paced off some steam for a good five minutes, grumbling to the black billy goat he discovered tethered just outside the front door, then picked his way carefully through the mud to inspect his truck for any damage done by the thieves who'd borrowed it. There were some scratches along the door, both from breaking in and from driving too close to tree branches.

Roman apparently had taken care of the wires beneath the dash.

Roman . . .

Was Dallas right? Oh, he knew he didn't care more for a doe than for his brother, but was he being too hard on him?

He slid in behind the steering wheel. Roman had been the last one to sit there. He hated flying with Harrison, yet he'd gone with him in the helicopter to retrieve the truck. It had been his responsibility while he was in charge to either retrieve it or have someone else do it. He'd handled it very quickly and saved Jackson the time and effort. Maybe the kid was growing up. Maybe he was old enough to take on a wife and baby.

Whoa! He was actually thinking of easing up on Roman? He wasn't ready for that much change. It was bad enough he'd actually given in and nibbled on some of Dallas's stolen food and sipped some of her stolen soda. That was enough change in his principles to last a year, maybe even a lifetime.

His job as sheriff, now that didn't involve a whole helluva lot of change. Law and order he understood; black and white were easily distinguishable; right and wrong never changed. He'd stick with what he knew.

PIPE TOBACCO. Black coffee. Those two smells defined Martha's Diner and they welcomed Jackson after he finished his morning rounds.

"Hey, Martha." He headed directly across the room for the counter.

She pushed a wisp of gray hair back toward her bun and bestowed a cheery smile on him as she refilled Jasper's coffee cup. "You're looking a heck of a lot better than the last time you were in here."

Jasper, sitting on a stool at the counter, snickered as he sucked the last remnants of Martha's famous fried chicken from his fingers. "Yeah, havin' a woman stay at the jail must agree with you, Sheriff."

Jackson straddled a stool, leaving one empty between him and the old moonshiner. He figured the CB bands were burning up with the news of Dallas staying at his jail. He didn't want to discuss her; he was having enough trouble keeping her out of his thoughts. "I hope you're in town to take that puppy back."

"Nah. I was over to the jail this mornin'." His wide grin revealed several new teeth—a fact not lost on Jackson. New dentures cost money, and Jasper hadn't been gainfully employed for the last twenty years.

"You wouldn't happen to have left a black billy goat behind, would you?"

"I see your gal's taken quite a shine to Sonnet," Jasper sidestepped smoothly.

"She's not my gal." Speaking the truth only made him realize how much he wished he could say just the opposite, that she was his, that she was staying. But he knew he could receive word, any minute now, that there was indeed a missing person's report on Mrs. Diana Radcliffe, and that her husband was on the way to claim her and take her home. Next to all that, the goat's questionable arrival paled in comparison.

"She could be your gal," Martha said with a twinkle in her eyes. "I've seen how she looks at you."

"Well, she's not."

"Methinks thou doth protest too much."

"Don't go spewing Shakespeare at me, Jasper. It's bad enough I have to think of you every time I look at that damn puppy. Why couldn't you have named it Rover?"

"If the shoe fits..."

"She's married," he stated flatly. "All right?"

"I didn't see a wedding ring on her finger," Martha noted.

"It probably fell off in the river." More comfortable taking care of business than listening to Martha's clucking noises of sympathy, Jackson turned toward the old moonshiner. "And speaking of 'shine, Jasper—"

"I wasn't speakin' of it, Sheriff."

"Why don't you just make it easy on yourself and tell me where you built your new still?"

"You look hungry, Jackson," Martha commented "How about something to eat?"

If Jackson was surprised by her interruption, he didn't show it. No sense letting the old man think he was off the hook just because Martha hovered around like a mother hen. He answered her without taking his eyes off Jasper. "I wouldn't turn down some of your fried chicken."

"Coffee?"

"Grape soda."

"Something for Dallas?"

"There's plenty of food at the jail."

Martha looked for a moment as if she'd like to stand there and prevent Jackson from interrogating Jasper, but she'd pretty well run out of questions to ask. She bustled off to get the order together. Jackson, waiting patiently, continued to stare at the old man.

"I don't have no new still," Jasper answered.

"Where'd you get the money for those teeth?"

Jasper grinned again, showing them off for the sheriff's inspection. "You like 'em? My boy sent me his tax refund."

"Uh-huh." Jackson frowned at the lone chicken leg on the chipped plate Martha set in front of him, along with a bottle of grape soda. "One piece is all I get?"

"'Fraid so."

"But, Martha—" he smiled and turned on the charm that had always worked on her in the past " —you always give me a leg *and* a breast."

"I'm saving up for the reception."

Totally resistant to his ploy to wheedle anything out of her this time, she glared at him, daring him to deny there'd be a wedding or a reception. In an exaggerated motion, she placed one hand on the towel over her shoulder, and he knew she would snap him with it if he so much as dared.

He grabbed the chicken leg in one hand and the bottle of soda in the other, swiveled to the side, and slid off his stool. "I think I'll take it to go."

"Hold on there," Martha said imperiously, bringing him to an instant halt as she'd been able to do since he'd taken his first baby steps. "You'll have to drink it here."

"Now why on earth would I have to do that?"

Jasper swiveled his stool away from them, distancing himself from their conversation.

"Because I'm recycling."

"I'll bring it back later."

"Oh, sure, you and fifty other people. You drink it now or leave it here, young man."

He didn't try to figure her out. He was still trying to decide what to do about his feelings for Dallas; he couldn't decipher Martha's little quirks right now, too. He tipped the bottle up and his head back, draining it in one breath and wondering if there was anywhere in town he could go where there wasn't a woman who had it in for him.

DALLAS THREW HERSELF full force into planning Julie's wedding. It helped take her mind off Jackson.

Of course, she'd just as soon sit there and daydream about him, but circumstances prevented her from being comfortable doing so. After all, wedding vows were sacred, as she was reminded while leafing through *The Wedding of Your Dreams . . . on a Budget*. It was much safer to picture homemade decorations and just the right angle for a photograph of Julie and Roman's wedding bands than to picture herself in a white dress walking down the aisle toward a certain dark-haired sheriff.

There it was again.

Try as she might to concentrate on the wedding itself, that photography thing popped up again. She tossed the third *Budget* book aside, stood up, and stretched her arms over her head. Sonnet was instantly on his foot, so excited that someone might actually play with him that he stumbled and tripped over the black waterproof bag Roman had left on the floor.

Laughter at the puppy's antics died in her throat. Suddenly, inconceivably, she knew what was in the bag. She could have doubted herself and said she knew what was *maybe* in the bag, but she didn't have any doubts. Three cameras, one of which was very old. What else? She wanted to see if she could remember before she looked, to see if maybe her past was going to start coming into focus for more than a few seconds at a time, to see if she could beat this thing.

Some rolls of film . . .

Well, that didn't take a genius. Try harder.

Some photographs. One of two little girls. The same little girls she'd seen in a fuzzy flashback yesterday when her past had been teasing her. She was on her knees on the floor in the next instant, fumbling with the zipper in her haste to open the bag. If there was a photograph of her daughters in there, she wanted it in her hands. Now.

Her fingers brushed over three cameras and an assortment of lenses, feeling comfortable with them, but in too much of a hurry to pick up anything and look it over. She had to find the picture. Rolls of film were held neatly attached to the bag's rigid sides by small, stitched-in, elastic bands, and she skimmed over them, too.

It was there, in a side pocket. It was old and faded, with tattered edges. Two little girls. The same two little girls she'd remembered the day before.

She frowned. Two, not three. Her bio said three. And it looked so old.

She turned to share her good fortune with Jackson, to tell him she'd remembered something concrete and ask him what he thought of this, but he wasn't there. And she missed him more now than when she'd been daydreaming about him most of the day.

The photograph beckoned, and she scanned it with a practiced eye. The girls were five and six years old—she didn't even wonder how she knew that—with blond ponytails and red plastic barrettes to catch the short ends where they wouldn't stay tucked in. One wore a pink shorts set, the other blue. They were barefoot. Little girls had been dressing the same way since Dallas could remember; it was impossible to determine the age of the photo by their clothes. But all the same, she knew it was too old for them to be her daughters.

She turned her attention back to the cameras, two of which were very expensive Nikons, the third an old Minolta that looked as if it had been lugged all over the world. She picked them up, checked them for moisture and residue. None. She adjusted the settings and tripped the shutters to make sure everything was in good working order. They felt familiar, comfortable, as if they were extensions of her mind.

Dallas knew enough about her memory loss by now to know that, when nothing else became clear, trying to force the issue only made the images recede further from her grasp. Instead she looked forward. This equipment would do just fine for taking pictures of Julie and Roman's wedding and reception. And while she was using them, maybe they would trigger her memory the same way the puppy had.

She'd even get some shots of Jackson to take with her when she went back to Connecticut.

"GOOD BOY!" Dallas sat at Jackson's desk, tossing cheese cubes to the puppy to catch in midair. He'd missed the first few, but he was getting pretty good.

The front door opened just enough for a yellow-slickered man to slip through. He was as thin and ancient as Jasper and was clutching something beneath his slicker. He peeked outside, glanced up and down Main Street, then pushed the door firmly closed. Dallas got the impression he'd like to lock it behind him as he tried, unsuccessfully, to assume an innocent air.

"Afternoon," he greeted. "Name's Otis." He ignored Sonnet as the pup stood up on its hind legs to sniff at the bulge beneath the slicker. He moseyed around the jail, the pup circling him constantly, getting underfoot and nearly tripping him several times. "Where's the boys?"

"The boys?"

"Yeah, them Ridgefield boys."

"Oh." Since she'd turned the volume down on the radio traffic when its incessant chatter had nearly driven her nuts, she wasn't exactly sure where any of them were. "Out working, I guess. Why?"

"You think cats and dogs can get along?"

Surprised by his abrupt question, no quick answer leapt forward from her uncooperative memory. "I'm not really the person to ask."

"Ain't you the Budget Lady? Jasper said the Budget Lady was stayin' here."

"Well yes, I am, but—"

"You done wrote a book on it."

Her eyebrows arched. "On cats and dogs?"

"On the perfect pet for ever'body. On a budget, of course."

"Of course."

She remembered reading something in her biography about accumulating too many pets while doing research on a pet book. She was distracted by a hiss from beneath Otis's slicker.

"Ow! Dang!" he cursed.

Suddenly he jerked the slicker off and lunged backward—a spry maneuver for a man of his years—trying to pry a large yellow cat from his shoulder and neck. All he succeeded in doing was giving the large tabby a boost up to the top of his head, and he didn't have nearly enough hair up there to cushion his scalp from the claws.

Sonnet leapt up repeatedly, trying to get to the cat. He eventually tripped Otis, who fell over backward onto the hardwood floor. In a flurry of fur, the two animals darted around the jail until the cat used the desk as a runway and makeshift springboard to the top of the file cabinet.

Dallas rushed to the old man's side. "Are you all right?" If he had a broken hip or anything, she didn't know how she was going to get help.

Blood from the claw lacerations trickled down his face and neck, making him look like a candidate for scaring children in a haunted house. He accepted her hand up, then dabbed at the blood with the white handkerchief he pulled from the pocket of his overalls.

"I reckon I'm a sight better off than that desk over there." He had the good grace to look guilty.

Dallas looked at the chaos created in the cat's wake. Papers that had been neatly stacked on Jackson's desk were scattered all over the floor, along with pens, pencils, and a zillion paper clips. Journals that had been on top of the cabinet were tumbled on the floor, some open, some not.

"I'd say it's a tie."

Otis inched backward toward the door, snatching up his slicker on the way. It looked like the cleanup was going to be left entirely for her to handle. He reached into his overalls as he asked, "You think cats and birds can get along?"

"You'd better not pull a bird out of that pocket," she warned.

Out came another fresh white handkerchief to sop up more blood. He grinned mischievously and ducked out the door. A second later, he poked his head back in. "I forgot to tell ya. His name's Macbeth."

"Terrific."

Dallas put Macbeth into the bathroom, stacked the papers and journals into neat piles, and wondered as she got down on her knees if she could teach the puppy to retrieve paper clips as easily as he'd learned to catch flying cheese cubes. When she was done with that, she got up and brushed off her jeans. She had acquired an accumulation of puppy hair, cat hair, and spatterings of dried mud.

Jackson had been gone for hours. He'd probably return soon. She reminded herself that she should be more concerned about meeting a husband who was a stranger to her than thinking about Jackson, but the reality was that the whole idea of a husband still sounded like a foreign notion to her. And wasn't the fact that she hadn't been notified yet an indication that she was right? In this day and age of communications, with radios and cellulars running on batteries, she felt she should have heard something by now—if there was anything to hear.

As she continued to brush off her jeans, her eyes fell on the peach-colored dress Julie had brought her. It was still laying over the back of a chair. Jackson had seemed quite interested in it when he'd first seen it, studying it, stroking it with his fingertips. Would he stroke it again if she put it on? She grabbed up the long dress and the oil lamp and slipped into the bathroom without letting the cat out or the puppy in.

"What is that smell?" she muttered, frowning at the yellow cat who sat on the floor and licked its front paw.

Her red teddy still hung on the back of the door and it looked as bad and stiff as she'd thought it would. She didn't need to put her nose up to it to know it reeked of river water and dead fish. She dropped it into the trash can beneath the sink. She'd throw it into the outside trash later.

She sat on the closed toilet while she unbuttoned the tiny, pearl buttons running down the front of the dress, thankful her fingers weren't as sore or stiff anymore, though they still bore scabs. The peach color would highlight her auburn hair. The tiny green flowers would bring out the green in her eyes. She was pleased to learn that she apparently had some fashion sense.

She didn't have anything to wear under the dress, of course. And she didn't much care. She'd wash before she changed, so at least she'd be clean.

Chapter Ten

Jackson entered the jail just in time to see Dallas back carefully out of the bathroom. It didn't occur to him to wonder why she was backing out. He only noticed she'd changed clothes, and the rounded curve of her rear was emphasized nicely.

The dress did everything he'd thought it would. Its long length hid the scabs on her legs. It draped softly over her hips and thighs. It nipped in loosely at the waist, hinting at the trim figure that the jeans and flannel shirt had totally hidden.

She turned then and walked into the main room. While the flannel shirt had been large enough for her to tuck a book inside, the peach bodice clung to every curve she possessed. And he wasn't disappointed that he'd had to wait. It was worth it to see the slight bounce of her breasts that told him Julie still hadn't brought her a bra. Maybe he could learn to like Julie yet.

"Oh, hi," she said softly when she noticed him standing there. Her smile was shy, as if she hoped he liked the change. She set the oil lamp on his desk.

When he'd first seen the dress laying over the chair, he'd known the green flowers would bring out the emerald in her eyes. He was right.

"Did you hear anything yet?" she asked eagerly.

"It's Saturday. I don't expect a response from your publisher until the weekend's over."

He admired her calm reserve as she gave a simple nod, and he wondered how most women would fare in her shoes. Would they cry because they couldn't remember where they'd come from, lamenting because it surely had to be better than this hick town dealing with flood problems? Would they complain because they only had borrowed clothes to wear?

As a matter of fact, he wondered how he'd do if he suddenly couldn't remember his family.

"I thought we could eat over at the diner," he suggested. He should have added *Then you can go home with Martha for the night,* but something stopped him. He didn't want her to go with Martha for one thing. For another, he wondered whether she was wearing her red teddy under that dress.

So much for distancing himself from her all day. Instead of getting her and the fact that she was married out of his mind, it had only served to make him want her more. That old proverb about absence making the heart grow fonder. Only he didn't think it had as much to do with his heart as his libido.

"Sounds good," she agreed.

He knew he didn't have a bat's chance in hell of finding out about that teddy. It was flaming red; it seemed as if he should be able to see a shadow of it through her dress, but he couldn't. At least not in this light. It'd be another story at the diner, where it was all lit up thanks to Martha's generator.

"Is everything all right?" She looked down to check all her buttons.

"Oh, fine." He smiled to reassure her. He tried to look away, but he didn't have much luck with that.

"I'm afraid these shoes don't go with the dress very well."

He heard the nervousness in her voice and he wanted to put her at ease. "I didn't even notice them." And it was true, too. "Maybe we can find you some sneakers later."

He led the way to the door, only to find she'd detoured by way of the black bag Roman had brought in yesterday.

"I remembered something," she said. "The puppy was jumping around and stumbled over this bag, and all of a sudden I knew what was in it."

"You knew?"

She nodded.

"You mean you guessed right?"

"No, I knew. I didn't guess at all. I knew there were three cameras. I knew one was really old. I knew there was a picture of two little girls."

She retrieved the photo from the bag and held it out to him.

He took it from her gently. "It's old."

"I know."

He heard disappointment in her voice and wished he could snap his fingers and make it all better. Without her being married and having to go away, of course. He didn't want to knock the guy off or anything, but . . .

"I wanted to ask your opinion. I thought possibly they were my little girls, but I don't see how they could be."

"Anything else in there?"

"Rolls of film."

"Exposed or new?"

"Some of each."

She bent down and pulled out several canisters without hesitation. Surprise registered on her face almost as soon as he felt the same.

"You *know* the difference?"

She nodded, nearly speechless. "Yes. Oh, my God, how can I know something so precise and not who I am?"

He reached for her then, wrapping his arms around her and comforting her. "It's all right. I'm sure it's just a sign that you're starting to remember more and more."

"But film is so... unimportant."

"Maybe not."

She tilted her head back and looked up at him. "What do you mean?"

"Let's get those developed before we decide how important they are. Martha's nephew ought to be able to give us a rush job."

She pulled back. He was tempted to hold her longer, but he knew she had her own thoughts to wrestle with. Probably ones very similar to his own.

He held the door for her, closing it carefully so as not to catch her fingers as she pushed the puppy back inside. He could have told her again that Sonnet belonged outdoors anyway, but he didn't want to argue. He wanted to hold her again. To find some reason to kiss her. To get her to kiss him as she had in the library cellar. Now *that* was worth thinking about. Worth planning for.

It was a pleasant temperature outside, too warm for him to slip his arm around her with the excuse of keeping her warm. It was dark, with the moon only occasionally peeking through the mass of clouds. A perfect night to convince her to let him hold her hand so she wouldn't trip on something.

"It's only a block away. Would you like to walk?"

She looked up at the dark gray sky. "Sure. It feels good to get out."

They walked side by side. When they came to a section of the sidewalk that had been pushed up crookedly by a shallow tree root, he reached for her hand. "Careful now."

Safely over the bump, she didn't tug her hand back. Now he wanted to drape his arm over her shoulders and hold her against his side. If she let him do that, then what would he want? He knew the answer to that as well as any red-blooded, American man. Fortunately they reached the diner before he could tempt himself.

"Smells good," she said when he opened the door, letting the coffee and pipe tobacco aroma waft out.

"The food's even better. I recommend the fried chicken."

The diner was half-full of customers, scattered here and there at the square wooden tables as a waitress bustled around among them with a pot of coffee. He released Dallas's hand and gestured her toward an empty table.

"There you are!" Elvin Brooks croaked before the door had even closed behind them. He leaned forward in his chair, and Jackson knew if he waited for the man to get to his feet and shuffle over to him that he'd be away from Dallas too long.

"You go on," he told her casually as he headed over to Brooks's table. "I'll be along in just a minute."

"I talked to your no-good brother about someone snatchin' my chickens, just like you told me," Brooks grumbled. "And nothing's gettin' done."

"No need to get up, Mr. Brooks. I'm sure Roman's keeping an eye out for anything suspicious," Jackson tried to reassure him. "We all are."

"When're you coming out to dust for fingerprints?" He rocked forward a few times, then eased up to his feet slowly.

Jackson could think of nothing worse than dusting a stinking chicken coop for fingerprints. He'd rather be leaving prints of his own on Dallas's skin. "I think we can handle this without going to that trouble."

"Ah-ha! Just as I thought." He shuffled forward until he was in Jackson's face, then glared up at him. And he backed that up by pointing his bony finger at Jackson's chest. "My wife, God rest her soul, was a McKane. That's why you're not tendin' to your job like a sheriff should. Don't think I don't know it, Ridgefield."

"Now, Mr. Brooks—"

"What's the matter with you, boy? Your daddy knows right from wrong. He's a fair judge, too. Didn't he teach you nothin'?"

Dallas listened to their exchange from the table she'd selected over by the far wall. Several of the patrons were watching with amused grins on their faces. Mr. Brooks looked to be about sixty, and Dallas thought he could hold his own in a verbal argument in spite of the fact that he moved in slow little jerks.

Others looked as if they were about to get up and side with the older man. McKanes, she supposed. Jackson had complained about them before in connection with Julie and the upcoming wedding. She'd chalked it up to a personal grudge against Julie. Now she was suddenly aware that the clan Jackson had complained about might be more real than she'd imagined. And more extensive.

She counted ten frowning men and women. They'd stopped eating and were paying rapt attention. She counted an equal number of mildly amused people. They were all scattered through the diner, not sitting on opposite sides as if they couldn't stand each other. Yet she felt an undercurrent that said otherwise.

Dallas instantly sided with Jackson. She knew this argument was none of her business, but if anybody was going to do his job, she knew it was Jackson. She'd never met anyone who had such an unshakable knowledge of black and white, right and wrong. And it felt strange for her to know someone so well.

She didn't even know she'd risen to her feet until Julie rose and laid a hand on her arm.

"Sit over here with Roman and me," she invited softly.

"But—"

"But nothing," she whispered. "He's the sheriff. He can handle this without anyone else getting involved. Leave him be."

Dallas noticed McKane eyes all around the room watching Julie. And her. Measuring them. She let Julie lead her over to her table and she lowered herself into the chair Roman held for her. She saw every one of them decide to keep a wary truce and follow their example.

"What's this all about?" she whispered to Roman and Julie.

"It's an old family feud," Roman replied.

"Yeah," Julie added. "So old, nobody even remembers how it started."

No more words were exchanged; she'd missed the end of their conversation. Jackson gave Mr. Brooks a reassuring pat on the shoulder, steadying the older man's chair as he inched back down into it.

JACKSON WAS BORED, or so Dallas hoped. He sat at the small table, his food barely touched, his arms folded across his chest. He leaned back in his chair, and Dallas eventually deduced that he was once again trying to keep his hands safely out of Julie's reach. Martha whizzed by, grabbing up empty soda bottles.

"Hey, I'm not finished," he objected as he snatched it back from her grasp with lightning reflexes.

"It's warm. Let me get you another."

"It's fine." He glanced around the room. Most of the crowd had left, so no one was waiting for their table. "What's the big hurry?"

"Hurry? No hurry. What makes you think there's a hurry?"

"You're right." He handed her the bottle back.

"I am?"

"I'm ready for coffee."

"There is no coffee."

"Martha, I can smell coffee."

She tittered. "Oh, my, that's from years of brewing the stuff in here. Nope, all I have is bottled soda, bottled juice, and bottled tea. Can I get anybody else another drink?" she glanced inquiringly around the table.

Dallas declined, along with Roman and Julie.

"You're sure now? You must've worked up quite a thirst with all these wedding plans." Her voice underlined *wedding plans* verbally.

"Oh, sure," Julie said. She nudged Roman. "We'll each have another tea."

Martha bustled off toward the kitchen.

"Now, where were we?" Julie mused.

Spread out on the table in front of her were lists. One was made up of things for Roman to do before the wedding, one was for herself, and one was marked off into blocks for various other people.

"I was just asking if you know when you're going to do this yet?" Dallas repeated.

"Let's see... I wrote myself a note about that." Julie dug through her purse and pulled out an envelope, the back of which was covered with her writing. "Oh, yeah. Madame Celeste says she needs to know your birthday."

"That makes two of us," Dallas replied.

Julie frowned sympathetically. "Nothing yet, huh?"

"Nope."

She sighed. "Well, then, she said the next best thing was that she meet you in person."

Jackson hung his head. "Please tell me you're not going to bring her into my jail."

"She offered to stop by," Julie replied too sweetly. She turned back to Dallas. "She's so wonderful! She may even be able to tell you something about yourself."

"Really?"

"Just last year she helped the sheriff find a little boy who was lost in the national forest."

Dallas looked at Jackson, surprised to hear he'd used a psychic's help when he didn't seem to believe in her abilities.

"Not me," he said defensively. "It was Sheriff Gruder over in Clark County." He glared at Julie. "And he was found less than a quarter mile from the campsite he wandered away from."

"Still—"

"And only two hours after he'd been missing."

Dallas expected Roman to jump to Julie's defense, but he just sat back and let her handle Jackson on her own. Nor did she seem to mind this time.

"Here you go." Martha put a fresh bottle of one thing or another in front of all four of them. "Drink up."

"But I didn't want—" Jackson started to say.

"I already opened it. Drink it." She pulled up a chair and squeezed in next to Julie, perusing her lists. "What'd you decide to do about flowers?"

"The bridesmaids have already started making them. They drove over to Mason and got peach and mint tissue paper."

"Ooh, that'll look so pretty with their dresses. How'd they ever find those colors in that small of a town?"

Julie smirked in Jackson's direction. "Madame Celeste told them they'd find it there."

"What about booze?" Roman asked. "The liquor store's flooded."

"Oh, don't you worry about that," Julie said as she patted his hand. "Martha makes a wonderful punch."

"Punch? Men don't drink punch except at christenings. Right, Jackson?"

"Hey, leave me out of this."

"Oh, I almost forgot," Julie smacked her open palm against her forehead in a comical gesture. "Not enough blood to my brain, I guess. Your mother said your Uncle Henry would marry us."

Jackson and Roman groaned in unison.

"What?" Julie asked warily.

"Not Uncle Henry." Roman slumped back in his chair.

"Better have a backup," Martha acknowledged.

Julie looked at Jackson for an explanation, since no one else was helping. She knew he was always good for depressing news.

He grinned like a Cheshire cat. "Uncle Henry is, shall we say tactfully, likely to forget to even show up."

"Oh." She brightened. "Then we'll just send someone for him ahead of time."

"And, even if you do get him here on the right day, there's no guarantee he'll remember how to marry anyone. He is, as I was saying, a bit forgetful."

"Forgetful!" Roman scoffed. "Boy, that's sugarcoating it. The man is senile, Julie. We can't have him marry us. That's all there is to it."

"I'm not telling your mother we don't want her brother to marry us."

Roman looked beseechingly at Jackson.

"I'm not telling her," he said firmly.

"But he's retired," Roman stressed.

"Get real," Jackson scoffed. "This is Green Valley. If the family asks Reverend Brown to lend his pulpit to the former pastor, he's not going to object."

Roman's head rolled backward as Julie muttered, "How bad can he be?"

No one seemed to be interested in answering that question. Martha and Julie were already poring over the lists again, tsking over how everything could get done quickly enough so that when Madame Celeste picked the day, they'd be ready.

Mr. Brooks inched his way across the room and hovered near Julie's shoulder. "I reckon I can help somehow. I got less work to do at home now that so many of my chickens is gone."

Dallas wondered how on earth he could help when he could barely get across the room, but Julie tore off part of her list. As she turned to give it to him, he stuffed his hands into his pockets. He hesitated, withdrew one slowly and tentatively reached for his assignment, inching backward as he did so.

"Oh, Mr. Brooks, have you felt the baby kick yet?" Julie asked as she reached for his wrist. Too late. He made his escape.

A middle-aged woman inched her way over to the table, a wary eye on Brooks as he departed. Her cautious gaze then shifted to Julie.

"Aunt Sally," Roman said, his eyes round with surprise.

"I'd like to help, too," she said to him. She took a deep breath and turned to Julie. "That is, if you'd like."

Julie beamed as she tore off another part of her list and handed it to her. "Roman and I would be honored, Aunt Sally."

Aunt Sally cringed at the familiarity, squinted at the list, and muttered, "A Ridgefield wouldn't do it this way," as she walked away.

Julie's face fell. "Oh, so you think she wanted to feel the baby kick?"

Roman grabbed her hand, holding it safely in his. "I think that might be pushing your luck, honey."

Redheaded Millie burst through the front door and headed right for their table. "I found some!" she announced. "I was saving them up for canning, but what the heck. I'll never get around to it."

Jackson perked up for the first time in over an hour. "Some what?"

"Oh, Jackson, hi." She pasted on a smile. "I see you've arrested a billy goat."

He ignored the subject of the goat entirely. "What did you find?"

"Some pots," Martha interjected. "I need more pots. Dallas, have you met Millie, our librarian?"

Jackson interrupted. "You have a lot of pots, do you, Millie? A single woman like you?"

"They were my mother's," she replied.

"And some cake pans," Martha added at the same time.

"You own a diner and you don't have cake pans?" Jackson asked with disbelief.

"Not near enough. I'm making a big cake. A really big cake. Lots of layers. Lots of tiers. Chocolate on one side, yellow on the other. It's gonna be the talk of the county."

Everyone tossed out ideas and pointers for the wedding and reception. Dallas noticed that everyone wanted to help in some way, even if it was only a small thing. Everyone pulled together, the way a large family would do. And everyone was obviously putting something over on Jackson, but, as yet, Dallas couldn't figure out what.

She thought the interaction felt wonderful, yet somehow foreign. Her biography said she came from a large, boisterous family. So shouldn't this feel familiar to her? This haranguing and teasing and helping? If the puppy Sonnet had inadvertently triggered a memory of another puppy named Penny, wouldn't a familial atmosphere like this act as a similar trigger?

Julie and Roman had asked her advice freely during supper. Even though she didn't remember writing a book on putting weddings together on a budget, they seemed to think she'd retained the information somewhere in the back of her mind. They'd listened carefully. They'd made changes in their lists with what appeared to be growing anticipation and excitement.

The bottom line was, she felt included. Part of a family. An important individual. And she felt so warmed inside by those thoughts that she was puzzled, apprehensive, almost compelled to draw back and distance herself. But she didn't.

She caught the tail end of Jackson's latest disparaging comment regarding Madame Celeste. Julie was just about to dress him down when Roman interrupted, a big grin on his face.

"Madame Celeste told us not to worry about you, Jackson."

"Is that right?"

"Yeah. She said you'd ease up when the right woman comes along." He laughed as if he knew a secret.

Jackson didn't think it was in the least bit funny. His first reaction was to wonder if Madame Celeste had mentioned that the right woman was already married. His second was to wonder what got into him that he would even consider listening to anything she had to say. Especially about his love life.

He'd found no report on a missing woman named Diana Radcliffe. It was possible her family didn't know she was in this area and therefore didn't know she was missing. Maybe they thought she was off on vacation somewhere. Or on a business trip. Women did that these days—left the husband home with the kids while they went to conventions and conferences.

"Oh, I almost forgot," Dallas said eagerly. "Roman, that bag you found is mine. The cameras all seem to work fine, and I've got plenty of film, so your wedding photos are on me."

They all spoke over one another.

"Terrific!"

"It was yours?"

"Do you remember anything else?"

"Why, you must do all your own photography in those books." Martha beamed like a proud parent.

"That reminds me," Jackson said as he pulled the five small black canisters out of his pockets and lined them up on the table in front of Martha. "Do you think Richard can get us some prints on these by tomorrow?"

"You bet he can." Martha jumped to her feet, scooped them into her apron, and bade everyone a good-night on her way into the kitchen.

Tomorrow was Sunday. Jackson vowed to try the publisher again first thing Monday, not that he thought they'd give him any more information than an agent's name. But even that would be a start. In the meantime, he was sick to death of this wedding talk. He'd been patient so far, giving a lot of consideration to the idea that Roman was indeed more important than a dumb doe, as Dallas had suggested. But he still thought his little brother was too young to get married.

IT'S JUST NOT NATURAL. Men don't think about weddings, Jackson thought, as he and Dallas walked side by side back to the jailhouse.

He supposed his exception to that had everything to do with listening to Julie and Roman's plans for two hours at Martha's Diner. And everyone else who'd stopped by the table and offered their opinions on everything from flowers to vows.

Men thought about sex. If not constantly, then a good part of the time.

And, after they fell in love, they thought about marrying. Not that he ever had. But he'd seen his youngest brother fret over the proper way to do it; even though Roman felt he'd had no choice in the matter, he'd still wanted to do it right.

Then the honeymoon took over a man's thoughts. Well, basically, that was back to thinking about sex. It must be the man's reward for living through the proposal and the wedding and the reception.

And, when he was done contemplating all the above, there was still a myriad of other related topics like children, grandchildren, mortgage payments, retirement plans and things like that.

But it wasn't natural for a man to mull over the actual logistics of the wedding. That was something little girls dreamed of and planned from the time they were old enough to chase little boys. Men got roped into paying attention to wedding plans, offering an opinion when asked, getting measured for a tux. Period.

So then why was he picturing Dallas in a white dress, walking up a rose-petal-strewn aisle in the only church in Green Valley? Why were words of love—vows, really—running rampant through his mind?

The answer was simple; he was losing his mind. All that lack of sleep had deranged him. Or too much caffeine had permanently impaired his reasoning ability.

What the hell was he doing falling in love with a married woman?

His mother would reach up and shake her finger under his nose and tell him he was going straight to hell. His father would rightly point out that he could no longer be trusted—by the residents of Twain County or anyone else—to uphold the law if he couldn't even be trusted with a stray woman.

And that, he rationalized, was the crux of the whole problem. She *was* a stray. She needed someone. And she'd landed right in his lap.

Not that he was complaining.

He made a dumb remark about how it had cooled off outside while they were at the diner, then followed that with a movement that draped his arm across her shoulders. She didn't step away. She didn't acknowledge it either, not with a smile, not with a lifted eyebrow, not even by slipping her arm around his waist.

But, if he wasn't mistaken, she leaned just a little bit closer. Her shoulder pressed against his side, tucked under his arm like a chick under its mama's wing. Trusting. Seeking protection, warmth, comfort. And he was helpless to resist.

The pup barked when it heard them approach.

The lamp on his desk had burned down low, but, after being outside, it threw off enough light to see them into the jail. Jackson tried to close the door behind the pup after he ran outside, but Dallas caught the door and left it open enough for Sonnet to squeeze back in when he was done.

Tiny squeaks drew Jackson's attention back to the desk.

"What the hell?"

A small white cage with two tiny lovebirds huddled together on their perch sat in the center of the desk. When Dallas stepped closer, murmuring soothingly, they darted to the other side of the cage, clung to the wires, and let loose with complaints that could be only described as shrill.

"I wonder what he named these?" Dallas cooed.

"Who?" Jackson asked with a low growl.

"Otis."

"Otis brought them?"

"Well, I'm not sure. He said something about cats and dogs and birds—"

"You *knew* they were coming?" First a lame pup, now they'd progressed to a children's zoo. "What next? Chickens?"

"I'll bet he named them Romeo and Juliet."

He wished she didn't sound so damn charmed.

"Did you see how they were cuddling together?"

"Birds don't cuddle." He headed for the peace and quiet of the bathroom.

It was in vain. No sooner had he opened the bathroom door than a yellow-and-red streak shot out, darted across his boots, and careened around the room. And that was mild compared to what it did when the pup returned, claws gouging the hardwood floor in hot pursuit.

Jackson's life didn't fly before his eyes, but his papers did. Along with pens, paper clips, journals, and bird feathers from the bottom of the cage raised from the two lovebirds' flapping wings.

"Oops, I forgot to tell you about Macbeth."

He knew he should shut his mouth before he inhaled feathers and choked to death. "You *knew* there was a cat in there?" He pointed an accusing finger at the cat, sitting up on his file cabinet, as if she didn't know what he was talking about.

She smirked. "Otis brought it."

He could barely hear her over the barking pup. He wanted to boot it a good one. "Otis! What the hell is he up to?"

She looked confused. "Up to? He's just trying to help these guys out until you find their owners."

"Ha!" Not a strongly professional term, he realized, but the best he could do at the moment. "Otis can't be trusted to 'just help out.' He's up to something. I don't trust him any farther than I can throw him."

"I'm sure the people who are missing these animals won't feel that way when they're all reunited. I can take care of them until then. You could find some dog food or something to help out."

"Help out? This is a jail, in case you've forgotten." He said it slowly, enunciating every word so there'd be no misunderstanding.

"It wouldn't hurt, Jackson."

"Well, hell, then. I might as well let you run the jail while you're here. Call it research. Or have you already written a book on that, too?"

He could have gone on for another five minutes—if he hadn't taken a closer look at the red streak the cat had dropped in his wake. It was bad enough he had to stare at Dallas's teddy every time he went into the bathroom. Now he was faced with it right there in the middle of the jail. And if it was on his floor, it sure as heck wasn't under her dress.

He promptly forgot whatever he'd been complaining about.

Chapter Eleven

Jackson woke up to the sound of the stove door banging shut and the aroma of strong coffee.

Not that he'd been sleeping much. He'd gone to bed in a pique last night, too angry to sleep.

It was his jail, and he was protective of his image, its image and the image of law and order that he was sworn to uphold. And law and order didn't carry much weight when it housed a pup named Sonnet, a cat named who knew what—and he didn't want to remember what—and two lovebirds most likely called Romeo and Juliet.

The truth was, he'd missed sleeping with Dallas. He'd stormed off to the back room and tossed and turned in the twin bed. Her scent was still on his pillow, in his sheets, in his mind, driving him crazy all night long.

He got up once to see where she'd settled in for the night. She was curled up on the cot in the cell. He hesitated at the door, thinking about picking her up and carting her off to share his bed. The pup was curled up in a ball in front of her, Dallas's arm thrown across its back the way Jackson would have liked to drape his arm over her again. In the library, that had been his arm over her breasts. Soft, warm, rising and falling with each breath.

Another ball at her feet lifted its head. How the hell she'd gotten the cat and pup to settle down together, he'd never know. She just had that way about her. The same way that made him want to go over there and crawl onto the cot behind her. Animals or no animals. But he didn't.

The jail just didn't seem like the proper place to make love to a woman. So he hadn't wakened her.

Now he wished he had, because waking up with her in his bed would have been a whole lot more fun than trying to figure out how to go out there and apologize for his unprofessional behavior and unchivalrous attitude. Maybe he could blame it on the weather.

He opened the door to see more light than he'd seen in a long while. Weeks maybe. Sunlight. It streamed through the windows, mocking his intention to blame his foul mood on three and a half weeks of rain.

His desk and file cabinet had been put back in order. The bathroom door was open, so he had to assume the menagerie was still compatible. The little chirps of the lovebirds were actually kind of pretty.

Hell, anything would beat three weeks of rain and a flood.

And Dallas? She stood at the stove, watching potatoes brown in a skillet, a shy smile on her face. "I hope I didn't wake you."

Relieved that she wasn't going to bite off his head, he grinned in return. "Nah. I thought I should get up before someone sends the pumper truck."

Her nose wrinkled. "You could smell it in there? It wasn't much smoke, and I opened the front door to air it out right way. I think I've got the hang of it now."

She poured him a cup of coffee and held it out. He took from her, his fingers lingering on hers longer than necesary. He set it on the stove. And, before she could ask why, he pulled her into his arms and covered her lips with his own.

She melted against him. He felt the softening of her bones, the warmth of her skin, the forgiveness for his behavior last night. He wasn't sure she'd forgive the thoughts he'd had all night. The dreams of her in his bed, as naked as the first morning she'd lain there while he'd swiped her blanket in exchange for the sheet.

He remembered perfect breasts, not too big to go without a bra the past couple days, not too small for anything he had in mind. Just well-rounded, firm. He could feel them pressing against his chest now, two mounds that burned a path to his groin and made him wish he wasn't standing.

He remembered a firm, flat stomach and abdomen, one that didn't look anything like he thought a mother of three would have. One that he pressed himself against now, growing harder by the second.

"Dallas..." Her name escaped from his throat, his lips, but he hadn't known he was going to say it like that. Like a man who hadn't much patience left. He inched backward toward the bedroom, taking her with him, careful not to break the spell.

Sonnet barked.

Jackson ignored him. They were at the doorway now. Her hands were in his hair, threading their way through it, igniting every nerve ending he had.

The front door swung open. "'Morning, Jackson. Did you know there's a goat out there?"

Jackson pried his lips from hers to tell Harrison to go take a long flight and take the goat with him, but, when he saw his brother's grim face, reality intruded as effectively as a cold shower.

"'Morning, Dallas." Harrison looked directly at Jackson then. "Something's come up." He stuttered over hi next few words as he realized how they might take his double entendre. "I . . . I mean, there's something you need . . . something that requires . . ."

"Oh, hell, Harrison, spit it out."

"I need to talk to you. Private-like."

"Can't it wait?"

Harrison's gaze flickered to the bedroom door, then back to his brother's face. "No. Trust me."

"I'm sure Sonnet and Macbeth need to go outside," Dallas offered.

"Who?" Harrison asked.

"Don't ask," Jackson told him as Dallas gathered up the pup and yellow cat. "You don't want to know."

Harrison grinned then as he noticed the caged birds, too. "Those names explain where all these animals are coming from. Now what do you think those three old boys are up to?"

"Diversionary tactics. But it doesn't make much sense them leaving their signatures all over everything, does it?"

"Well, nobody ever said rotgut was good on the brain cells," Harrison said as he pushed the door shut behind Dallas. "We just got word there's a man on his way to Green Valley." Harrison's eyes darted back toward the bedroom door where Jackson and Dallas had been wrapped around each other when he'd interrupted. "I don't quite know how to tell you this."

"You were going to pick him up in the chopper, but you wrecked it?" First rationalization, now he was stalling. Anything was better than finding out the film had been developed into dozens of photographs of her adoring husband.

"Nice try."

"Okay." Jackson sank into his desk chair. "Give it to me straight."

"It's her husband."

Damn!

Jackson shoved a pile of papers aside. "Why wasn't there a missing person's report filed on her?"

"I didn't get to talk to him direct, but she probably writes under a pseudonym."

It made sense, Jackson knew. He didn't want it to, but, heaven forbid, it did.

He'd dreaded this moment. A hundred different doubts raced through his mind, obscuring the fact that the potatoes had started to burn, and Harrison took care of them.

Maybe it was mistaken identity. Highly unlikely. If the physical descriptions hadn't matched, the guy wouldn't be on his way. Besides, not that many people were missing. Maybe he was her ex-husband. Then why would he have been the one to file a report? It would have been one of her family members. Unless the guy was still important to her. Well, they did have three kids together. Boy, talk about rationalization. For a man who'd never done it before, ever, he sure was a quick learner.

Harrison thrust a piece of paper at Jackson. "Here's the stats I got over the radio."

"Five-seven? I don't think Dallas is that tall."

Harrison looked at him as if he were grasping at straws.

"A hundred thirty pounds? No way."

"So what? The guy's off an inch or two, and ten or fifteen pounds over. Not everybody's good at guessing."

"A husband should know."

"Besides, she could've lost ten pounds waiting out on that island for you to come along."

"And I did, too. Just in the nick of time."

"Is that your problem?"

Jackson jerked out of his reverie. "What do you mean?"

"You saved her, so now you think she's yours or something?"

"Don't be ridiculous."

The front door inched open. "Okay if I come back in now?"

"What're you going to do?" Harrison asked Jackson quietly.

Dallas lingered by the door, far enough away not to hear his decision.

"It might be a mistake."

"Jackson, would you wake up and—"

"Let's wait until he gets here. I don't want to get her hopes up for nothing."

And he certainly didn't want to dash his own before it was absolutely necessary.

DALLAS PUSHED herself harder.

She'd remembered enough that she wasn't afraid to try to remember more. She used the *Budget* books, leafing through them over and over, waiting, hoping. Getting nothing.

What had she been hoping for? She knew without a doubt that she'd been on her way into the bedroom with Jackson this morning. She was trying, hoping to remember that she had every right to do exactly what she wanted to do. Exactly what her body wanted to do.

But not just her body. Though she was listening to that all right. But her heart was in this, too. Jackson had earned a place there. And not just by saving her life. By trying to help her find her past. By holding her when she needed to be held. By restraining himself when she wasn't ready, like at the library on the couch. By maintaining a sense of humor when she'd fumigated his jail. When she'd woken up with him that first morning and, in a righteous frame of mind, socked him out of her bed. When he'd stood over her last night, scratching his head and looking as if he'd like to strangle her two bed partners.

The front door blew open. Well, it didn't blow, really. The woman just gave it that effect as she threw it open and stood on the threshold, arms outstretched, eyes closed, her long, gauze skirt billowing gently in the breeze.

She was seventy-five if she was a day, and dressed like a flower child. There was a wreath in her long, flowing, gray-streaked brown hair. Crystals hung from her earlobes and neck and wrists, along with stones of hematite, malachite, lapis lazuli and several different quartzes. A huge, unpolished crystal adorned one finger. The rest were circled with silver and gold.

"Madame Celeste," Jackson informed Dallas with a wry touch of humor.

Dallas was seated in a chair close to his desk, so she felt safe asking quietly, "What's she doing?"

"Cleansing the room of negative spirits, I guess."

Dallas was left without a doubt that Jackson was clearly amused by the old woman.

Madame Celeste breezed in then, not bothering to close the door behind her in spite of the chilly air. "Hello, Sheriff."

"Madame Celeste. I'd introduce you, but I'm sure you already *know* who this is."

She bestowed a patient, understanding smile on his unfortunate, doubting soul. "Of course I do. But, Jackson, *she* might not know who I am."

"Oh, yes, she does." He met her glare with a sassy smile that his mother probably would have wiped off his face. "But what the hell? Dallas, this is Madame Celeste."

Dallas extended her hand. "How do you—"

She was jerked right out of her chair as the woman latched on to her hand, closing her eyes and swaying as she hummed.

"Julie asked me to pick a time for her wedding vows." Madame Celeste's clear gray eyes popped open. "It would help if I knew your exact time and place of birth."

"Sorry."

"No matter, child." The stones around her wrists clicked against each other as she waved her hand in the air, dismissing Dallas's amnesia as no real roadblock to what she sought. "Astrology can be quite an exact science if I have all the right information, but I'll get a viable impression shortly."

"You're saying it pays to be psychic, too?" Jackson teased.

"Hush. I hear your mother calling."

"That hasn't worked on me since I was five."

The phone rang. Madame Celeste stared at him pointedly.

He hesitated briefly, then squared his shoulders defiantly and picked up the receiver. "Hello?" The color drained from his face. "Mom! Hi. I didn't know the phones were working again."

"Now, that will take care of his negative vibrations," Madame Celeste said triumphantly.

"How did you do that?"

She smiled. "What Jackson won't admit is that I'm more psychic than astrologer. It's easier for him to cast aspersions on natal charts and transits by proving that those ridiculous predictions they print in the newspapers are a bunch of baloney. He can't do that with my more gifted abilities. Now, child, give me your other hand."

Dallas stood there mutely, not sure whether she was supposed to hold her breath, clear her mind, or count backward from one hundred. Could she even ask, or would that distract Madame Celeste, who now had her eyes closed again, her face tilted up toward the ceiling.

"Just relax," the old woman said softly. "Let your shoulders drop. That's it." She took a deep breath.

Dallas wondered if the old woman could read her thoughts regarding Jackson. Her very confused thoughts, ones that even she was having trouble sorting through.

"I can tell you've had a battering experience."

"You can read that in my mind?" Dallas asked in awe, suddenly dreading what kind of past she might be going back to.

"No, I can feel the scabs on your hands, silly. Now then . . ." Madame Celeste released Dallas's hands, whirled around and rooted through a cloth sack she'd dropped on the desk. She pulled out a long, flowered, gauze skirt, similar to the one she wore, and a lacy, off-white peasant blouse. "I brought you this to wear to the wedding."

"When?"

"Tomorrow afternoon, 2:47."

"Tomorrow?" Jackson roared as he banged the receiver down into its cradle.

Madame Celeste narrowed her eyes and studied the two of them. "Yes, I'd say tomorrow would be perfect."

"It's out of the question!"

She smiled at him as if he were still five years old and in awe of her. "It'll be tomorrow." She held the blouse up in front of Dallas. "Now, dear, I want to show you how to wear this. See, it's elastic around the top. That's so you can wear it off your shoulders and show off a little skin."

With a twinkle in her eyes, she glanced over at Jackson presumably to see if she'd distracted him with that visual image, which she had. She smiled secretly.

"And, dear—" she squeezed Dallas's hand "—in answer to your question, no, you're not married. You never have been."

In a flurry of gauze skirt, long hair and clicking stones, Madame Celeste was gone, leaving Dallas to stare at the door as it banged shut. If not for the material in her hands, she might have doubted the other woman had ever been there.

And all she could think about were her last words. *You're not married. You never have been.*

Terrific. But she wished Madame Celeste had hung around a little longer to explain the three kids.

"She reminds me of my grandmother." The words just popped out, surprising her as much as anyone.

"You mean there are two people on this earth like that?"

"No, not like that. Her face. She has a kind face."

"Kind of nutty," he muttered.

"She knew your mother was going to call."

He shrugged. "I'm sure she's been trying the phone every hour since the lines went down."

"You're that close?" *How wonderful,* she thought, wishing she could remember her own boisterous family.

"She's that determined to smooth the way for Roman and Julie."

"Let me guess..."

"As long as you don't claim to be psychic."

"Your mother's not a McKane?"

His smile told her she was right, though he refused to acknowledge it. Instead he turned toward Harrison's voice crackling over the radio, advising Jackson that the road to his cabin was above water now.

Was the old woman really psychic? Dallas hoped so. More than anything, she wanted to be single. She also wanted to be part of a large, boisterous family, the way her biography stated.

Could she have both? If she could, then she wanted her family to be just like the people she'd met in Green Valley. A little quirky, like Madame Celeste. Friendly and helpful, like Martha and Julie. A little sly, like Jasper and Otis, to keep things lively. And dedicated to each other, like Jackson was to his brothers. Everyone pulling together.

That wasn't too much to ask, was it?

DALLAS ROOTED AROUND the stove, trying not to disturb Jackson at his desk. He'd had his nose in a very legal-looking book for over an hour, hardly ever turning a page. She knew because she'd been watching him.

She opened every cabinet that looked big enough to hold a pot to boil water on the stove. They still didn't have any electricity at the jail, therefore the water heater in the bathroom was useless, and the wedding was tomorrow. She wanted to get cleaned up.

"What are you doing?" he asked when she resorted to filling the lone skillet with water and putting it on to heat.

"I want to wash up."

"That seems like the hard way to go about it."

Her eyebrows arched sassily. "You have a hotel within walking distance?"

He chuckled. "Not hardly."

"Then you must want me to go over to the diner and bathe in the kitchen sink."

His smile disappeared quite suddenly and his eyes darkened. "I think my cabin would give you more privacy."

"You look awfully busy." She held out her hand for the keys. "Draw me a map, and I'll come back for you later."

He stood, stretching his arms up over his head and giving his back a twist. "You'd never find it on your own. Besides, I need to get a fire going in the stove to heat up the bathroom.''

''No electricity?''

''Never needed it.''

''Never? As in, you don't have any at all?''

''Nope.''

''Not even a generator?''

He shook his head. ''I'm a simple man, Dallas. I don't need much.''

Jeez, she didn't know anyone lived without electricity any more. Not voluntarily, anyway.

He turned away under the guise of listening to something interesting crackling over the radio. It wasn't anything important he had to hear, but she didn't know that. He actually went so far as to write himself a note, all so he could duck his head and hide his face while he tried not to imagine her naked in his bathroom.

He already knew what she looked like naked. He'd seen her a whole two seconds. But he remembered. He didn't have a photographic memory; his was better. He'd deleted all her cuts and scratches and bruises, and gave her back the smooth skin he knew she'd had before she'd been tossed around in the river. Her legs would be perfect, shapely, long enough to wrap themselves around his hips, strong enough to hold him tightly to her.

''Something wrong?'' she asked when she came back into the room after dumping the water out of the skillet.

That was when he knew that faraway groan he'd heard had been his. And that was when he looked at what he'd been writing on the notepad in front of him.

Her husband is coming. Keep my hands to myself.
Her husband is coming. Keep my hands to myself.
Her husband

He quickly ripped off the sheet of paper and crumpled it into a ball as he rose from the desk.

"Nothing's wrong." He didn't need to see the curious look on her face to know he'd growled the answer out like an angry bear.

He started to throw the paper into the trash can, thought better of it, and tossed it into the fire in the stove. Which was pretty much what he'd like to do with any man who called himself her husband.

JACKSON HAD BEEN RIGHT. Dallas never would have found his cabin on her own. The drive out of town was simple enough, but she would have missed the first turn onto a little, narrow gravel road; it looked like a driveway, with two paths of rock for the tires and weeds growing in the track between.

They wound around for fifteen minutes, going through areas where the branches hung close and brushed gently along the sides of the truck. The lowest spot was still underwater, but shallow enough for him to drive straight through it.

The cabin was better than it sounded. For a simple man, Jackson exhibited good taste in choosing a cedar-and-glass A-frame. The surrounding area was free of virtually any sign of man interfering with nature. In fact, the cabin was the only human-related item within view. Everything else was virgin forest.

"Make yourself at home," he said as he got out of the truck. "I'll get a fire started. The bathroom and the water supply'll be toasty in about half an hour."

Dallas slid out of the truck to the sounds of birds chirping and insects buzzing, and the white flash of tails as three deer bounded off through the forest. She picked her way through the mud, left her duck shoes on the porch next to Jackson's boots, and stepped indoors.

He busied himself at the stove while she perused the inside of his cabin. It was basically one room, with hardwood floors, paneled walls, and a tongue-and-groove ceiling. A loft soared overhead, set off by a balustrade that she suspected was handcarved.

He'd managed to break up any possible monotony by sprinkling the floor with rag rugs, the two sofas with handmade quilts, and the walls with family photographs and bookcases. His books were all nonfiction, she noted. Nothing so frivolous as a good adventure for the man who believed in truth above all else. She found herself examining the titles for a *Budget* book, since he'd known so many of her titles, but there were none of those, either. Not a big surprise.

She was thumbing through his high school yearbook when he gently took it out of her hands.

"You don't want to look at that."

"Yes, I do. I want to see what you looked like in high school."

"I looked like a kid. Bathroom's warm."

She made a grab for the book, but he was too quick. "What are you hiding, Jackson?"

"Nothing."

"Uh-oh," she said with a laugh that said she knew she was on to something. "Careful, or your nose'll start to grow."

"I put some towels on the sink and a set of the smallest sweats I could find."

"Come on, let me see."

"No, you'll laugh."

"No, I won't. I promise."

He glared at her until she quit snickering, though it was hard, and she had to bite the inside of her lip to do so.

"Absolutely not." He raised up on the balls of his feet and put the book on a shelf she couldn't possibly reach.

"Not fair, Jackson."

He grinned broadly, acknowledging he'd won. She shrugged, as if it didn't really matter and she'd lost all interest, when in fact she'd go out of her way to get a peek at that book later if it was the last thing she did before she left here.

"I already poured the hot water into the tub."

"What?"

"I poured the hot water into the bathtub for you."

"I heard you. I just don't understand."

"No electricity, remember? No water heater other than the stove. It's only a couple inches, but I've got more on the stove in case it starts to cool off too much."

"You do this all the time?" She didn't want to sound as if she thought he was a caveman, but *really*.

"Heck, no. I just take a cold shower."

"Even in the winter?"

"Sure. I knew you wanted warm water, though. This way you get more than a skilletful."

There were four pots simmering on top of the stove as she walked past it into the bathroom. He was right; with special ventilation, the tiny room was toasty enough to encourage her to get out of her clothes. And the mirror was large enough to reflect half her body, not just small portions of her anatomy through a web of cracks like the one in the jail.

A few black-and-blue-and-green bruises, mostly on her legs and one over her right shoulder blade, caught her attention right away. When she pressed on them gingerly, they didn't hurt nearly as much as they looked like they would.

She had scabs on her elbows and hands and knees, but
hey all looked to be on their way to a healthy recovery.
Which was surprising, considering the smell of the water
he'd been immersed in and the dead animals she'd seen
loat by.

When she heard Jackson puttering around the small
itchen in the corner of the main room, she looked at her
eflection in the mirror with a new perspective. Take away
he bruises and scabs, and she was left with a figure that she
would rate as a little on the thin side, probably from not
ating right for the past few days. But overall, not bad.

And then she realized what was missing. Stretch marks.
None on her breasts. None lower, where her waist and abdomen would have flared out for months at a time. If she'd
ad three children, wouldn't she have some telltale signs?

Suddenly she doubted the whole Budget Lady identity.
She must be a look-alike. She'd always heard everyone on
arth had at least one double. Did she remember that, or
vas she making it up to lend credence to her train of
hought? She didn't waste any more time with that issue.
he'd also heard of people sent unjustly to prison because
hey'd been mistaken for a look-alike criminal.

But everyone in Green Valley seemed so certain that she
vas the Budget Lady. Everyone but her. She decided to go
n gut instinct alone. Budget Lady or not, she hadn't had
hree babies. And if that part of her biography was wrong,
vhat were the odds that the husband part was wrong, too?

Pretty good, as far as she could figure. As far as she
vanted to, anyway. Her inner voice warned her not to jump
o conclusions—after all, the kids could be adopted, not
iological. But she chose to ignore that line of thinking. It
vas making itself heard because she'd been convinced for so
vany hours that everyone was right. In her heart, she knew
hey were wrong. She might have felt suddenly empty that

she'd just lost a whole family she'd longed to meet again—
a husband, children and boisterous siblings. On some ele-
mental level, she knew she needed them. But, right now
with Jackson moving around in the other room, her rational mind was elsewhere.

It was listening to her heart. And it told her Jackson was
no longer off-limits.

HE KNEW THE INSTANT she stepped into the tub. She let out
the slightest of gasps due, no doubt, to exposing some of
those cuts of hers to the water. When he found himself lingering just outside the door, like a voyeur, he propelled
himself into the kitchen area. Before he knew it, he was
opening a can of chili and dumping it into a small pot on the
stove.

If he kept real quiet, he could hear the water splashing as
she wet herself down, then rinsed. She'd have to lie down to
get her hair soaked before she shampooed it. That presented quite a picture. In his short tub, she'd be flat on her
back, her arms overhead as she spread her hair out in the
water, her knees bent up in the air.

"Jackson?"

He swallowed. Hard.

"Jackson?" she called louder.

He inched over to the door, jamming his hands into his
trouser pockets to keep them off the knob. "Yeah?"

"Can you come in for a minute?"

He closed his eyes. He took a deep breath. When his
forehead banged against the solid door, he told himself it
was just as well.

"Jackson?"

"Are you decent?" *Please say no.*

"Yes."

His hand flew to the knob, opening the door before he could think twice. She was out of the tub, standing with a towel wrapped around herself... tucked between her breasts...accenting the valley between them. Her hand flew self-consciously to her hair.

"I couldn't rinse all the shampoo out."

"Oh. I'll...uh...get some water."

At the stove, he tested a potful to make sure it wasn't too hot. At the same time, he took a deep breath and counted to ten. He remembered what he'd written on that notepaper. *Keep my hands to myself.*

If he managed to do that, he'd nominate himself for sainthood.

When he reentered the bathroom, she was sitting on the closed toilet, bent forward with her head over the edge of the tub. It was a position designed to drive him mad as the towel, too short to begin with, rode up high on her thigh. As a matter of fact, part of her very lovely bottom was probably naked against his toilet lid at that very moment.

"Hey, you're missing my hair."

He aimed better, letting the warm water cascade over her dark hair and into the tub.

"Let me check it," she said.

He stopped the flow as she ran a thumb over her scalp in several spots, eliciting clean squeaks.

"Does it look all out to you?" she asked.

"Uh-huh."

She angled her head slightly so she could look up at him sideways. "How can you tell if you're not looking?"

"I looked." *Too much if you ask me.*

"You're sure?"

"Uh-huh." *As sure as I can be without running my fingers through your hair.*

"Well..."

Go ahead. Ask me to.

"Okay, then. Thanks." She twisted her hair over her head, wrung it out, then sat up straight.

The towel slipped a little over her breasts, inching downward. Was that a shadow he saw, or the very edge of a dusty rose areola?

She grabbed another towel and wound it around her head like a turban.

Keep my hands...

"Oops," she said as she made a grab for her main towel. Too late.

... on her bosom.

Jackson bolted from the room.

Chapter Twelve

"Gimme another jar."

Elmer spoke in a hushed tone, the way he always did whenever he and Jasper and Otis ran their still. Four hours a week he had to worry about getting caught. The rest of the time, their mash pretty well took care of itself. All they had to do was give it an occasional stir, and there wasn't much risk of getting caught in the amount of time that took.

No, it was running the still that set them up like sitting ducks.

They had a better setup this time, though—more secure, more private—and that made Jasper noisier than usual. They'd boated their cornmeal and sugar in earlier, when the river was higher, and hidden them in a nearby cave. The river had fallen steadily since then, making the cave nearly inaccessible. They hiked jars in as they accumulated them, holding on to trees to keep from falling off the steep hill and into the river below. One of the Ridgefield boys would have to literally roll down the hill and land at the mouth of the cave to find the evidence.

The mash barrel was a bit more exposed, of course, but even it blended into the woods. It had an old, aged board over it to keep out small animals and insects, a piece of burlap over that, and they'd topped it off with a couple of cut branches. Not much chance of it being seen unless someone tripped over it.

Unfortunately, Jackson had a knack for literally sniffing out their stills; he'd learned it from an old revenuer years ago. But the breeze here was limited by the terrain itself. And Jackson had other things on his mind.

"Are we gonna have enough jars?" Jasper asked.

"Pipe down, would ya?"

"You worry too much, Elmer."

"I'm not partial to jail cells."

"Relax. I told ya the sheriff took the woman to his cabin, Roman's escortin' some man into town to identify a missin' person, and Harrison's busy with those two dairy cows I tied up outside the jail." He snickered. "That'll keep 'em busy for a while." He didn't think Harrison knew diddly about cows that were hours past their milking time.

They heard leaves rustle along the hillside as someone approached. They slunk back toward the cave. Jackson might find their still and bust it up, but if he didn't catch them red-handed, they'd still be free men.

"It's me," Otis called out in a hoarse whisper.

"Why didn't ya say so sooner?" Elmer complained.

Jasper cackled and stuck his thumbs into the shoulder straps of his overalls. "Ever'body still busy?"

"No, that's why I hightailed it back here. We gotta hurry," Otis said.

"Can't rush 'shine," Elmer grumbled.

Jasper's eyebrows arched up. "Jackson left the woman?"

"Yep," Otis said with a nod. "He bolted outta his cabin ten minutes ago like it was on fire."

"Would you two quit your yakkin' and gimme a hand?" Elmer demanded in a low voice. "It's not like we can leave this unfinished. The weddin's tomorrow."

MARTHA BREEZED BY Jackson's shoulder carrying a plate of biscuits and gravy over to Elvin Brooks and humming "The Wedding March" as she went. For the first time, Jackson didn't mind thinking about the wedding. Anything—even listening to Martha's lively *da...da...da-da*—was better than being shut up alone with a naked Dallas.

Not that he minded Dallas. What he minded was what he wanted to do with her. He minded that Roman was due in Green Valley sometime today with her husband.

Life had been so simple four days ago. Right was right and wrong was wrong, and never did they cross. At least nowhere near him. The flood had kept him up a couple of days in a row, but it was nothing disastrous. No lives had been lost. No looters had descended on Green Valley. Most of the valley flooded every few years, anyway. The wedding had been called off.

And then Dallas came. Right had become difficult to determine. Wrong had started to look right. Under her influence, the wedding had taken on all the power of a flood. Impossible to stop, delay or talk it away. Would life ever be the same?

No.

Oh, the river would go down. It always did. There'd be a massive cleanup, and then life would go on until the next time.

Otis and Elmer and Jasper would still be making moonshine. He and his deputy brothers would go on trying to find their still, smash it up when they did, and wait for them to build another one. They never did manage to get them in front of dear old dad, the judge.

Martha's Diner would still smell of black coffee and pipe tobacco. She'd still make the best fried chicken anyone had ever tasted—not like those fast-food franchises out along the highway.

Harrison would still fly the helicopter like a kamikaze on a mission and drive his car like an Indy 500 wanna-be whenever he thought he could get away with it. He didn't want another ticket from Jackson any more than Jackson wanted to give him one. But he'd get one if Jackson caught him.

And he would still crave Dallas. She'd be gone, of course. Back to her life in Connecticut, turning out Budget Lady books every year. Celebrating birthdays and anniversaries and Christmases in the bosom of her family.

He didn't want to think of the man who would be in her life. Probably some little, wimpy, accountant-type guy, with a bald spot and bifocals and a gut, who wore striped shirts with plaid pants. Not that that's what she deserved. But—he grinned to himself—it'd sure make her look back fondly on the sheriff she'd left behind in Green Valley.

And he'd be an old... What was the male version of a spinster? *Bachelor* didn't carry the same connotation. *Crusty old bachelor,* maybe. Yeah, he'd be pretty crusty all right.

He heard the front door of the diner open behind him. He knew, without turning to look, that it was Roman and *him,* because Martha stopped moving—a first—and a heavy silence fell over the room. No cup clattered in its saucer. No fork scraped along a china plate. Nothing.

Footsteps approached. Two sets. He set his cup of coffee down on the counter and took a deep breath.

Roman broke the silence. "Jackson?"

Damn, he sounded sympathetic. Jackson didn't need anyone's sympathy. He'd be damned if he'd live the rest of his life with everyone in town tiptoeing around him with long faces. He swiveled his stool around.

Six foot two, two hundred pounds, dark hair. Dark eyes the color of a Hershey bar stared back at him.

Roman chuckled nervously as he looked from his brother to the stranger. "Almost like looking in a mirror, isn't it?" His voice was laced with compassion.

Jackson made a conscious effort to remember to shut his mouth and swallow. Hard. His hand rubbed agitatedly over his whiskers. He'd meant to shave at the cabin when Dallas had finished in the bathroom, but he'd bolted out of there too fast after the towel incident. Of course he'd gone back for her, but then he'd hustled her out of there as quickly as possible—not fully trusting himself.

This guy needed a shave, too. Poor slob had probably been worried sick about his wife.

But did he and this man have to look so much alike? Just at first glance, of course, but enough so that Dallas had probably felt comfortable with him because, subconsciously, he looked like the man to whom she was married.

"You want me to take him over to the jail?" Roman offered, breaking the silence again.

Jackson's stool thumped behind him as he got off it and let it swing back into position. It was the only sound in the diner. Probably the only movement, but he wasn't looking around.

"No. Uh... yeah, sure." He raked his hand through his hair. "Let me go in first and tell her, okay?"

And he was out of there. Almost as fast as he'd left the cabin when he'd resolved to keep his hands to himself.

He drove the short distance to the jail. He could have walked and prolonged it, but it was better to get it over with. Besides, he wasn't sure if he didn't do it right away that he'd go through with it at all. The puppy, finally outside where he belonged, barked at him when he drove up.

"Oh, shut up," he muttered as he strode by it.

He entered the jail, closed the door behind him, and leaned back against it. What was he going to say to her?

Maybe he should have told her as soon as he'd known, but he'd hoped and prayed it would all be a big mistake.

"Dallas?" he called out when he realized she was nowhere in sight.

"Back in the bedroom. I'll be right out."

"Okay."

"Are you alone?"

"Yeah." *For now.*

"I hope you don't mind my borrowing one of your shirts..."

Oh, my God.

He was speechless as she entered the main room of the jail, clad only in one of his tan uniform shirts. The top three buttons were open, with the collar spread wide. The sleeves were rolled up to her elbows. The tails flapped around her bare thighs, teasing him with a glimpse of golden-tanned skin as she walked.

"What the hell are you doing?"

"It got too hot in here for the sweat suit. And I'm saving the clothes Madame Celeste gave me for tomorrow."

He heard the innocent words. He saw the sly smile teasing the corners of her lips.

"If you think this is hot, you ain't seen nothing yet," he muttered.

"It fits pretty well, don't you think?" She pirouetted for him. Her dark hair waved out and caressed the shoulders of his shirt.

"Dallas..." Was that strangled sound coming from him?

He watched helplessly as she padded barefoot over to him, stopping just in front of him as if waiting for inspection. Her eyes twinkled merrily, as if she knew every lustful thought flying through his mind and was relishing every second of it.

"Of course, if you mind," she said as her hand reached up to the buttons, "I can take it off."

"No!"

"No?"

"Uh..."

"No, as in you want me to leave it on? Or no, as in you want to do it for me?"

She inched away, backward, and he was drawn along with her, following her like some lovesick puppy dog. Like Sonnet, who was barking up a storm. Someone was coming.

"No, as in your husband is outside."

Color faded from her cheeks. "My..." She tugged the buttons closer to the holes where the shirt had gapped across her collarbones. "But I'm not married..." Her voice trailed off at the end, even as her eyes darted toward the door. She'd been so sure. "Madame Celeste said—"

He growled. "Madame Celeste is a fraud. She's just a crazy old lady who doesn't know when to shut up."

"But, no. I felt like she was right. I looked in the mirror." She knew she was rambling, but her thoughts weren't coming in coherent sentences just then. The bio, for example. "It wasn't me. I don't have any children."

She felt moisture pool in her eyes, threatening to spill over and run down her cheeks. She stepped forward and plastered herself to his chest, and his arms barely touched her.

"Hold me." She closed her eyes; a tear squeezed free and trickled downward until it dampened his shirt. "Just for a few minutes."

His strong arms closed around her. They were warm, protective, comforting. She circled his torso with her own arms, letting her hands lie flat along his broad back, drinking in his strength as she pressed herself to him.

She'd been so sure she wasn't married. Sure enough to make a play for him, to tempt him to take her in his arms and hold her for reasons other than staying warm on a library couch overnight. Sure enough to throw caution to the wind and go after what she wanted. And she wanted him.

The front door of the jail opened behind him. She squeezed her eyes shut tightly, not wanting to end her last moment in his arms, afraid to see the reaction on her stranger-husband's face when he found her half-dressed in another man's arms.

He cleared his throat.

Jackson turned around to face her husband, pushing her around behind him to hide her half-dressed state. Why the hell was Roman getting so efficient all of a sudden, bringing the man here so quickly? Didn't he know—

Of course he didn't. Even Jackson hadn't suspected that she'd make such a move.

He noticed Roman hadn't bothered coming into the jail.

"Well, Sheriff? I've traveled a long way. I'd like to take my wife home with me now." The man's voice rasped as if he'd spent too many nights awake over coffee and cigarettes, waiting for some word of her.

He felt Dallas peek around his shoulder.

"Uh..." Jackson glanced down at her legs, then back at her husband. "We gave her more clothes than this. Really." It was then, of course, he remembered that she'd never gotten any underpants anywhere. And that meant...

"I really don't care what she's wearing."

"Go put the sweatpants back on," Jackson ordered with a low growl in her ear.

"I'd just like to get my wife and go."

"You're not my husband, are you?" Dallas queried in a tone that said she already knew he wasn't. It bordered on surprise, and she sounded so sure of herself.

Jackson's emotions bordered on shock. He looked from one to the other and back again. He hoped he didn't look like a stupid straight man in a movie.

"Well of course I'm not," the man snapped impatiently. He glared at Jackson. "Sheriff, if you could please take me to my wife now."

Jackson pointed at him as he looked at Dallas. "He's not . . . ?" A grin broke out on his face. It matched the one on hers. He looked at the man for confirmation. "She's not . . . ?"

"Are you really the sheriff in this godforsaken town?" the man demanded. When he didn't get any answer, he added, "I sure as hell pity the people who elected you." The door slammed behind him, muffling his, "Never mind. Don't bother helping me. I'll find that kid deputy again."

Dallas was grinning up at him, inching her way backward toward his desk. He noticed the front of her—his, rather—shirt gaping open again. Who would've known his uniform shirt could look so sexy? So tantalizing?

No, it wasn't the shirt that was sexy and tantalizing. It was the occupant.

"Five minutes ago you thought you were married," he said as he followed her all the way to the desk until her hips bumped up against it.

She reached for the buckle on his gun belt. "Ten minutes ago I knew I wasn't."

His hand automatically went to his gun.

"Relax. I'm not going to shoot anything."

"Just the same." He tossed it up onto the file cabinet, well out of her reach as long as she stayed where she was.

She reached for the buttons on his shirt, starting at the top. "I've got better things in mind."

He glanced over his shoulder at the front door.

"Sonnet's standing guard."

"He's a puppy."

She grinned. "He hasn't failed me yet. How do you think I knew when you were coming?"

"I don't think this is such a good idea."

"That's your problem, Jackson."

"What?"

"You think too much."

He was having great difficulty doing it, too, as she slipped his shirt off his shoulders. When he made one last attempt to bring her to her senses, when he started to back away from her, she levered her hips back onto the top of his solid oak desk and wrapped her legs around his thighs.

His undershirt was the next to go, quickly replaced by her mouth on his smooth chest. Her lips were cool against his hot skin. Her tongue was moist where she flicked it over one nipple, then the other.

Her hands were flat on his back and, with her legs hugging his as they were, pressed him toward her. The maneuver spread her thighs wider as he closed in. The shirttails rode higher, nearly exposing their secrets.

He gave in then, as his hands involuntarily threaded themselves through her hair, his fingers savoring the texture of her tresses. And then he started on a downward trek. Not too fast. Not too slow.

He framed her face with his hands, tipping her head back and holding her still while his lips descended on hers, tasting her like he'd never done before. Sweet. Sexy. Hotter than an afternoon in July.

"Dallas," he murmured as his lips trailed off hers and over her cheek. So smooth.

His shampoo smelled different on her than it did on him. It mingled with her own chemistry, producing a scent that was light and flowery. Something uniquely Dallas. Something that teased his senses and made him want to know more.

His fingers found their way to her buttons, freeing them in short order, all except the last one, giving his hand the freedom to cup her breast and tease her nipple into an even harder bud. The bottom button of the shirt still concealed her secrets. Had she dug through his dresser and borrowed a pair of his briefs at the cabin? He wanted to know. He didn't want to rush it.

She tugged him closer, though he hadn't thought it was possible. He slipped one hand behind her back, tugging her forward to the edge of the desk, letting her feel how hard he was. How ready.

And with her pressed so intimately against him, he couldn't stop his hands any longer. One stayed behind her back to support her. The other landed on her thigh, finding it silky smooth and inviting higher exploration. Upward it roamed, hesitating, teasing, prolonging their foreplay.

"Thank God," he murmured when he discovered bare skin all the way up, when his thumb dipped between her thighs and discovered crisp curls.

"What?"

"I didn't know if I could make love to you if you were wearing a pair of my briefs."

The last button flew open under his fingertips, giving him a clear vision of what she was offering.

Her response was a breathless chuckle. "Afraid they'd be a big turnoff, huh?"

"You have no idea."

She unbuckled his belt, letting her hand slide down over his erection. "Oh, I don't know. I'm pretty sure your briefs won't turn me off. Maybe I'd better check."

His trousers parted under her fingertips. Her legs held him as she tugged them roughly down over his hips, along with his briefs, freeing him.

"We should go in the other room," he whispered.

"We shouldn't waste the time." She leaned backward, taking him in her hand, taking him with her.

He followed willingly. His arm swept across the desk, sending his In and Out baskets clattering to the floor. Papers flew everywhere. The yellow cat, who'd been dozing beside the desk, hissed and streaked across the room to a safer spot.

Jackson couldn't help himself, he took over. It was his nature to seduce, not be seduced, though he wouldn't turn her down if she tried it again. He pushed her shirt out of the way, baring her to him.

She was so perfect. He saw no cuts, bruises or scabs, only perfection. Only silky skin, open arms and green eyes that beckoned him to make her his.

He'd never been so aroused in his whole life. Was it because anyone could walk into the jail and catch them? Was it the desk, out in the open, where he usually did his paperwork? Or was it her?

His hands caressed her, learning all her secrets, and he knew it was she who made him feel as if this were his first time, as if he couldn't bear to wait.

But wait he did. Until he knew, from the deep throaty moan he drew from her, that she was ready, too. Until her breath was hot in his ear. Until she dug her fingernails into his back.

He pressed himself into her... and there was no more waiting. They had used up all their patience. It was time for giving and taking and sharing. Touching and grasping and squeezing. Deep moans of release, sighs of ecstasy.

And winding down. How he would have loved to have been in a bed where he could roll her over on top of him and fall asleep with her weight pressing down on him, reassuring himself all night long that she was still there. That she wasn't going anywhere.

He kicked out of his shoes and pants and briefs, slipped his arms beneath her back, and stood up straight. The movement disoriented her, making her wrap her legs around him tightly again as she clung to him.

"What...? Where...?"

"To bed," he answered. "So the next time we do this, you won't be getting any bruises on your backbone."

She giggled in his ear as he carried her to the back room. "But it was fun."

"Yes—" he said chuckling "—it was. And it doesn't have to be over."

And he prayed that, for once, Madame Celeste knew what the hell she was talking about when she said Dallas had never been married.

They'd probably know something when Martha's nephew finished developing the film.

Chapter Thirteen

Jackson woke up with a heavy weight on his foot. He grinned wickedly, thinking it was Dallas's leg thrown over his that was holding him down. Until he remembered that he'd had to get up in the middle of the night and let the damn, howling puppy inside. And that hadn't been enough for the little monster; he'd scratched on the closed door and whined pitifully until he got to be *in* the bedroom with Dallas.

He kicked his foot where it lay under the covers, hoping to tumble the troublemaker onto the floor where he belonged. Instead of the rewarding *thump* he'd anticipated, though, he got a hiss, and the yellow cat padded up to what must have looked like a more comfortable spot—his chest.

It was way too much for a man who believed dogs belonged outdoors and cats belonged in the barn.

"Get the hell off me," he growled through clenched teeth. "Now!"

Dallas, lying tangled with him in the twin bed, jumped, startled out of a sound sleep.

"Shh, it's okay," he crooned. He tightened his arms around her, encouraging her to stay close and go back to sleep.

The cat sported a toothy grin.

Dallas curled against his body, chuckling. "I never thought I'd see the day you'd voluntarily let an animal live indoors, not to mention sleep in your bed."

He was about to tell her exactly what he thought of all this when it occurred to him that sharing his opinion might not be in his best interest. Not right now, anyway. He chose a safer tactic. "I think I deserve a reward."

"I think you do, too."

She rolled on top of him, upsetting the cat on his chest and the puppy on his feet. It was almost reward enough for him to hear the two of them thump onto the floor. But not quite. The sweet torture she had in mind was infinitely better. And she made it last a long time.

IT'S RAINING."

Jackson peered out the window. "It's sprinkling."

Dallas looked down at the peasant blouse and long, gauze skirt that Madame Celeste had given her to wear to the wedding. The duck shoes could withstand the weather. She didn't know about the clothes.

"My mother says it's good luck for it to rain on someone's wedding day," Jackson said.

"Your mother undoubtedly owns an umbrella and a can of hair spray."

His gaze raked her from head to toe, and she knew he didn't find fault with anything he saw. Not even the duck shoes. Not that he got that low. His eyes hovered near the vicinity of her neckline for a tad too long before he cast an appreciative eye over the whole picture. She was glad she'd found a new teddy tucked into the pocket of the skirt when she'd gone to get dressed. Otherwise, she'd think by the heated look in his eyes that anyone would be able to see right through her blouse. The fact that Madame Celeste had known she might prefer a teddy over a bra and panties hadn't escaped her notice.

"Will your mother be at the wedding?"

"Hmm? Oh…yeah." He grinned as if he knew he'd been caught looking and was hoping his charm would earn her patience. "Are you kidding? Roman's her first son to get married."

"Even though Julie's a McKane?"

"You're forgetting—she's pregnant and she says it's Roman's baby. Mom won't turn her back on a grandchild."

"Julie also says that the feud is so old, no one even remembers what it's about." It was a blatant hint, but she didn't care.

"I'm sure that's not true."

"You don't know, do you?"

"It was important to my great-grandfather."

"It's important to Roman that both families get along now." She glanced at the wall clock. "It's almost two. I guess we should go."

"It's only a block away. And *Madame Celeste—*" his tone mocked her name "—said they weren't supposed to start until, what, 2:47?"

"But—"

"And where the hell did she come up with a time like that?"

"Something to do with the moon entering a new—"

"No!" He held up his hands to stop her. "Don't tell me. I don't want to know."

She glanced at the wall clock again.

"It's too early." The twinkle in his eyes hinted at other things they could find to occupy an extra half hour. "We could stay here a little longer."

Dallas refused to blush in response, though she suspected, from the heat suffusing her face that she didn't have much control over it. "Julie might need help getting ready. Plus, I want to take some pictures before the ceremony."

They listened to the rain dripping off the roof outside, the wall clock ticking away the seconds.

Jackson mulled over her suggestion, then brightened. There *was* something he could do with the extra time. Something vital. "Yeah. Maybe you're right. I could have a little talk with Roman while we wait."

"Jackson..."

He ignored the gentle warning tone in her voice, the censure in her eyes that told him she knew exactly what he was up to. "He might be having second thoughts."

"Don't you dare talk him out of this."

"Me? No, I'd just be supportive."

"Yeah, I bet."

"Come on." He grinned unrepentantly as he shouldered her camera bag. After all, this was *his* youngest brother's life they were talking about. "We'd better get going."

She, who'd been in such an all-fired hurry before, now lagged behind. "I have to let the puppy in."

"He can stay outside during the day."

"It's raining."

"It's sprinkling!"

"I know, but it might pour while we're gone."

She opened the front door. The puppy and cat ambled in together, not at all discouraged by his pointed glare. In fact, the cat seemed to be gloating as he aimed directly for Jackson's dark brown trouser leg and rubbed himself up against it, leaving a sprinkling of yellow fur behind.

Jackson wondered if Roman would have half the trouble married to a McKane woman that he was having in four days with Dallas. He also wondered if Roman would have half the fun.

"WELL, ROMAN, how do you feel about all this?" Jackson asked when he finally cornered his little brother in the back of the church.

They were surrounded by their parents, brothers, aunts, uncles, cousins, friends, and townspeople. There was no getting away from everyone as they visited and chatted and laughed and shared the latest gossip; no one went to sit down. It had been tricky, but he'd managed to sequester Roman long enough to ask the all-important question.

"I don't mind telling you, Jackson," he whispered as he tugged at his collar, "I'm nervous as hell."

Their mother, short, stocky and broad-bosomed, was chatting in a small group next to them, seemingly paying them no mind until she reached over and slapped his arm with a rolled up church pamphlet. "Watch your mouth, young man. You're in the house of God."

Roman edged away.

Jackson followed, a hopeful glimmer in his eyes. "Having second thoughts?"

"No. Are you?"

"Me?"

"Yeah." The steady look Roman cast in his direction was nearly enough to make him think the tables had turned. "Getting involved with a woman who might be married doesn't seem like something you'd be comfortable with," he said pointedly.

"She's not married."

"Uh-huh."

"And while we're on the subject, what about that guy you brought to the jail yesterday—"

"We thought maybe she wrote under a pseudonym."

"Didn't it ever occur to you to ask the guy if his wife was a writer?"

"I thought they'd taken care of that—" His demeanor changed. "Oh, I get it. You're still trying to convince me I'm not old enough or responsible enough to get married. You're still trying to talk me out of this, aren't you? Isn't that kind of like the pot calling the kettle black, Jackson?"

"Shh!" Jackson glanced nervously over his shoulder to see if anyone had heard.

Too late. Their mother descended on them, no matter that she was barely five feet tall to their six feet. Roman laughed with glee to see his older brother take a step backward and adopt a sheepish look. Only their mother and Martha could put him on the spot like that.

She waggled a finger beneath his chin. "Jackson Ridge-field . . ."

"Yes, ma'am?" He wondered how much she'd heard.

"Stuff it."

"Stuff it?"

"You heard me. Leave your brother alone. Go keep an eye on Uncle Henry."

He winced. "Oh no, please not Uncle Henry. I should be making sure Dallas isn't feeling left out—"

"That young woman of yours is doing just fine on her own," she snapped, making him wonder if she'd actually met Dallas and knew what had transpired between them. "Go make sure Uncle Henry's got the right page marked in his book this time. We wouldn't want him doing a funeral service for your brother's wedding."

His father watched silently, taking it all in, weighing the pros and cons of stepping in. He'd been a judge too long to just jump into anything that others could work out for themselves. He'd known from the time Jackson had taken his first steps that the boy had a way about him. An up-right, unbending way. He'd taken him to court with him, time and time again, from little on up, hoping the art of compromise would rub off on him.

He watched his eldest son now, hoping to see a change. And what he saw disturbed him. Jackson, the most rigid Ridgefield in the history of the clan, had been that way thirty years too long. He'd heard he might be softening up around that new woman in town—Dallas, he thought her name was—but he didn't see any evidence of it. It was time to take Jackson down a peg or two, for his own good. As soon as he could figure out how.

Jackson looked around for Uncle Henry. There was no telling if he would even remember to hang around and of- ficiate a wedding in, he glanced at his watch, another twenty-two minutes.

Suddenly, Madame Celeste breezed in through the double doors, crystals refracting, stones clicking. Right behind her came a woman who was obviously a stranger to these parts. She was blond, in her thirties. Her navy pumps and navy purse matched her navy business suit. Instead of a blouse, she had a flashy silk scarf tied in a fancy knot. She reeked of East Coast and high-powered meetings. Of course, most meetings on the East Coast were probably high-powered compared to anything that went on in Green Valley.

Madame Celeste turned and conversed with her. A relative, Jackson wondered?

And then he remembered his own relative and how he was supposed to keep an eye on him. He went in search of Uncle Henry.

Squeak.

Dallas snapped shots of the church and its tissue-paper flower decorations. Following directions Julie had found in *The Wedding of Your Dreams...on a Budget,* they'd whipped up peach-and-mint-colored bouquets and festooned them with lacy ribbons. They adorned the end of each pew on the center aisle, and the sanctuary appeared to be a garden in full bloom. Between the bouquets, the dozens of candles lending a romantic glow, and the rainbow of colors thrown in as the sun came out and hit the stained-glass windows, the small church felt alive with promise.

Squeak.

She ran down to check the basement of the church, where the reception would take place. The main hall was one big room, set up with dozens of small tables for casual dining, draped in white linen and centered with peach-and-mint green candles. Peach-and-mint tissue flowers hung from the ceiling and the backs of the chairs. The gift table nearly overflowed with silver-and-white packages. The smell of fried chicken filtered through from the kitchen, making her mouth water.

One table was set aside for the froth-topped, peachy-colored punch and a three-tiered white cake. The only other people down in the basement were Otis, Jasper and a similarly ancient friend that she was sure must be Elmer. They hovered near the punch bowl, in spite of the fact that everyone in Green Valley knew the liquor store had been flooded and its entire stock destroyed. Everything seemed to be in order, as long as they didn't sample the cake—which they looked just sneaky and boyish enough to try—and she ran back upstairs.

Squeak.

There it was again. Her duck shoes made a horrendous noise on the tile floor.

She checked out the other women's feet. They'd worn their sneakers in and carried their pumps, then left their sneakers near the door when they'd changed.

Squeak.

There was no way she was going to have everyone staring at her on Julie's wedding day. She tiptoed back to the double doors and off to the side where the sneakers awaited. The first pair she selected was too large. The next pair too small. She felt like Goldilocks and Cinderella rolled into one. She picked up the pace and found a pair that fit before anyone noticed what she was doing. Especially Jackson. If he saw her, he'd think she carried a specialized gene for stealing—all for a good cause, of course.

She walked away from the scene of her crime. *Ah, silence.* After the ceremony was over, she'd get back there before everyone left and leave the sneakers none the worse for wear.

Julie was in a room set aside for the bridal party to get dressed. Her three bridesmaids, her mother and Martha were with her. Julie, already in her white, off-the-shoulder gown, was hunched over on a window seat, looking quite pale and uncomfortable.

"Ohh!" she moaned.

"She's in labor," Martha explained when Dallas entered.

"Is she going to be able to go through with the wedding?" One look at Julie's pinched face, and Dallas doubted it.

"First babies take forever," a perky bridesmaid chirped. She sounded as if she'd had five; she didn't look old enough to be out of pom-poms.

"Not McKane babies," Martha said in an aside to Dallas. "Those little darlings pop out like biscuits."

"Maybe we'd better get the minister in here and get this over with then," Dallas suggested.

"Nooo!" Julie moaned. She caught her breath and looked at her watch. Her eyes pleaded with Dallas for more time. "It's too early... not 2:47... yet."

"But, Julie, dear—" her mother began.

"Madame Celeste said 2:47, Mother."

Madame Celeste breezed into the room. "Oh, dear. I was afraid of this."

Everyone glanced at their watches, except Dallas, and she peeked over Martha's shoulder. Twelve more minutes.

"I'm afraid I've made a slight miscalculation."

Julie and her mother glared at Madame Celeste.

"Well, actually, it wasn't a miscalculation, considering the information I had at the time. But now I've received new information—"

No one asked where from.

"—and, Julie, dear, you mustn't begin the wedding until 3:23."

A collective groan echoed throughout the room and all eyes turned to Julie. She panted. She mopped her brow. "Okay."

"But, Julie..." Dallas heard herself say when no one else would. All eyes were on her now. She couldn't tell if they were hoping to get on with the wedding or if they were daring her to question Madame Celeste's time frame.

"I'm not going to get married before 3:23... And that's..." Another contraction grabbed her, and she moaned through it. "...final."

Madame Celeste, her job done, turned and favored Dallas with a lascivious wink. "I'm so happy for you, dear. I *knew* it was only a matter of time."

She tugged the shoulders on Dallas's peasant blouse to an off-the-shoulder position and then breezed out the door with as much fluttering as when she'd entered. Which left everyone staring at Dallas, who was blushing red to the roots of her hair, instead of the crazy old woman who saw too much.

"UNCLE HENRY, what did you do with your book?"

Jackson looked high and low. He'd only left the man's side for thirty seconds when he thought he'd heard some awful noises coming from the room set aside for the bride and her party to get dressed. Julie must be having a heck of a time getting into her gown to make sounds like that.

"Ah, there it is." He picked it up off the shelf above the coatrack and put it back in his uncle's hands.

"You make a fine-looking groom, Jackson," Uncle Henry said with admiration.

"I'm not getting married, Uncle Henry. Roman is."

"Roman? But he's just a lad."

"Tell me about it," Jackson muttered.

"I'm twenty-one, Uncle Henry," Roman corrected him on his way toward the dressing room to see what was going on.

"Who was that?"

"That was Roman, Uncle Henry."

"Oh, my, he's quite tall for his age, isn't he?"

Jackson could see he was going to have to stand by the man's elbow every second during the service. He'd probably have to whisper Roman's and Julie's names in his ear at the appropriate times. He'd suggest calling it all off and waiting for a lucid minister, but they'd probably lynch him from the steeple.

"Jackson!" Dallas weaved her way through the crowd, which still hadn't moved into the main part of the church. One look at her face, and he knew Julie had bigger problems than squeezing a few extra pounds into her wedding gown. "Have you had any medical training? Julie's in labor, and I don't think she's going to take much longer."

"Harrison!" he bellowed, mindless of being in church. There was no way he was going to deliver a McKane baby. Not in this lifetime.

Harrison took his own sweet time finishing up a conversation with Millie before he ambled over to Jackson and Dallas. "Yeah?"

"Fire up the helicopter. Julie's in labor, and I want you to fly her to the hospital."

Roman charged up, his tie loose, his collar unbuttoned, his hair disheveled as if he'd been wringing it. "I'm going to be a father!"

"So we heard," Jackson muttered. "I'm sending Harrison for the helicopter so you two can head for the hospital before it's too late."

"Harrison?" Roman screeched, a terrible sound for a man about to become a husband and a father, but he didn't seem to notice. "No way. Uh-uh."

"She's a McKane, Roman. Everyone knows it's the only way she's going to get to the hospital in time."

Roman jerked his thumb over his shoulder in Harrison's direction. "She's not riding with him."

"Roman . . ."

He shook his head agitatedly. "No way. She's safer here."

Harrison took offense. "I haven't lost a passenger yet."

"That's because no one in their right mind will ride with you. Not unless they're worse off where they are."

"And she might be. She shouldn't be having a baby here."

"Why not? She wants to wait until—" he glanced at his watch "—3:23. That's—"

"What the hell happened to 2:47?" Jackson demanded.

"Last minute recalculation. Besides, if it's a close call, you've delivered babies before."

"One baby."

"Six."

"The other five were puppies, you ninny. And I was fifteen."

Roman stood up tall and straight, buttoned his collar and tightened the knot on his tie. "The wedding starts, as planned, in—" he glanced at his watch "—oh, my God, in ten minutes!"

"She should go to the hospital," Jackson argued.

Roman turned on his heel, grabbed Harrison by the arm, and said, "Come on. It's time we get into position."

Harrison followed him, nervously asking, "To get you married or to catch a baby?"

Jackson was speechless. Which was a good thing, because he wouldn't be making any friends if he said what was on his mind as he watched what went on in the next ten minutes.

Someone brought a chair in for the bride to sit on during the ceremony, since she obviously wouldn't feel like standing. The ushers herded everyone into the pews. They pointed Dallas toward the second one, reserved for her and Martha. His father escorted his mother up the aisle to the first row on the groom's side. Julie's mother ran in at the last minute, peach-and-mint tissue flowers fluttering in her wake as she charged up the aisle to the first pew on the bride's side. Both sets of parents pointedly kept their eyes averted from the other. Roman, Harrison and two more groomsmen lined up in front, waiting.

He sighed and took the older man by the arm. "Come on, Uncle Henry."

"Shouldn't we wait here for your bride?"

"It's time to marry Roman and Julie."

"Oh." He sounded confused.

Jackson led him up the side aisle and around to the front of the altar to await the bridal party.

Three twenty-one. Three twenty-two. Three twenty-three. A hair-raising scream ripped through the church.

"IT'S A BOY," Madame Celeste proclaimed to the group gathered in the hall.

"It's not even here yet," Harrison noted.

"Who's not here?" the East Coast woman asked curiously.

"Any minute now," Madame Celeste promised. "The bride's having her baby. I knew you'd be here today and I know she's having a boy. As sure as the fact that it's done raining."

Harrison stuck out his hand toward Ms. New York, knowing he wasn't going to get an introduction any other way. "Harrison Ridgefield, ma'am."

She cast an appreciative eye over him, then lay her hand gently in his. "How *do* you do?"

"And you are?" he hinted, equally charmed.

"M.J.—"

"Quick, Harrison!" Madame Celeste interrupted. "Jackson needs you. Get in there."

He walked into a room of intense concentration. Martha supported Julie's head, Julie's mother mopped the soon-to-be-mother's brow, and both women encouraged her to push again. Dallas stood by with a large towel draped over her arms, waiting for the new arrival. Roman lay on the carpet next to his wife, holding her hand, his other arm thrown across his face, trying to hide the fact that he didn't feel too well at the moment.

Julie was down to her white slip and a lot of sweat. Jackson was posed to catch her son, trying to remember everything he'd learned about delivering babies, which didn't amount to a whole hell of a lot.

"I heard you needed me?" Harrison said when no one seemed to notice he'd entered the room.

"Get . . . the minister," Julie ordered between pants.

"Push," Jackson ordered.

"Get ... the darn ... minister ... in here. Now!"

Jackson was pleased to note that Harrison could move as fast on foot as in the air. He had Uncle Henry there in a blink, opened his book to the right page and got him started near the end of the service. Roman managed to sit up. His mother pushed her way in through the door with a determined air.

"Right here," Harrison whispered. "Do you, Roman..."

"Do you, Roman Ridgefield, take..."

"Julie McKane," Harrison helped the addled minister.

"Julie McKane ... Oh, my. A Ridgefield and a McKane? Say, do your parents know about this?"

Julie screamed again.

"Hurry up," Roman pleaded.

Harrison pointed to the next phrase.

"To be your lawfully wedded wife. In sickness and—"

"Yes!"

Uncle Henry beamed at Julie's enthusiastic response, then waggled a finger at her. "Be patient. I'll get to you in a minute." He tried to resume his place, but couldn't find it.

Harrison's finger skimmed the page. "Here, Uncle Henry."

"Do you ..." He looked up at Harrison for help.

"Julie McKane."

"Oh, yes, I remember now. Do you, Julie McKane, take—"

"Yes, for crying out loud! Hurry up."

"I now pronounce you ..." Harrison hinted.

"Oh. Am I that far already?"

"Yes, Uncle Henry."

"Oh, well then. I now pronounce you husband and wife. You may kiss the bride." He closed the book, noticed what was transpiring in front of him, and looked to Harrison for clarification. "I thought they just got married."

Jackson tuned them out, glad he wasn't delivering a baby whose surname would be McKane. "It's a girl!" he announced, with no small amount of pride. There was something about delivering a baby that did that to a man. "What's her name?"

"A girl!" Both grandmothers beamed proudly. Their smiles froze in place when each noticed the other for the first time.

"A girl?" Julie asked with confusion.

"A girl?" Roman echoed.

"I know the difference, guys. It's a girl." Jackson slipped the little bundle into Dallas's waiting arms, watching as she quickly wrapped up the baby to keep her warm. Quite without warning, he pictured himself handing her a baby that was their own. Down the road, of course. Say, nine months to a year?

Dallas glanced at him as she cleaned up the infant and he made use of the soap and water Martha had brought before she'd even let him near Julie. They exchanged a secret smile, and he wondered if she was having the same thoughts he was.

"Did the doctor tell you it would be a boy?" Dallas asked the new parents.

"We didn't ask the doctor," Roman said.

"We didn't have to," Julie explained. "Madame Celeste said it was a boy."

Jackson gloated. "Seems she was wrong. Funny how that works. You got yourselves a little female Ridgefield."

"She's a hyphen," Julie said.

"That's her name?" Jackson asked with a frown. "Ahyphen?"

"Jeez, Roman, your brother is such an idiot."

"Careful, Julie. That idiot's seen you at your worst."

She sighed loudly and glared at Jackson. "She's a Mc-Kane-hyphen-Ridgefield, not just a Ridgefield."

He knew he looked astounded. He had to remember to close his mouth before his jaw hit his chest. "This isn't California. What the hell's she going to do with a hyphen in Green Valley?"

"Remind everyone that feuds are stupid. That there's always a compromise," she retorted pointedly. She glared at both grandmothers, who inched closer to the baby from opposite directions.

He snapped his jaw shut rather than say what was really on his mind and start another feud on top of the old one.

From the distraught look on Dallas's face, he wasn't sure she was too happy to be there just then. "What's the matter?" he asked quietly over her shoulder as she tended the baby. "Is she all right?"

"She's perfect."

"What's wrong, then?"

"It's a girl."

He grinned. "We all know that already."

"Madame Celeste said it was a boy."

"Madame Celeste was wrong."

"I know. That's what's wrong. What if she was wrong about everything else, too?"

"Like what?"

"Like she said she knew I'd never been married."

"And you believed her?"

"Of course I did," she snapped.

"Careful. Your cranky side's showing again." He knew his grin was making her angry, but he couldn't help it.

"It was easy to believe her because I'd already come to the same conclusion myself."

She'd decided, on her own of course, that she couldn't ever have been married and still feel the passion she did for Jackson. Julie's unshakable faith in Madame Celeste, along with the woman's pronouncement that Dallas never had been married, had allowed her a comfortable margin of assurance on the subject. She'd felt a momentary pang of doubt when Madame Celeste was proven not to be infallible, but that's all it was. Momentary.

Wasn't it?

Chapter Fourteen

Dallas wandered through the empty church on a path that took her all the way from the back, and up the center aisle. All the pretty decorations, and no one to use them. She'd seen professionally decorated churches for other weddings; she could even recall one, though she couldn't identify any of the people she remembered seeing there. As beautiful as those churches had been, she'd choose this one to get married in.

And she'd choose Jackson as her groom, if it was up to her. She'd known she was in love with him before she'd made love to him. She'd even convinced herself that she was single and available, on the shaky grounds that what she felt in her heart was correct.

But Jackson was a by-the-book kind of man. He believed in right and wrong, black and white, no shades of gray, no in-between. She couldn't very well grab him by the collar of his shirt, march him up the aisle, and wring an "I do" out of him when it would go against everything he believed in to marry a woman who might—just the slimmest maybe—already be legally married to someone else.

It would definitely be harder than trying to convince him to take a bite of her cheese crackers with peanut butter. And she couldn't very well just draft a hasty apology to a possible husband, promising to pay for damages the way she had with the vending machines.

No, Jackson could never bend that far. And she wouldn't ask him to. She'd get all the facts first, then work everything out, even if it took months. Though the thought of months without him seemed cold and endless. Then, when she was free to promise him she had no other attachments, she'd like to come back here. *Then* she could propose and drag him up the aisle of this church.

There was something about the small structure that felt cozy, intimate, as if a wedding here would be a family affair. Though in Green Valley, *family* apparently had few boundaries. Townspeople felt free to sit in on wedding plans and freely offer advice. Their goodwill and best wishes were palpable. Julie and Roman were off to a fine start, even though they'd already left for the hospital and were missing what was about to be the best party of the year, in Dallas's estimation.

"Dallas?" Jackson spoke quietly as he traced the same steps she'd just taken up to the altar rail. "The party's about to start."

She turned and smiled up at him. "I just wanted to enjoy the decorations. Julie didn't get to."

He reached into his pocket and pulled out a manila envelope. "Martha's nephew got the film developed."

Her smile froze on her face. "What are they? Did you see them already?"

He opened it slowly, driving her nuts as he took too long with his struggle to put his answer into words. "I think you'll have to see them for yourself."

She chewed her bottom lip and held out her hand. The photograph on top was of two boys, standing on the roof of a small, flooded café, holding fishing poles with their lines in the river. Below them was a sign reading Catfish, All U

Can Eat. It was obviously an old sign—some of the paint was peeling and flaking—and had nothing to do with the flood, but that made it all the more poignant.

"I've never seen pictures like these," he said in awe as she flipped through several more. "I look at them and I *know* there's a flood there, but...that's not what I notice. It's the boys in that first one." He pointed at another that she'd stopped to study. "And the crawdad party in that one—God, I wish I'd been there," he admitted with a chuckle.

She sat in the first pew and looked at every photograph.

"Do you recognize them?" he asked hesitantly.

"I don't know." They seemed eerily familiar, like a vital part of her that was temporarily disconnected or out of order, yet she knew it had worked well before. "I hate rain. I hate thunderstorms. I have a career writing budget books. Why would I take pictures of a flood?"

"I wish I could tell you."

"Maybe they're not mine." Even as she said it, she knew it was wrong. It was like trying to deny she had two arms. Thinking about it, struggling to remember, didn't do any good. It always accomplished just the opposite as far as her memory was concerned. Flashes came when she least expected it, which meant if she was to remember anything, she'd have to quit trying. "How about we go to the party?"

"Sounds good to me." He looked around the inside of the church, the same way she had. She took advantage of his perusal and admired his profile as much as she had the decorations. More so. The man radiated character.

"I've never seen anything so beautiful," Jackson finally said.

"Everyone pitched in," she replied.

He grinned. "I wasn't talking about the church, though it's nice, too. Too nice to go to waste, don't you think?"

She smiled then. "You know someone else who's engaged?"

"I know someone who'd like to be."

She might be in love with him, but she'd only known him for four days. She could hope he meant himself, but she really didn't want to make a fool of herself and jump to conclusions. "Oh?"

Her breath caught in her throat as he stepped closer. He framed her face with his hands. They were warm on her skin, strong yet gentle. She wondered if she detected just the slightest tremble.

His head dipped toward hers, drawing her involuntarily up onto her toes to meet him halfway as his lips closed over hers. His arms engulfed her in an embrace that held them together as one. She thought she heard organ music begin softly, but figured it was just the angels playing a trick on her mind.

He tore his lips from hers. "I can't wait any longer, Dallas."

"I know," she whispered, feeling hot blood rush through her veins. "Me, neither. You think they'll miss us if we leave now?"

She was surprised to hear him chuckle. It was soft and low by her ear, then rumbled through his chest and into her heart.

"Well, that, too," he admitted with a wry grin. He pulled away just far enough to lock eyes with her. "But I meant I can't wait to ask you any longer."

"Ask me what?" Whatever they'd been talking about before that kiss, she couldn't remember. And who could blame her? The man kissed like a pro.

"Will you marry me?"

"Oh." She remembered, all right. She also knew he couldn't possibly mean now. Could he?

She sank back down onto her heels. She pulled back a step as a frown creased her forehead.

Jackson let her have a few inches of breathing space, but no more. He couldn't have read her that wrong, could he? He was madly, deeply in love with the woman, and all she could say to his proposal was *Oh?*

"It's your family, isn't it?" he guessed. Before she could reply, he rushed on. "I know you've been thinking about them ever since you read your biography. I know how important family is. I should have known you'd want to have them here for your wedding, but—"

She lay her fingertips on his lips, cutting off his words. He kissed them and was rewarded with her soft smile. The same one he'd fallen in love with. It was so sweet, so feminine, a little bit shy, and so... Dallas.

"First of all, I'm pretty sure I don't have any children, and, as for the rest of my family, yes, I'd want them at my wedding," she began. "But they're not as important as you are."

He took that as a hint. He hoped. He couldn't bear to wait to hear any more. She might object. "The church is all decorated and ready."

"Yes, I know."

"The reception is waiting downstairs, along with a roomful of friends and family."

"Your family," she said ruefully.

"They'll be yours, too." He loved the way her eyebrows arched as she realized he was right. "I know they can't replace yours, of course, but their hearts would be in the right place. And there's twice as many as there used to be... the Ridgefields and the McKanes are actually talking to each other."

"Jackson—"

He closed his eyes and said a quick prayer, then opened them again to see her gazing up at him intently.

"Yes, I would love nothing more than to marry you. But..." she tacked on quickly, just as he opened his mouth to shout the rafters down.

"But?"

"Have you forgotten?"

He took a deep breath and let out a lusty sigh. "You mean our little legal problem?"

"That's a unique way of putting it." She glanced at the decorations one more time. "Maybe we can make it look like this again when I come back."

He pulled her to him again, not willing to let her go anywhere. He never wanted her to leave, not for even a minute. "Come back?"

"I should go to Connecticut and make sure everything's legal."

"But, Dallas—"

She wrapped her arms around behind his back, holding him tightly. "It's all right, Jackson. I know how you are. I know you need to know I'm free to marry you."

"Oh, hell."

She looked surprised, as indeed he was to hear himself say it inside church.

What was even more surprising was what he felt, what he thought. "What good is having a father as a judge if he can't bend the law for his own son once in a while?"

"Jackson!"

Her whisper carried a tone of shock, and, when she pulled free by a couple inches, he noted that so did the expression on her face. The back of her hand landed on his forehead.

"If I feel feverish, it's just because I'm so damn hot for you, lady," he said with a growl as he pulled her into his embrace again. Her lips were soft, pliant beneath his as they met his with lustful energy.

"That's no reason to throw your priorities away," she said when he gave her a millimeter of space.

"I love you. What better reason is there?"

"Jackson, no."

Reality intruded then. He heard organ music. He heard whispers behind him.

"Jackson, I love you so much that I could marry you in a second without my family being here. Whoever they are. But I can't let you sacrifice your priorities."

He started to object.

"Think about it. How could you go on being sheriff every day if you knew you'd stepped over the line? You'd hate me."

"No. Never." He shook his head, wondering why God wasn't helping him out here. He'd been good his whole life; he deserved a break.

She was right, he knew. He'd only needed her to instill a little caution in him to realize that if he insisted on going through with this, he would be putting her at risk. If it turned out she were a bigamist, she could go to jail. He didn't think his dad would send her, but a Connecticut judge might.

The whispers stopped as high-heeled shoes clicked across the marble floor. He turned himself and Dallas around to face what he thought might be his mother, but turned out to be Ms. New York.

"Excuse me if I'm intruding," she began.

Jackson didn't say what he was thinking; he was afraid even thinking it in church would get him into trouble.

"With all the excitement, I haven't been able to find the right time. Maybe I should start by introducing myself. I'm

M. J. Braniff, Diana Radcliffe's literary agent.'' She held out her hand.

He felt Dallas's spine go stiff, and he kept his arm around her shoulders even as she shook the other woman's hand.

"Am I really Diana Radcliffe?" she asked in a quiet voice.

As long as there hadn't been a positive identification, he knew Dallas was able to hold out hope that she was single. She'd even said she'd convinced herself that Madame Celeste was right because she wanted her to be right.

"Yes," M.J. answered with a warm smile. "You really are. I...we...couldn't help overhearing." Her cheeks turned pink. "It seems I'm the only one here who can tell you you're not married."

"I'm not?"

"She's not?"

"No, she's not."

"You're absolutely sure?"

"Positive."

Jackson gave Dallas a rib-crushing hug. "Say yes," he begged.

"Yes."

"Even without your family?"

"I'll borrow yours."

Jackson wasn't convinced, though. He wanted everything perfect for her. He turned to M.J. "Will her family raise a big fuss if she gets married without them?"

"No one will object, I promise."

He grinned at Dallas, then turned and yelled, "Uncle Henry!" His voice echoed throughout the church. "Get your book!"

"What about a license?" Dallas asked.

The judge stepped forward. "All taken care of."

"Since when?" The words slipped out of Jackson before he could think twice.

"Just take my word for it."

"But—"

"Hell, Jackson, everybody's got a skeleton in their closet. A little bone or two won't kill you. How much longer do you want to wait to marry this gal?"

Jackson grinned. "What's taking Uncle Henry so long?"

Harrison stepped forward, Uncle Henry in tow. "I got 'im. We're ready when you are."

DALLAS STOOD in the midst of a flurry of activity in the room set aside for the bridal party. She hadn't even been asked about whether she wanted to wear Julie's unused wedding dress. Martha and Millie and Madame Celeste quickly ripped open a couple of seams and folded the edges in, and she was just as quickly pinned into it. It seemed no aspects of a budget wedding were beyond the capabilities of these small-town women who worked together like a family.

M.J. looked familiar to Dallas. Images took the shape and form and color of warm, fuzzy memories.

"You're a friend of my grandmothers, aren't you?" she asked in one of the less-hectic moments. She stood on a low stool while the other women finished turning her into a bride. *Jackson's bride.*

"Yours, too," M.J. replied, chewing the inside of her lip.

"She's dead, isn't she?" Dallas didn't feel sad, exactly. She suspected she'd gone through her grieving period a long time ago.

M.J. nodded reluctantly, clearly concerned about how much bad news Dallas could handle. "About ten years ago."

Dallas wanted to ask if her children were okay. If they were boys or girls. If they missed her. "How are the—"

"She needs something old," Jackson's mother announced as she entered the room with the persona of a commanding general. She smiled up at Dallas and held out her hand. "Here are my pearl earrings, dear. They were my mother's. I gave Julie her brooch." She hesitated. "You do have pierced ears, don't you?"

Dallas didn't even have to check. "Yes. Thank you, Mrs. Ridgefield."

"Now, none of that. It's Mom to you." She patted Dallas's hand. "Oh, my. I wait thirty years, and then I get two daughters-in-law in one day." Her smile was radiant. "Okay. Something new."

"I think the dress counts," Martha said.

"No," Dallas objected. "It's just borrowed."

They all looked at each other.

"The teddy!" Madame Celeste blurted out.

Dallas blushed, thankful she'd had it on when they'd started stripping her for the transformation. She caught a glimpse of M.J. squeezing her way out of the room.

"Okay, the dress is borrowed," Mom said. "Now for something blue."

"Julie's garter?" Julie's mother suggested from the doorway.

Jackson's mother smiled. "Grace . . . how sweet of you."

Dallas barely listened to the women buzzing around her, letting them handle it all. A lot hadn't felt right to her in the past four days. Most notably that her biography said she was married.

But getting ready to marry Jackson, now *that* felt right. Even without her family present. She'd find a way to explain it to them—when she remembered or met them, whichever came first. If they loved her, they'd understand.

"It's peach and mint, but it's got a touch of blue in it."

She felt herself supported by Martha and Millie as Madame Celeste did the honors and slipped the new garter up her leg to just above her knee. She could have done it herself, but they were in too much of a rush to get her started down the aisle.

"You wouldn't be in a hurry to marry Jackson off for some reason I don't know about yet, would you?" she asked nervously.

They laughed and giggled and ushered her to the back of the church.

"He wasn't covered with warts or something as a child, was he?" She'd never gotten back to that yearbook of his to see what he looked like in high school. Not that it would matter.

They pointed her toward the altar, then rushed up the aisle to take their own seats.

Harrison offered her his elbow with a warm smile. "I'm supposed to give you away."

She looked up into his eyes, the same charming, twinkling, Ridgefield brown that Jackson and Roman also shared.

"It was me or Elvin Brooks."

"I'll bet you didn't even toss a coin."

"No, ma'am. Jackson said if he had to wait for Elvin to get you up that aisle, he'd have a coronary."

The organ struck up the wedding march. The congregation stood and beamed. As she started up the aisle on Harrison's capable arm, Julie's bouquet in her hand, all she noticed was Jackson waiting for her at the front of the church. He stood tall, confident and proud, the way she always thought of him.

Well, not always. She felt her cheeks grow hot and knew she better steer herself away from bedroom thoughts . . . for another couple of hours at least.

At the foot of the altar, she took Jackson's arm and cuddled up close to his side. She jumped when a pin jabbed her in the hip, and she quickly put an inch of space between them. An inch too much as far as she was concerned.

She didn't hear Uncle Henry's first few words, but since Harrison quickly raced over to his uncle's side and started turning pages, she suspected it hadn't been the start of a memorable wedding.

"Oh. Here?" When Uncle Henry got the nod from Harrison, he began again. "Dearly beloved, we are gathered here today, in front of family and friends . . ."

It was true. These people had become her friends. Who else would whip her into a wedding dress in fifteen minutes flat? And they'd become her family. Who else would make sure she had everything a bride was supposed to have on her wedding day?

"Do you, Roman Ridgefield . . . Oh, you're Jackson, aren't you? Do you Jackson Ridgefield, take Julie Mc-Kane—" He was interrupted again by Harrison. "Dallas Radcliffe? But I thought . . . Oh, the heck with it. Do you, young man, and do you, young lady, take each other in holy matrimony, et cetera?"

"I do," Jackson replied.

"I do," Dallas said at the same time.

"Then I pronounce you husband and wife, and you may kiss the bride."

They reached for each other, Jackson's lips descending onto Dallas's.

"And be careful."

They hesitated.

"The last couple I said that to had a baby before they knew it."

"SMILE," Millie repeated for the tenth time. She flitted around the main hall in the church basement with both her camera and Dallas's, determined to get pictures of every memorable moment. "Once more now."

"Don't you have enough yet?" Jackson asked.

"I'm just so glad you didn't cut yourself shaving this morning!" she teased. "Let me get one of you taking off her garter."

He obediently knelt on one knee in front of Dallas, who sat on a folding chair in front of a dozen tombstones and lifted her hem with a shy smile.

"Cute shoes," he said as he slipped the garter off her leg, letting his free hand wander as high above her knee as he thought he could get away with in front of a crowd. "Is that your 'something borrowed'?"

"Ah, no. Actually, I got them from the pile in back of the church."

He hesitated for only a second. "You stole them?"

"Well, my duck shoes were squeaking up a storm every time I took a step and Julie's didn't fit."

He sighed. "I'm going to have to retire and find a new occupation. How can I be sheriff when my wife's a known thief in two counties?" He tried not to smile to soften his words, but he couldn't help it. "I told you not to make a habit of it."

Her smile carried no trace of remorse. "I'm a new woman, I swear. It'll never happen again."

"I know." He pulled her up to her feet and wrapped his arms around her, much to the objections of the single men who wanted a chance at the garter. "Because I'm going to make sure you have everything you ever need."

"That'd be you, then," she said softly.

He tossed the garter haphazardly over his shoulder, ignoring the scuffle behind him. "And your children," he said. "Let's go find your agent and see about collecting them."

My children. What if her instincts were wrong... Was Jackson ready to be a dad?

As she followed him through the room, her hand still in his, she realized she didn't need to ask him. It was a dumb question. He'd accepted kisses from every female from eighteen months to eighty. Jackson loved family and he would love her children.

Snatches of memory returned intermittently, flickering in and out, taking form as they searched for M.J. She remembered the two little girls in the old, faded photograph were her sisters, killed in the same California mud slide that had taken her parents and their home. No wonder she hated rain. No wonder she photographed human triumphs at disaster scenes.

"You okay?" Jackson asked with concern. "You look like you've seen a ghost."

"None I haven't seen before," she murmured.

As quickly as her next breath, she knew she wasn't only Diana Radcliffe, but the other Radcliffe in the library's card catalog, as well. And she knew, if they'd searched for and found that other book, it would have had a photograph on the cover of a twelve-year-old girl standing in the rain, cuddling a beagle puppy, a National Guardsman beside her with his gentle hand on her shoulder. If she'd seen it days ago, would she have recognized herself at that age?

"There you are," Jackson said when he, with Dallas in tow, finally found the agent arm-in-arm with Harrison.

"Jackson, wait," Dallas said, but he was hell-bent on getting something he thought she needed just as her memory of her biographical children decided to come into focus.

"Congratulations," M.J. said. "Oops, I'm not supposed to say that, am I? Best wishes, then."

"We'd like to go pick up Dallas's children as soon as possible."

She had to stop him. She had to tell him herself. "Jackson—"

M.J.'s eyebrows puckered. "What children?"

"Well, you're going to think this is silly, but since Dallas can't remember anything, we read her biography in the *Budget* books . . ."

He smiled charmingly, and Dallas wondered if she could stop him by fainting or screaming. Or both. Short of jumping on his back and clapping her hand over his mouth, he was going to be about as easy to stop as a freight train.

"Oh, that!" M.J. laughed lightly. "That's all made up."

"What?" Jackson's single word sounded deadly calm. Too calm.

"We thought it would boost sales if the buyers thought she was married and had a house and family. Diana—oh, I guess I mean Dallas—wrote it herself. Didn't she make up just the cutest story?"

Chapter Fifteen

Dallas hadn't just spent four days with Jackson for nothing. She knew exactly what he was thinking.

Lies. All lies.

And she certainly knew how he felt about that. From the hard, cold look in his eyes, she knew she'd just been slotted into the same class with Julie, Jasper, Elmer, Otis and the entire McKane clan. Not his favorite people.

Memories filtered back to her. Memories of discussing the biography with M.J. before she wrote it. The publisher had asked for a short blurb on her, requesting something personal because the buying public wanted that small attachment, to feel as if they knew Thelia's granddaughter, to trust that she knew what they *thought* she was writing about.

Memories of how she'd written *Studio Quality Portraits... on a Budget*, donated the proceeds to a women's shelter in Thelia's name, then let the publisher hire a ghostwriter to keep it afloat while she pursued her photography career.

Memories of her telling M.J. that she'd written the bio she wished was true. She wanted that "boisterous family" and the houseful of children.

And she wanted the husband to make it complete. She wasn't wrong for wanting it. She wasn't wrong for writing it. But she understood now why she sometimes felt an invisible wall between her and Jackson, and why she hadn't ever settled into a long-term relationship. She was afraid of losing it all. She'd already lost everything she'd ever loved. Her parents, her sisters, her grandmother. And, if she didn't go about fixing this fast, she knew she could lose her brand-new husband.

"Come on," Martha said, grabbing each of them by the arm. "You're supposed to be the first ones through the buffet line." She propelled them forward, toward chicken that had smelled mouthwateringly delicious only a few moments before. Now it turned her stomach.

"Wait," Dallas stalled. "I need to talk to Jackson first."

"Oh, my, you have the rest of your lives for that," Martha said loudly, with a laugh that drew chuckles from nearby friends and relatives.

"Come on, son," her new father-in-law said to her new husband. "We're hungry."

Jackson grabbed two plates and shoved one at Dallas. "After you, *darlin'*," he murmured so quietly that only she could hear the ice in his voice.

Yes, he was thinking exactly what she thought he'd been thinking. She had to talk to him. Now.

"Hey!" Elvin Brooks croaked.

He shuffled across the room toward Jackson faster than anyone had ever seen him move, though it was still slower than Dallas's limp when Jackson had first pulled her out of the river. Four days ago... It seemed like a lifetime. Long enough to fall in love.

"Where the hell did all these chickens come from? Sheriff!" Brooks wedged himself between the new bride and groom, glaring at Jackson. "Look at all these chickens!" he demanded, pointing at the long table laid out with dozens of steaming-hot dishes and huge baskets full of crispy, golden-brown fried chicken.

"What's the hold up?" someone toward the back of the line called out. It was followed by good-natured grumbling that everyone was hungry and the people in front had better get moving if they wanted their share first.

Martha gave an exasperated sigh, wedged herself in next to Brooks, and plunked a breast down on Dallas's plate, a drumstick on Jackson's. She gave the two of them a gentle shove to get them moving. Brooks got a glare that he matched and shot right back at her. Madame Celeste followed, helping herself to a leg and a thigh. Millie was in line right behind her.

"They're gonna eat the evidence!" Brooks bellowed as Millie reached for a piece. He propelled himself forward, his bony fists clenched and shaking with anger. "Sheriff, I demand you investigate where all these chickens came from before the evidence is destroyed!"

"You want me to investigate fried chickens?" Jackson asked with disbelief. "*Before* the evidence is destroyed?"

"Excuse me, Mr. Brooks." Dallas tried to elbow the older man aside, but for an elderly guy who creaked when he moved, he stood his ground like a brick wall. "If anybody gets to talk to Jackson before we eat, it'll be me."

Brooks turned and gave her an unwanted view of his narrow back.

"What evidence, for God's sake? Unless you've got bands on these drumsticks," Jackson pointed at the leg on his plate, "there is no evidence."

"Sheriff, you know as well as I do there haven't been any food deliveries into Green Valley for over two weeks. So where'd all these chickens come from? I'll tell you where. My place! I'm missing two dozen prime hens. And—" he shoved his way down the line, slapping at people's hands as they reached into the baskets of chicken "—if you don't get busy, all the evidence'll be gone."

Jackson eyed the large drumstick on his plate, the big breast on Dallas's. He arched an eyebrow at Martha. "Mr. Brooks does raise the plumpest hens I ever saw."

"Oh?"

He scowled at her innocent expression.

"Well, Sheriff?" Brooks demanded.

"Well, what?"

"Aren't you gonna arrest her?"

"No, I'm not going to arrest her." He glanced at his father as if wondering how he would handle this in his judging capacity, then narrowed his gaze back to Martha and Brooks. "I'll leave it to the two of you to work out on your own."

"But—"

"Now, listen hear—"

"Peaceably! I'll arrest the first one that lands a blow."

Dallas gave up trying to get his attention while they were in line. If she could just get him to the table, alone for a few minutes, she could explain why she'd written a make-believe bio.

She put some homemade potato salad on her plate, then a piece of golden corn bread, without even noticing what she was selecting. It didn't matter. She wouldn't eat a bite of it. She nearly tripped over the hem of her dress in her hurry to get seated. Jackson followed more slowly—not in any hurry to be alone with her, she noticed—and looked around as if wondering how he could eat at a different table without creating a scandal.

"I won't bite," she snapped, then was immediately ashamed of herself. That was no way to win her husband over.

"Really? Is that the truth, or just something you made up?"

She was relieved when his mother, full plate in hand, explained that he was supposed to sit at the head table beside his new wife, as if he couldn't figure that out for himself.

"Put your plate down and then go get some punch," she advised her son with a warm smile.

"I don't want any—"

"Do it." Her tone brooked no argument. She smiled again. "And get some for your bride, too."

Dallas used her two minutes alone to figure out how best to explain herself. By the time he set two glasses of frothy punch on the table, she was ready.

"I know what you're thinking," she began, "but really, Jackson, this is stupid."

"Better eat," he said without looking at her. "You're getting cranky."

As they were joined at the table by others, precluding any private discussion, she'd never felt so cranky in her whole life.

The head table had been reserved for Julie and Roman's wedding party. Now it filled up with Harrison, Jackson's parents, Uncle Henry, and Madame Celeste. Jackson had mixed feelings. He wanted them there to keep him from saying something to Dallas that he'd regret later. He also wanted them to go away and leave him alone with his new bride so they could decide whether to annul this mess or get a quickie divorce.

The very thought cut him to the core. Yet how could he compromise his aversion to anyone telling lies? He couldn't figure this out without some peace and quiet, and he wasn't getting it here.

As Julie's parents walked by with their food, Jackson's mother jumped to her feet. "Grace, we have two empty seats here. Would you like to join us?"

"We'd be honored," Grace and her husband answered in unison.

Harrison clinked his knife on the edge of his punch glass. The entire roomful of people took up the clinking, adding their own ringing to Harrison's, big smiles on the faces of every blasted one of them. Jackson sighed and turned to Dallas. They all chuckled as if he were putting on an act.

"What's going on?" she whispered.

"Tradition," he mumbled, as his lips touched hers briefly, then pulled back.

Groans of dissent ran rampant through the room. They all clinked louder, and he knew they'd keep it up until they got what they wanted.

He dipped his head, touching Dallas's lips with his own again. He intended to make it brief, just long enough to make them all stop that confounded racket, but something happened. He could call it chemistry or he could call it electricity, or any other damn thing he could think of, but he couldn't pull himself away. He couldn't let her go.

He felt her stiff spine soften and relax as he circled her with his arms. Her hands pressed against his back, holding on for dear life. He almost lost himself in the moment, and then he wondered if this was her honest response or something she fabricated for appearances?

He inched away from her, setting her back from his embrace. He tried cooling his passion with a deep breath of air, but that only served to assail his lungs with her scent. Thank God everyone had stopped clinking. He shot Harrison a glance to warn him against trying it again.

Harrison grinned and elbowed his father. The judge grinned and obliged, starting the next round of a roomwide call for another kiss between the bride and groom.

"This is tradition?" Dallas murmured before his lips closed over hers again.

"Mm-hmm," he hummed against her lips.

She didn't taste like chicken or potato salad; she hadn't taken a bite. She tasted of Dallas. Her lips were moist with punch. He frowned and pulled back from her.

"I need to talk to you," she whispered. "To explain."

He grabbed his own cup of punch, sniffed it, then tasted half a mouthful. "What the hell?"

All of a sudden, no one was paying him any attention. The clinking stopped; the knives dropped to the table. Everyone showed exceptional interest in the food on their plates, much more so than a few minutes ago. No one risked his attention in a call to kiss the bride again.

He took another sip. "Dad, have you tasted this?"

His father drained his cup and grinned. "Martha makes a fine punch, doesn't she?"

"Martha and three old moonshiners, you mean. I sent Roman out to destroy their still..." His voice trailed off as he realized the implication of what he'd said. He groaned. "Roman." It all fit into place. The flooded liquor store. Roman's denial that there was a still to be found. The impending reception for his and Julie's wedding, where some sort of liquor was expected.

"Where are you going?" Dallas blurted out as he shot to his feet, sending his chair sprawling behind him.

"To find Roman."

Martha, who'd been sitting across the table from Brooks, suddenly jumped to her feet. "Why?"

"Probably to arrest him," Jackson muttered through a clenched jaw.

"The punch was my doing," Martha blurted out, stepping forward. "If you have to arrest someone, it should be me."

He wadded up his napkin and threw it down onto the linen tablecloth. He wanted to say "If you insist," but he knew he couldn't arrest Martha. She'd always been like his second mother. Jasper, Otis and Elmer, on the other hand...

Jasper stood up, a smirk pulling his wide mouth into a victorious, toothy grin. "You can't arrest us, neither," he said.

"Why the hell not?" Other than the fact that he had no proof, Jackson wondered what reason the old man would offer in his defense.

"'Cause we didn't sell no 'shine, Sheriff." He cleared his throat. "As I understand it, someone *donated* it to Martha for her fine punch." He winked and raised his cup in a toast to her. Everyone in the room took the excuse to swallow more of the evidence.

The judge spoke up. "It's not illegal for a man to make a little moonshine now and again, Jackson."

"Only enough for his personal use," Jackson retorted.

His father shrugged. "Who's to say what's personal? Or if they exceeded the quantity allowed under the law?"

Jackson felt his jaw drop and snapped it shut. He heard clinking again. He didn't know who started it, but it ran through the room like a plague. He glared at all of them when, unexpectedly, Dallas rose beside him.

He was lost as soon as her hand reached his chest and ran up to the bare skin of his neck. With the soft touch of her fingers on his firmly set jaw, she gently turned him to face her. He was powerless to resist. She rose up onto her toes and aimed her lips for his, drawing the moment out long enough to make him lose patience. He grabbed her and pulled her against him, taking possession of her mouth, drowning in her kiss, going down for the third time.

The crowd was pleased with the kiss, but a discreet cough from behind him suggested he save *something* for the wedding night.

Since learning of Dallas's deception, he hadn't thought there would be a wedding night. Now he knew he couldn't live without one. And, if he arrested Martha, the town would probably throw him into the cell instead—alone.

He looked around at the celebrants, an entire roomful of moonshine-swilling citizens waiting to hear his decision. "I sure as hell hope the State Troopers don't raid this place."

A sigh of relief whispered through the crowd. Conversation picked up again as they returned to their meal.

His father gave a nod of approval. "Celeste was right," he murmured in an aside to his wife. "Dallas is going to be good for our Jackson."

DALLAS STILL WASN'T able to eat. First because she'd been scared she'd lose Jackson over the fake bio bit. Then because that last hot kiss of his had made her forget about food, guests, everything.

No, not the guests, she amended. They filled a need in her. They were the boisterous family she'd wanted for so many years. She got a warm, fuzzy feeling that her years as a loner, as an award-winning photographer who flew from one disaster to another, were over. That, or the spiked punch was taking its toll. And they were proposing another toast.

"To Martha and Elvin's new joint venture," Madame Celeste said as she rose to her feet and held up her cup.

Martha's mouth dropped open, but she quickly recovered.

"To the new, homestyle, fried-chicken eatery they're going to open out on the highway."

Dallas took notice of the fact that Jackson seemed to be enjoying the punch just fine now. She leaned toward him and whispered. "Everyone's busy. How about if we slip upstairs and have a little talk?"

He nodded in agreement but, from the grim expression on his face, she didn't know whether he was going to be receptive to what she had to say. They rose together, but Dallas was hampered by the long, full skirt of her dress hanging up on the chair.

"They're ready for their first dance!" Martha announced just as Dallas got free.

Everyone clapped. A man wearing his Sunday suit grabbed his fiddle and started right into the most beautiful notes Dallas had ever heard. Too beautiful to resist melting into Jackson's arms. One dance, that's all it would be. Then they'd find a quiet spot to talk.

Jackson waltzed with grace and style, floating Dallas around the floor with the ease of ice dancers. And, no sooner than that number was done, there was another. And another. They were joined on the dance floor by other couples, but any and every time she tried to lead Jackson off, they were called back.

"This is ridiculous," she snapped beneath her breath.

"What?" he whispered in her ear.

She lifted her head so he could hear her. "I want to go somewhere and talk to you. To explain that the bio wasn't a lie."

His arms stiffened as he missed a step and they jolted into another couple. "A rose by any other name—"

"If that's more of Jasper's Shakespeare, just stuff it for a minute."

He arched his eyebrows at her.

"Besides which, you're quoting it in the wrong context."

"Are you an English teacher, too?"

"Shut up and listen, Jackson. I don't know how much time I'll get to say this. That biography I wrote wasn't a lie. It was a dream." She looked into his eyes and saw the temptation to start quoting the rose thing again. "My dream," she whispered. "My parents and my sisters were killed when I was twelve."

"Killed—?"

"Hush. Just listen. I've always felt an emptiness in my heart for them. For family. My grandmother was the only relative I had left, and she died ten years ago. So when the publisher asked me for a bio that depicted a normal, family-type life, I wrote what I always wished I'd had."

He pulled her close, and she let him, as they moved slowly around the dance floor.

"So... You want three kids, then?"

She could feel his lips moving in her hair, just above her ear. She remembered how they'd felt everywhere else as he'd learned the secrets of her body. "I want you, Jackson. I never lied to you and I never will."

She felt the change immediately. These were the arms she remembered. This was the embrace she wanted to dance in for the rest of her life. To sleep in. To make love in. Speaking of which...

"How soon do you think we can leave?" she whispered.

His grin was as naughty as she could hope for, given the fact they were surrounded by dozens of couples and young children.

Madame Celeste swayed by them. "I see five children," she intoned as if a vision had just presented itself to her.

Jackson chuckled. "Sounds like you won't be traveling much, darlin'."

"I'll do nature photography in our backyard."

Madame Celeste droned on, "They're all very artistic and they love to travel at high speeds."

Jackson twirled them away from her. "Green Valley's going to need a new sheriff when the first one hits sixteen, then. I don't want to have to ticket my own kids."

Dallas laughed lightly. "They're going to drive like Harrison and you think they'll wait until they're sixteen? I can see it's going to be my job to bring you into the real world."

"Everyone here seems to think if anyone can get me there, it's you."

"What do you think?"

They were locked in each other's arms and didn't even notice they'd quit dancing.

Jackson looked around at the guilty moonshine-punch-drinkers and stolen-chicken-eaters. "I think I should arrest everyone of these people for something, but Dad would just let them all off."

"Wise man."

"So, if I kick and scream too much—" His lips hovered over hers.

"I'll hold you close," she promised.

"How close?"

She plastered her body along the length of his, knowing the full dress billowed around them, hiding his reaction to her.

"Careful, darlin', or I'll have to arrest us."

"Ooh, then we can go to jail." She wiggled closer. "I know a great desk . . ."

She tossed him a teasing smile, not caring if more old memories ever returned; she was already working on new ones.

Weddings by DeWilde

Since the turn of the century the elegant and fashionable DeWilde stores have helped brides around the world turn the fantasy of their "Special Day" into reality. But now the store and three generations of family are torn apart by the divorce of Grace and Jeffrey DeWilde. As family members face new challenges and loves—and a long-secret mystery—the lives of Grace and Jeffrey intermingle with store employees, friends and relatives in this fast-paced, glamorous, internationally set series. For weddings and romance, glamour and fun-filled entertainment, enter the world of DeWilde...

Twelve remarkable books, coming to you once a month, beginning in April 1996

Weddings by DeWilde begins with
Shattered Vows
by Jasmine Cresswell

Here's a preview!

"SPEND THE NIGHT with me, Lianne."

No softening lies, no beguiling promises, just the curt offer of a night of sex. She closed her eyes, shutting out
temptation. She had never expected to feel this sort of re-
lentless drive for sexual fulfillment, so she had no mecha-
nisms in place for coping with it. "No." The one-word
denial was all she could manage to articulate.

His grip on her arms tightened as if he might refuse to
accept her answer. Shockingly, she wished for a split second that he would ignore her rejection and simply bundle
her into the car and drive her straight to his flat, refusing to
take no for an answer. All the pleasures of mindless sex,
with none of the responsibility. For a couple of seconds he
neither moved nor spoke. Then he released her, turning
abruptly to open the door on the passenger side of his Jag-
uar. "I'll drive you home," he said, his voice hard and flat.
"Get in."

The traffic was heavy, and the rain started again as an
annoying drizzle that distorted depth perception made
driving difficult, but Lianne didn't fool herself that the silence inside the car was caused by the driving conditions.
The air around them crackled and sparked with their
thwarted desire. Her body was still on fire. Why didn't Gabe
say something? she thought, feeling aggrieved.

Perhaps because he was finding it as difficult as she was
to think of something appropriate to say. He was thirty

years old, long past the stage of needing to bed a woman just so he could record another sexual conquest in his little black book. He'd spent five months dating Julia, which suggested he was a man who valued friendship as an element in his relationships with women. Since he didn't seem to like her very much, he was probably as embarrassed as she was by the stupid, inexplicable intensity of their physical response to each other.

"Maybe we should just set aside a weekend to have wild, uninterrupted sex," she said, thinking aloud. "Maybe that way we'd get whatever it is we feel for each other out of our systems and be able to move on with the rest of our lives."

His mouth quirked into a rueful smile. "Isn't that supposed to be my line?"

"Why? Because you're the man? Are you sexist enough to believe that women don't have sexual urges? I'm just as aware of what's going on between us as you are, Gabe. Am I supposed to pretend I haven't noticed that we practically ignite whenever we touch? And that we have nothing much in common except mutual lust—and a good friend we betrayed?"